Reasonable Doubt?

Julie Haiselden

Kind Regards,

Julie Haiselden

Copyright © Julie Haiselden (2019)

Published 15th April 2019

ISBN: 9781090488992

All rights reserved.

The characters and events in this book are fictitious. Any similarity to real persons, dead or alive, is coincidental and not intended by the author.

This novel is dedicated to all the readers who have enjoyed my books and have given me encouragement to continue to write.

Contents

Chapter 1 – Iniquities from the Past 5

Chapter 2 - Flies in the Ointment 30

Chapter 3 – Making Waves 49

Chapter 4 – A Serious Misjudgement.......................70

Chapter 5 – A Motive for Murder.............................89

Chapter 6 – The Truth about Malchington Bay......112

Chapter 7 – Spadework..137

Chapter 8 – Peeling the Layers................................158

Chapter 9 – Evasion and Discussion 182

Chapter 10 – Flight in the Night 203

Chapter 11 – Questions and Explanations 225

Chapter 12 – Back to the Drawing Board...............247

Chapter 13 – The Cornered Rabbit 270

Chapter 14 – Secrets and Lies 291

Acknowledgements 321

About the Author 322

2012

Chapter 1 – Iniquities from the Past

He folded the piece of paper neatly in half and put it in the envelope. After sealing it, he placed it on the hall table as he left his detached Edwardian house. He looked back wistfully and hoped his wife could forgive him. With his shoulders bent against the wind, he walked purposefully in the direction of the wood with a guilt-laden heart.

*

The following morning, a large florid man in a shabby office in Balham opened his newspaper. The headline caught his attention immediately.

"Headmaster Found Dead at Local Beauty Spot

The body of Dr Cornelius Hopsmith was found yesterday morning by a dog walker in Bilsbury Copse, Floxley. Dr Hopsmith was Head of the £20,000 a year Moreford College until his recent resignation following an exposé in a tabloid newspaper. A source has also revealed that he had subsequently been suspended from his regular radio phone-in programme on XBC5, pending an official investigation."

When he realised he was up the proverbial creek without a paddle, Hopsmith had sent wine and theatre tickets to the shabby Balham office. He'd then tried a charm offensive over dinner, suggesting that he could pave the way for all sorts of media work via contacts he had made through his popular "Ask the Head" radio feature. Indeed, he had been making quite a name for himself on the celebrity circuit, with an ever eager public avidly watching him bake soufflés on a morning cookery show and turn his hand to portrait painting. They also followed his adventures as he and his family took part in the weekly-aired "Let's Get Away" lunchtime programme, espousing the virtues of a camping holiday in France. When these overtures failed, he knew his star was no longer ascending; in fact it was plummeting earthwards.

'But my wife,' he'd implored; 'she has no idea; believe me when I tell you I'm filled with remorse and utterly ashamed. Name your price; I can't give you much now but if you give me some time...'

They were always "filled with remorse and utterly ashamed" when their dirty little secrets got out. It was a pity because a couple of hundred thousand might have made a difference. The ten year dalliance with the maths teacher, who subsequently took his own life in dubious circumstances, might have been overlooked. Arguably, the Head's unimaginable grief over this tragic event might have been the reason behind the drug-fuelled night of debauchery with a group of underage rent boys. Maybe it would have been possible to believe the headmaster was a contrite, reformed character and worthy of another chance. Unfortunately for Dr Hopsmith, with no reasonable sum of money on offer, ethical obligation had won through.

'Integrity is not for sale, Dr Hopsmith and I would have thought you, as a man entrusted with instilling moral guidance into the hearts and minds of the young, would have appreciated that,' he'd replied with mock incredulity. The look on the teacher's face had been priceless as he realised his reputation was in ruins.

Yes indeed, another win for truth and justice.

*

Just as the journalist in Balham was congratulating himself regarding his latest scalp, three hundred miles away in the Cumbrian village of Blenthorne, local entrepreneur, Lizzie Lockwood was shutting the post office door behind her. She'd decided as she left home that she just had enough time to send a parcel to her son and had exchanged a few words with Hilary Cole, the postmistress, before glancing at the clock on the wall behind the counter. Her departure was hasty, if not actually rude, as she hurtled out of the building.

She stopped herself from breaking into a run as she crossed the road in the direction of the pub. Knowing her luck, she'd probably trip over anyway. She reached the back door of the Blenthorne Inn and opened it quietly, trying not to draw attention to herself as she pulled her fingers through her unruly dark mane in a vain attempt to bring it under control.

Unfortunately, she was rumbled by the ageing barman who was crossing the hallway.

'Morning, Bert, blimey, I'm so sorry; late on my first day back,' gabbled Lizzie, feeling the need to apologise.

'It's your pub,' Bert muttered without breaking step as he lumbered into the public bar with a box of cheese and onion crisps.

Lizzie pushed the office door open and walked in; she was about to repeat her apology but didn't get the chance.

'Oh my word; you're a sight for sore eyes. Lizzie Lockwood back at the Blenny! Come here,' said Maggie Blake as she reached out and clutched her friend in a vice-like grip.

'Not quite; I'm a barmaid for a few shifts a week, it's your domain now,' said Lizzie as she disentangled herself from the pub manager.

'I'm delighted you've got time to pull a few pints. Do you realise, I haven't seen you for nearly a month! It's so good to have you back. How are you? And how's life with Gary?'

Lizzie felt herself blush, completely belying her attempt at nonchalance.

'I'm fine and yes, Gary moved in as planned a couple of weeks ago and so far, nowhere near as feral as I feared.'

'It's still early days, so he'll be on his best behaviour; wait till he gets comfortable.'

Lizzie was bound to agree with her friend.

'I never get anywhere when I try a little gentle probing about your relationship,' observed Maggie, wistfully.

'I know all about your "gentle probing". It's nobody else's business, so stop fishing. What I will say is that he has the most amazing business acumen. If he'd gone down the management route, he would be running a multi-national by now instead of my modest portfolio.'

'So what's happening with Hope Cottage; any occupants yet?' asked Maggie, referring to the property Lizzie had recently purchased and renovated.

'Yup, everything's in place with the authorities and three women moved in last week. I've sorted some work to help each of them get back on their feet. If all goes to plan, then I hope to do the same for another three parolees next year.'

'Only you could emerge from the slammer with the firm intention of helping as many of your cohort as possible.'

'"The slammer?" really, Maggie, you watch far too much American telly. I didn't buy the cottage for altruistic reasons; it's a good investment and it makes sense to use it for a practical purpose. As for my stint behind prison bars, I want to forget it; if people will let me. I know five years is a long time but it's all done and dusted now.'

Lizzie left the office and walked through into the bar area. She hoped her wish to draw a line under the past would be respected; all she wanted was for her life to be settled and above all, uneventful.

She was blissfully unaware that "uneventful" would be the last adjective that could be used to describe events in the weeks ahead. As she greeted her first customer that day, she had no idea what lay in store for the quiet community of Blenthorne.

*

Just as Lizzie Lockwood was pulling her first pint, a petite fair haired woman checked the directions as she set off on the final part of her journey north. She had been to the Lake District before but until recently had never heard of her destination, let alone visited it. Blenthorne was; *"an idyllic Lake District retreat about half an hour's drive from Keswick, perfect as a base for walking or relaxing"*, if the area guidebook was to be believed. For her, it wasn't so much the place as one of the residents she was keen to see.

She checked her appearance in the mirror in the ladies' lavatory at the motorway service station and was satisfied with what she saw. She combed her neatly bobbed hair and reapplied her subtle lipstick.

She had reached a crossroads in her life; back from abroad with no money or job. Then an idea struck her; why not look up an old acquaintance who was now apparently residing in a place called Blenthorne? Thank heavens for social media or she might never have tracked him down.

She filled the convertible's tank as she contemplated her reception. She did think about phoning ahead but didn't want to be fobbed off. She decided the element of surprise would play in her favour. After all, what could he say once she was standing on his doorstep? Unfortunately she didn't have his actual address but she was sure he wouldn't be too hard to find in a modest village.

Another hour and she would be there and would find out if her host was as accommodating in the fells of Cumbria as she herself had been on the coast of Devon. She climbed back into her vehicle and put her foot on the accelerator.

*

Andrea Pearce was standing in the upstairs kitchen at the Blenthorne Inn. It took her time to do things and she cursed herself for being forgetful and slow. Everyone in Blenthorne was so kind and patient and she knew she was lucky to be functioning at such a high level. She had met Lizzie in prison. Now, Andrea could not imagine her life without her friend and mentor.

Lizzie had told Andrea of her plan to set up a project, in conjunction with the authorities, to help resettle ex-offenders and was so pleased when she offered her a place, which she assumed would be at Hope Cottage with the others. Never in a million years did she imagine she would live in this lovely flat and be able to have Mia come to live with her. Not only did she have a home and her twenty-one-year-old daughter but a part-time job as well, again arranged by Lizzie. She could never repay such kindness.

A sound disturbed her thoughts, a car swishing loudly into the carpark, churning up the gravel. Now what was she looking for? Oh yes, the potato peeler, she pulled it from the drawer with a small sense of triumph and was just about to attack a carrot when Mia appeared behind her.

'Mum, there's a woman downstairs looking for Gary Carmichael. I told her he's not here but she's very insistent and wants his home address.'

'Isn't Lizzie there, or Maggie?' asked Andrea, hopefully.

'No, Maggie's working in the public bar with Bert; you know she can't really leave him on his own when there's a darts match on. Lizzie won't be here until her church meeting has finished, around eight thirty or so.'

Andrea again felt irritated; yes, that's right. After the accident, the doctor had explained her condition to her but it was all very complicated; he kept referring to her having had a "TBI" as a result of a car crash but she found it difficult to remember what the initials represented. She asked him to write it down in the end; *"TBI – traumatic brain injury"*. She had coping mechanisms but even now, sometimes she could recall things and sometimes she couldn't.

'I think Gary's scheduled to take a walking party out on the fells tomorrow so he won't be around then either. What's the woman's name? I'll have to call him.'

Mia gave her mother the details and returned downstairs while Andrea rang Gary Carmichael, who professed not to know the stranger. She then went downstairs to speak to their unexpected guest. She noticed Mia's boyfriend was standing by himself at the bar as usual. Surely he must get bored hanging around while Mia worked. Now, where was the woman she was supposed to be seeing? She looked enquiringly at Mia who inclined her head towards the table by the window.

'Ms Anderson? Hello, I'm Andrea Pearce; a business associate of Gary Carmichael.'

That was stretching a point but sounded impressive and she felt quite pleased with herself.

'We weren't expecting you but maybe I can help?' She offered her hand and it was taken limply by the slender woman. Andrea slid into the chair opposite.

'As I've already explained to the young woman at the bar, I'm an old friend of Gary so if you would be so kind as to give me his address, I'll be on my way.' She managed a condescending smile.

'I'm sorry but he's unavailable this evening and has commitments for the next few days so if I can't be of assistance, then maybe it would be best if you made an appointment for one day next week?'

'I hardly think I need an appointment.' The deep blue eyes stared back at Andrea without blinking.

Andrea tried to keep her voice steady. 'Well, it seems to me, Ms Anderson, if you're a friend, you would already have Gary's address and probably his mobile number…' her voice tailed away.

The newcomer sighed and smiled insipidly. 'Oh, for heaven's sake; tell him it's Helen from Malchington Bay and I think you'll find he will make time for me.'

Andrea felt her pseudo air of confidence begin to evaporate in the face of this persistent and determined woman. She glanced over towards the bar and was delighted to see that Jono Johnson had just walked in. He was not only her employer at the adventure holiday company based in the village but a great friend and support. Thankfully he picked up on her imploring look immediately.

He walked over and introduced himself. Andrea grabbed the opportunity to leave in as dignified a manner as possible and went into the office situated behind the bar and called Gary a second time, armed with information regarding Malchington Bay.

Gary said he'd be there directly. Andrea was perplexed. How did he come to know such an assertive and overbearing woman? She was passive-something-or-other… aggressive, yes that was it! She had to be someone from Gary's past. Why had he seemed disinterested initially, only to change his mind when Malchington Bay was mentioned? Helen from Malchington Bay; there was something, but what? Lizzie might know but Mia had said she was somewhere else, now where? Drat, she couldn't remember. It was no good, her curiosity had got the better of her and she would have to look up the place on her laptop.

Five minutes later Andrea closed the article with a click. Now she remembered. She called Lizzie's mobile to forewarn her. This newcomer was definitely no ordinary visitor.

*

Gary Carmichael arrived at the Blenthorne Inn not quite knowing what to make of this unexpected turn of events. The name Anderson had meant nothing to him when Andrea called the first time. Helen was using a different surname when he knew her.

Jono Johnson stood up as soon as he saw Gary walk into the lounge bar. He smiled and inclined his head towards his companion. He then left the woman at the table and walked over to the bar.

'Helen, it must be what… five years? What brings you here?' Gary asked, trying to keep the irritation out of his voice. In fact, seeing her again had disorientated him more than he cared to admit.

'And it's very nice to see you too, Gary,' smiled Helen, softly. 'I'll have a large dry white wine, if you're buying.'

Over the following three quarters of an hour, Gary Carmichael sat with Helen Anderson in the lounge bar of the Blenthorne Inn and listened to her tale. To the casual onlooker it might appear they were congenial companions.

'You've certainly travelled a long way, do you have accommodation booked?' he asked pointedly.

'I'd rather hoped you would offer to let me stay with you,' said Helen, dropping her head and peering up at him through long eyelashes.

'I'll see if the hotel in the village has any vacancies, they offer very good terms,' said Gary, firmly.

He heard a welcome voice and twisted slightly to look over his shoulder.

'Hello, you must be Helen? I'm Lizzie Lockwood, owner of the Blenthorne Inn.'

Gary felt an immediate wave of relief sweep over him. The cavalry had arrived. Lizzie sat down in a chair at right angles to Helen and within a few minutes had taken matters into her own hands. Gary made his excuses and went through to the office, breathing a silent sigh of relief. After ringing the owners of Fell View Hotel he sent Lizzie a surreptitious text.

'I'll explain later, room booked at hotel.'

Half an hour later Lizzie joined him.

'It sounds like you were practically engaged!' said Lizzie as she sat down in the chair opposite the desk and looked expectantly at her partner. 'Helen tells me you met in Devon?'

'Yes, it was several years ago, during the time you were serving your sentence. I went to Devon for the funeral of an old colleague and met Helen while I was there.'

'You pulled at a funeral?'

'What? No, not really; it's a long story.'

'I'm listening.'

'A very long story…' Gary lapsed into silence and stared into space. 'I will tell you but not now, it's rather complicated.'

'Okay, let's be practical; she doesn't have any sort of hold over you does she? I'm not sitting in judgement; you were single at the time so whatever happened, that's no one's business but yours but if there's more…?' Lizzie looked at him enquiringly, letting the end of the sentence hang in the air.

After a short, awkward silence, Gary swallowed and shook his head.

'After I got your message about the room, I sent her to the hotel, she's not happy but at least that gives us some time to decide what we're going to do about her,' said Lizzie grimly.

'Not sure we can do anything. She's a free agent to go where she wants and she's quite adamant that she wants to make a fresh start as far away from Devon as possible.'

'Did you know she has an interview at Triple Dale tomorrow for the matron's vacancy?' asked Lizzie, referring to the residential home in the next village. 'Maggie suggested giving the owner a call; we're in the am-dram group together so I know him quite well.'

'Yes, she told me. Lizzie, she's had a rough time; if she gets the job, that's fine. As long as she understands there is nothing else for her here.'

'Why would she think there might be?' asked Lizzie, looking at him sharply.

'I suspect she's lonely and afraid of what the future may hold. People clutch at straws at times like these.'

Lizzie experienced a feeling that had been absent from her life for a long time, one of utter dismay. Surely fate couldn't be as cruel as to allow her a brief taste of happiness only for it to be snatched away again. Could it?

*

The spring flowers danced in the breeze as Helen Anderson left the residential home in Rowendale just after eleven o'clock the following morning and climbed into her convertible. The interviewer was a professional recruitment consultant rather than the owner of the care home. He had said he would make contact in the next few days. It was something of a triumph that she was being considered for a managerial role at all. The job for which she had just applied wouldn't have been worth a second glance previously but times had changed and she could no longer aspire to a prestigious position, given her tarnished history.

She was particularly disappointed with her reception in Blenthorne. She had thought Gary Carmichael would be reasonably malleable had he been single but sadly he wasn't; although what he saw in Lizzie Lockwood was a total mystery.

Helen made her way back to the hotel wondering how she would spend the remainder of the day. She was extremely irritated to receive a text message less than an hour after her interview to say she did not fit the person specification for the role of residential home manager and therefore her application would not be taken forward to the next stage of the selection process.

She swore as she threw her phone onto the bed. Stuff them and their piddling second-rate job.

*

Gary Carmichael was in reflective mood as he caught up with some paperwork at the home he now shared with Lizzie. He had renewed his friendship with Lizzie after her release from prison and she had offered him a job managing her business interests, which coincided nicely with his retirement from the police service. He had no experience of the world of commerce and suggested that Lizzie gave him a trial period. However, he loved what he was doing and Lizzie appeared suitably impressed. Their personal relationship seemed to develop almost effortlessly. If he was pushed on the subject, he would say he had never been happier.

He hadn't thought about Malchington Bay for years but it had had a profound effect on him at the time. On the surface, it seemed like any other sleepy seaside town but what he'd uncovered during his time there had shaken the town to its roots. Even he, as a police officer with nearly thirty years' experience, had trouble believing the evidence he found.

The press had had a field day, sensationalising what they referred to as; *"Murder in Malching"*. Despite never facing any charges, Helen's name had been splashed everywhere, so it was hardly surprising she'd tried to get as far away from the place as possible. He wasn't sure why he felt so uncomfortable.

The relationship, if you could call it that, had happened before he knew there was any prospect of getting together with Lizzie. While he had had feelings for her for years, she was firmly committed to her second husband, Jim. He knew she wouldn't hold his brief liaison with someone else against him. So why hadn't he told Lizzie about Helen?

What he hadn't expected was for Helen to turn up here in Blenthorne. His thoughts were disturbed by his phone ringing in his pocket.

'Helen's here in the pub. Shall I tell her you're on the fells with a walking party?' asked Lizzie in a hushed whisper.

'No, she'll only hang around waiting for me and you'll be stuck with her for the rest of the day,' he said in resignation.

He walked to the Blenny with a sense of foreboding. It was clear that Helen Anderson, as she now wished to be known, wasn't going to be side-lined.

She was sitting demurely at a corner table. Over the next forty minutes, Helen asked him if he knew of any local vacancies, as she'd decided a change of career would be appropriate. Reading between the lines, he realised she hadn't got the position in Rowendale.

He explained recruitment was in the hands of the individual establishments with which he was involved. Maggie took care of the pub and Carl, the executive chef at Lockwood's, looked after the restaurant. Jono had Andrea as his administrator at the adventure holiday company, so that only left the hotel where she was staying, in which Lizzie had a small stake. His answers didn't please his companion.

'But you must at least know of someone. I'm a first rate manager, in addition to my other skills. Don't you have any contacts? Really, Gary, I have to say I'm disappointed.'

The glance she gave him demonstrated, lest he was in any doubt, just how disappointed she really was.

After a slightly dramatic pause she added simply, 'I thought you cared about me.'

He looked uncomfortable, winced slightly but said nothing.

It was left that Gary would give the matter some thought and contact her at the hotel. She had then asked if she could borrow some money. Feeling he had little choice, he gave her the cash he had on him which amounted to just under forty pounds.

After they parted company he went through to the public bar and spoke to Maggie.

'What? You want me to give her a job? Are you mad, what would Lizzie say? She does own this place, unless you've forgotten? That woman will never go if we let her get a foothold here,' she turned away, her annoyance evident even from the back view.

'She might just get bored and leave,' he said hopefully.

'Or she might just hang around and make your life hell!'

He assured Maggie he just felt sorry for Helen; she was down on her luck and needed a break. He suggested that maybe he would speak to Mark at the hotel in the morning.

Maggie answered tersely that he must do as he felt appropriate but made it quite clear without uttering a further word, precisely what she thought of the idea.

*

A week later, Helen Anderson started work at Fell View Hotel as housekeeping supervisor. Robin Corey and Mark Stevens had interviewed her after Gary mentioned she was looking for work. She felt quite pleased with the outcome. Not least as the job had accommodation and board thrown in.

She needed to re-establish herself and this job would do for now. Robin and Mark were pleasant and friendly. They professed themselves to be heartily sick of ongoing petty pilfering and told her of their difficulty in retaining reliable staff when larger establishments and central locations offered better salaries than they could afford.

Helen sympathised with their predicament and had assured them both that she understood their dilemma and managing staff would not prove difficult for someone with her professional background.

They had seemed impressed with the image she projected and offered her the job immediately. Of course, it meant moving from her guest room to the staff quarters at the back of the hotel but at least she still had her own room, albeit a small one.

Over the following weeks, she familiarised herself with the running of the establishment and hoped she was making a favourable impression. She was beginning to quite like the place and the owners often asked her to join them for a supper drink at the end of the day; they were always interested in listening to her ideas.

What she didn't tell them was that she had already identified the source of the pilfering and advised the culprit no further action would be taken, providing it stopped; always good to have leverage.

She thought Gary was getting used to having her around; he might not exactly be warming to the situation but he certainly wasn't as distant as when she first arrived. He had agreed to meet her at the pub and his manner changed after she repaid his loan, courtesy of a small advance on her first salary.

It was at the end of her fourth week as housekeeping supervisor that she returned to her room, post in hand. It was unusual for her to get mail as not many people knew where she was.

She sat on her bed, ripped open the envelope and read the contents of the letter. It was short and succinct.

After reading it, Helen stared at the floor in disbelief. She shivered as she crumpled the paper and threw it in the bin. A few minutes later after pacing the floor she walked to the bin, retrieved the letter and smoothed it out. She then refolded it, replaced it in the envelope and laid it on her bedside table.

What should she do now? Was this missive a one-off or the start of a hate campaign? Who could want her out of the way so badly? The obvious answer was staring her in the face. Maybe it was time to pay a call on Gary Carmichael's current paramour, Lizzie Lockwood.

*

The subject of Helen's thoughts had just left the doctors' surgery in Rowendale a couple of miles from Blenthorne. Since her incarceration, Lizzie's asthma had worsened. She knew her symptoms were exacerbated by stress and she'd allowed herself to get very worked up about the "Anderson Situation" as Maggie had dubbed it. She'd misplaced her blue inhaler, possibly she'd left it in Dorset when visiting her mother; she'd tried ringing for a replacement but the specialist nurse had insisted on seeing her.

The nurse had asked about recent anxiety and Lizzie had certainly had her fair share. Both Jim's death and that of her father, had hit her hard. Her relationship with her mother was tempestuous and she had anticipated the future with trepidation but as it transpired, her mother had only survived her husband for just over a month. In addition, her son, Alex, had separated from his wife and had decided to hone his culinary skills in France. Lizzie had rhetorically asked herself recently, what else could happen? She now had her answer in the shapely form of Ms Helen Anderson.

Her thoughts were interrupted as her phone pinged. She noticed she had missed a call from an unknown number.

She pulled up on the drive to see a sleek convertible parked adjacent to the kerb outside her home. She looked over briefly and then turned away, not wanting to appear nosy. She heard the car door open and a voice she instantly recognised calling her.

'Lizzie. May I have a moment, please?'

Lizzie took a deep breath and made herself turn slowly.

'Helen, this is a surprise! Would you like to come in?'

'How kind, as long as I'm not delaying you. I did try to ring just now but I didn't get an answer so I thought I'd just pop round on the off chance.'

'What can I help you with?' Lizzie swallowed the urge to demand how Helen had managed to get hold of her number. However, her curiosity was immediately satisfied.

'Mark gave me your number as he said you were the person to speak to if I had any particular ideas for improvements at the hotel. The guys value your opinion, as I'm sure you know.'

'We've been friends and business partners for a long time, so it's natural I suppose. Do go through,' she said as she unlocked the front door. 'Front room is first on the left.'

'Oh, you call it the "front room", how quaint!' Helen paused in the doorway as she surveyed her surroundings. 'It's very um… homely. I always think the interior of a property reflects the personality of its owner, don't you?'

Lizzie felt her hackles rise as she followed her unexpected guest into the room. All sorts of expletives sprang to mind but thankfully, none fell out of her mouth. She tried a bit more deep breathing in an attempt to regain her composure.

Sitting stiffly opposite each other, they talked for a few minutes about possible changes to the hotel's housekeeping needs. What piffle, as if the boys would need her input!

'Really, Helen, you sound like you have it all under control,' said Lizzie firmly, as she rose from the sofa. 'The "guys" as you call them, are very lucky to have you.' She gestured towards the door, hoping the vexatious woman would take the unsubtle hint.

'You're so kind. I do hope we can be friends. Anything between Gary and I was over long ago.' She flashed Lizzie a dazzling veneered smile as she rose to take her leave.

Finally, she'd said what she came to say. Lizzie hoped her countenance didn't alter as she watched her erstwhile uninvited guest walk confidently down the front path. Helen Anderson was trouble and Lizzie wished fervently that she had never set foot in Blenthorne.

As events unfolded, she would not find herself alone in that sentiment.

Chapter 2 - Flies in the Ointment

Whilst the village of Blenthorne was adjusting to the arrival of its latest long term resident, the overweight occupant of the shabby office in Balham was also taking an interest in that part of the world. Whilst he was still basking in the glory of the Hopsmith exposé, he was certainly ready for another challenge. Maybe this was it?

He stubbed out a cigarette as he looked at the open file on his laptop. Yes, it was clearly her. The name was different but he was in no doubt. Strange how the simplest thing can get a person noticed. An innocent photo in a little-read local rag, who on earth would see that? She must have thought she was safely tucked away from prying eyes but that was the beauty of the worldwide web. He had unearthed some juicy information regarding this lady a while ago, but when he went to confront her, she'd vanished! Disappeared abroad for several years but now, lo and behold, she was back. He was indebted to the anonymous letter writer. Fortune favoured the righteous he told himself. He looked at it again.

"Dear Sir
I recently saw your article about the school headmaster. You are clearly someone with a strong moral compass – in which case, you may be interested in this. Helen Bell-Martin or Anderson, as she now calls herself, is living in the village of Blenthorne in Cumbria and working at Fell View Hotel. I enclose a copy of a piece which appeared in

the local paper. You may recall that Helen was involved in a scandal at a nursing home in Devon and I thought you might want to look into this further.
A Well-Wisher."

She's clearly ruffled a few feathers in her new home he thought contemplatively. It was definitely worth a bit of digging.

He checked how far it was to Blenthorne. He called over to his assistant, Keith, and asked him to book a room at Fell View Hotel from the following night, for an open-ended stay. He would do a bit of background research today to reacquaint himself with the case, catch a bit of shut-eye and then travel up overnight, hopefully arriving about mid-morning.

Helen smiled at him from the page, seemingly without a care in the world. He was fairly certain he could wipe the smug expression off her face in the not too distant future.

*

Helen Anderson had been in Blenthorne for nearly four months. She had found herself a comfortable niche at the hotel and was working hard to make herself indispensable.

It was a pleasant enough place and most of the locals were getting used to seeing her around. On a personal level, things hadn't worked out as she'd hoped. It had been her plan to ingratiate herself with Gary

Carmichael because she did actually really like him, God knows why, damnable man. So quiet, calm and above all decent; how on earth he had got under her skin she had no idea because she never got emotionally involved. From time to time she had thought of him since their paths crossed in Devon. Wondered what he was doing, if he was happy and settled. Well, she certainly had her answer to that! Not for the first time, she wondered if she was losing her touch as he remained aloof. Never being one for false modesty, she knew she was much younger and significantly more attractive than Lizzie Lockwood, who was not only approaching her mid-fifties but ungainly with no sense of style. For some reason Gary seemed to hang on her every word. Presumably he was in receipt of remuneration for running her portfolio; maybe she was paying for more than just his business skills.

Unfortunately, it seemed the connection she thought she had forged with him in Malching wasn't going to pay dividends, for now. Still, she was making sure her profile was sufficiently high that he couldn't ignore her completely because she had a bit of pride.

However, she was nothing if not pragmatic and not being one to wait wistfully in the wings, had made the most of her opportunities at the hotel. She employed her usual modus operandi of asking pertinent questions in a quiet, soothing but nonetheless persistent way until she found the Achilles heel of her intended target. In Mark Stevens' case it was hair. He had been a stylist before leaving the profession to run the hotel with his partner, Robin Corey. Whilst Robin looked after the business side of the enterprise, Mark took care of the day-to-day running of the establishment.

Over a few weeks she had cunningly managed to weave references to Mark's former occupation into their conversations and gently suggested they add a makeover to the hotel's gold standard wedding package.

In addition, he could offer some regular guests the opportunity of having their hair exclusively styled at the hotel during their stay, rather than visiting the rather drab little establishment in Rowendale. She drip fed her idea to him and each time he had cited the impracticality of the suggestion. However, Helen realised with an insightfulness she had acquired long ago, he was excited by the prospect.

Once he was sold on the idea in principle, he started being practical; pointing out that above anything else, there was nowhere to site a salon. Helen appeared to give the matter a lot of thought and then drew his attention to the large attic space that had hitherto been used only for storage.

'Hang on though, what about this place? It doesn't run itself,' he'd said, shaking his head.

'Oh absolutely! It's a complex operation and I'm amazed how you keep everything running so smoothly; that's true professionalism. If I could take any of the weight, Mark, you only have to ask. As you know, my background is in nursing home management, but the principle's the same, I'm sure.' Helen looked at him in wide eyed innocence in the hope of appearing sincere.

'Of course, you would still have full control and I would only ever be your assistant. I'd be drawing on your expertise every day I imagine, I mean you're a natural, that can't be taught, it's instinctive.'

Good God! If she laid it on any thicker she would make herself sick. After a lot of damned hard work she finally managed to convince Mark the whole idea was his brainchild. The things she had to do to earn a crust. She had feigned total surprise when Mark had told her that he and Robin were extending their top-of-the-range wedding package to include hairstyling, courtesy of the hotel's resident proprietor. They'd decided this was a rich vein of revenue which they should be exploring.

The result of her endeavours meant that the renovation of the roof space was nearing completion and a reporter from the local paper had been round to interview Robin and Mark. Somehow, she found herself in the vicinity when the photographer arrived and the guys had insisted she be in the shot, bless them. When the reporter asked about her role in planning the new venture, she'd played it down, obviously. She was nonetheless delighted to see when the article was published, the caption under the photo read; *"Fell View Hotel Management Team"*. Goodness knows where they'd got that idea from!

She apologised profusely, saying that she just couldn't understand how the reporter had made such a mistake. Both Robin and Mark assured her they didn't mind in the slightest and in fact, they would be delighted if she would consider taking on the role of assistant manager.

'What; you really want me to be part of the team?' Helen clasped her hands to her chest in amazement.

Her training started immediately. She balked at the idea of employing someone to take over her housekeeping duties; why would she want to relinquish control of any part of the empire she was building?

She ordered herself three black tailored suits and an impressive gold-effect magnetic name badge bearing the hotel logo with her name and the title "Executive Manager". If anyone asked, she would say it was a mistake and should have been "Assistant Manager" but no one did.

Most gratifying of all, was being asked by Robin to accompany him to a finance meeting with Gary. She spent an hour getting ready to make sure she looked her best. *There you are, Gary; see what you could have?* She wondered if he even noticed. At least he had been polite and wished her well in her new role.

Sadly, there were flies in the ointment. It had quickly become apparent that the peculiar letter wasn't a one off. They followed a now familiar pattern, usually saying something like:

"I'm watching you"; *"you can't fool everyone all of the time"*; *"leave here now"* and more menacingly; *"I know what you did in Malching"*.

She hoped the perpetrator would get bored but the letters continued to arrive regularly and it really was getting very tiresome. She wondered about having a word with Gary. He would be able give her some advice but she didn't want the whole Malchington Bay business brought up again. On balance, she decided to say nothing.

No sooner had she decided she could brazen it out, a second fly worked its rancid way to the surface. This appeared in the form of freelance investigative journalist and award-winning writer, Percival Lynton Whitaker from Balham.

Before him went a reputation for rooting out unpleasant truths as well as sensationalising and distorting facts to sell his tawdry articles to the highest bidder. He had a couple of regular articles with which he was synonymous.

There were his "Reasonable Doubt?" exposés which looked at past crimes and potential suspects and asked the public to be judge and jury regarding the guilt of those who had never faced trial. This was followed by thousands of readers and all sorts of rags queued up to run his sensationalised rubbish.

Then there were the "Back in Time" articles, where he took pride in uncovering the shabby behaviour or poor judgement of figures in the public eye or sometimes, ordinary people who had done nothing other than make a simple mistake. Suddenly, hitherto unsuspecting folk from all walks of life found themselves the subject of his unwanted attention.

His latest coup resulted in the suicide of a school headmaster a few weeks previously; although it did seem the wretched man had a lot of baggage. Getting stoned and paying for sex with teenage boys wasn't quite the attributes one would look for in a headmaster when choosing a school for one's child. And therein lay the problem; the occasional authentic exposé gave validation to all the other articles. Whitaker could do no wrong in the eyes of the public and it very much looked as if she was to be his next target.

He arrived on a Wednesday when Helen was in reception, covering sick leave. She smiled politely as he approached, welcomed him and asked if she could be of assistance.

'I do hope so; I'm Percival Whitaker and I'm given to understand that Helen Bell-Martin works here? From the photo I saw in your local paper the other day, I do believe I've just found her!' smiled the overweight journalist, somewhat breathlessly, as he proffered his right hand with nicotine-stained fingers.

'I've taken an interest in you ever since that dreadful business in Devon. I thought you were long gone but when I saw you, it was so fortuitous; almost like it was preordained. All I want is a little bit of your time and to offer you the chance to give your side of the Malchington Bay story. I'm a purveyor of truth, no more, no less. Dear lady, may I say the years have been kind to you.'

Her professional smile never left her face as she took his hand briefly. Damn and blast! Why had she been so stupid as to allow herself to feature in that promotional photograph?

'Mr Whitaker, on behalf of the management team, may I welcome you to Fell View Hotel. Do you have a reservation with us?'

'Yes indeed. My assistant booked a room for me so I'll see that first, followed by a stiff drink in the bar and an informal chat with your good self.'

'Unfortunately, Mr Whitaker, I'm going to be on duty until midnight and as I'm sure you'll understand it's highly unprofessional for a member of staff to meet a guest socially. We've allocated you a room which boasts an excellent view of the fells but if you would like something larger, I can easily move you and the additional cost is minimal.' The journalist replied he was going to be busy while he was in Blenthorne, so both the view from the window and size of room were immaterial.

Odious, arrogant man! She had successfully fobbed him off for a few hours but wondered how she was going to avoid him in the days to come? Maybe she should speak to Gary after all and whilst he wasn't her biggest fan, he had a profound sense of fairness and hopefully he wouldn't be indifferent to her plea for help if Whitaker got nasty.

Would she ever get a break? Everyone made mistakes but hers stuck to her like glue no matter where she went or what she tried to do.

*

The following day Helen set about her duties early. She liked to be at her post before the morning staff arrived. She checked her appearance in the mirror before leaving the small office. Trim, neat and tidy as always. She used minimal makeup, just a little lipstick and foundation subtly applied; the exception she made was her sky-coloured eyeliner which was strong and vibrant to highlight the depth of her deep blue, almost violet eyes.

She greeted the breakfast waiting staff warmly and in particular Mario Sanchez, the maître d'hôtel. They had a pleasant working relationship but no more than that. Mario's wife Dawn, kept him on a very tight rein and being ten to fifteen years his junior, clearly held his interest and attention at all levels.

She hoped she could continue to avoid Percival Whitaker but realised to do this indefinitely wouldn't be practical. Maybe she could give him a brief interview and he would leave. She realised how futile that thought was almost before it was formulated. He was a muckraker who wouldn't be satisfied until he had some unsavoury or salacious half-truths to bandy about for as much profit as possible. She decided to contact Gary, not specifically to ask for his help but to warn him that the journalist was sniffing around and would no doubt want to speak to him about his time in Malching.

She messaged him and his response was succinct and dismissive.

'What can he have discovered that's not already out there? Appreciate the warning but think I'm equal to the task of dealing with a third-rate hack. You're letting your imagination run riot. Ignore him.'

For an intelligent man, he was incredibly naïve.

*

When he was a small boy, Percival Lynton Whitaker's nanny had called him "Percy L" and that's how he thought of himself. He was Percy. Percy was a model citizen who paid his bills and never parked on double yellow lines. He was kind to animals and gave generously to charity, particularly when it was tax-deductible. Nevertheless, when needed, he could adopt all manner of different persona depending on the circumstances because, to do his job, he relied on his wits. When talking to the public he had to judge each situation on its merits; when to drop a little indirect innuendo, provoke a little controversy or spread a little gossip. He prided himself on being adept at catching his prey out even when they were on their guard; just a pause, a bit of non-verbal leakage or the odd inadvertent inflection was enough. Once he was on the right track he would sense it immediately.

He decided to be "Percy Patience" during his first days in Blenthorne. He got to know some of the locals, visited the shops and post office, bought drinks in the pub and gleaned what snippets he could about Helen Anderson. If he mistakenly dropped the name "Helen Bell-Martin" into the conversation after a few drinks, it was merely the alcohol loosening his tongue. After such an occurrence, he was quick to apologise and ask his companion, whomsoever that should be on any given occasion, to please disregard what he had said.

Having established a conspiratorial understanding with his drinking companion, "Percy Patience" became "Percy Persuasion" and he was soon able to get all sorts of pertinent questions answered, on the mistaken assumption that whatever he was told in return, he too would hold in confidence.

He had tried to extract some gossip from the pub manager, Maggie Blake but she was keeping schtum. He didn't push it; he knew when to back off. The barmaid, Mia wasn't particularly forthcoming either; a nice enough girl and quite attractive. He hadn't spoken to her mother, Andrea Pearce. She looked like she might be a penny short of a pound.

A rich source of information had presented itself in the jovial form of Colleen Plumley, a small round lady in her late fifties. She was the curator of a museum in Leeds, prior to taking early retirement. She had been born on a farm owned by her mother's family a few miles out of the village and since returning to Blenthorne, had been collating local documents and artefacts. She had begun displaying many of her treasures in a converted barn on the Barton estate and was attracting an ever increasing number of visitors. It appeared her hobby was rapidly turning into a successful business enterprise. Colleen prided herself on keeping up with the news and having no immediate family, she had little else to do socially, save interest herself in the lives of others.

It seemed she remembered the "Malchington Bay business" and after several gins, told Percival Whitaker that she was certain there was more to it than met the eye. Helen Anderson had been in the village for a few months and seemed very professional. However, in Colleen's opinion, her interest lay less with hotel management and more in a dogged yet thus far unsuccessful pursuit of Gary Carmichael, who oversaw several businesses in the area on behalf of his partner, Lizzie Lockwood. It was Colleen's belief that during the time Gary had spent in Malchington Bay, he had had a liaison with Helen

Anderson. When pushed, she admitted she had no evidence on which to base that assumption but why else would Helen have come here? Of course, Colleen didn't think Helen would stand much chance of success, not with Lizzie Lockwood on the scene but one never knew, did one? Had he met Lizzie yet? He shook his head.

'Now she's got a colourful past, if you get my meaning,' said Colleen confidentially.

He realised there was little point in trying to steer her away from the topic so let her tell him the whole story. In fact, he remembered the case well. Lizzie had pleaded guilty to voluntary manslaughter of a young woman, although there was a school of thought that she was covering for someone, probably the husband. Bottom line was, she'd served a prison sentence and had been released. He was looking for people who'd evaded justice, not those who'd confessed, even erroneously. He doubted he would hear anything new so switched to autopilot while his cheerful companion continued to talk, leaving a filter in place just in case there was something to whet his appetite. One had to sift through a mountain of gravel to find the tiniest nugget of gold.

As it happened, he was pleased that the diatribe hadn't been a complete waste of time; it might be that Colleen's musings had thrown up one or two interesting lines worthy of further enquiry. He contemplated kissing her for a split second but thankfully stopped himself before his exuberance got the better of him. Could be a runner; he'd take a closer look at Lizzie Lockwood, time permitting but first things first.

As for Helen Anderson, she was proving as elusive as ever. So far, he had managed to exchange no more than a few words with her. He had compiled a very interesting little dossier of her time in Malchington Bay as well as her earlier life. Obviously, it wouldn't be the end of the world if he published the article without an interview with the subject herself but it would carry much more weight if he could include some primary data. There was no rush; his bed was comfortable, the company bearable and the scenery pleasant. He could wait for as long as it took.

He was just leaving the pub after a convivial evening with a few locals and some visitors who were walking in the area, when he looked over and saw several people coming from the direction of the church hall. It must be choir practice night he thought absentmindedly, as he suppressed the desire to belch. He needed to urinate; should have gone before he left the pub. Could he wait until he got to the hotel? He was becoming a slave to his prostate; better to find a bush to be on the safe side. He stumbled slightly on uneven ground as he made his way from the path to the hedge beyond, hoping he wouldn't encounter any brambles or stinging nettles.

Through a tipsy haze, he could hear a hubbub of voices talking and laughing; he'd wait for the melee to disperse. Just when he thought they were probably far enough away for him to pee in private, one voice in particular caught his attention, a voice that struck a chord, one which took him back many, many years. There was something familiar... what was it? The cadence, the syntax... a phrase... now who did it remind him of? Oh goodness, yes, of course! But surely not? It couldn't be, could it... then again... he paused to fully absorb the impact of the possibilities this could create. Good Lord! He could hardly breathe for excitement. All thoughts of a full bladder were forgotten as he turned away from the bushes, found the path and strode purposefully into the night.

He reached the hotel with his mind racing. He would need to check his records but he was almost sure he was right, in spite of the alcohol he had imbibed. He never forgot a face or a voice. He needed to get to work. It was quite amazing how quickly one could sober up. The stimulation he experienced created an incredible adrenaline-infused high which surged through his body, creating a better effect than an entire bottle of whisky without the mind-numbing consequences. On the contrary, his thought processes were clear and sharp.

It was all so long ago; he had been a keen young reporter at the time, desperate to make an impression with his editor.

What a story it had been. In fact, it was fair to say, covering the events of that cold November evening nearly three decades ago had shaped his career. Not for him the tedious existence of the local hack, covering flower shows and reporting on novelists making book signing appearances in the ever hopeful attempt to turn their pitiful little ramblings into best sellers. Real life was at times far more thrilling than anything the most fertile or strange imagination could conjure up. Investigative journalism would be his niche.

In the beginning, his reporting had been genuine and sincere. But time and events had hardened him. He had witnessed several killers literally get away with murder due to a slick legal team; all the more reason for him to become a crusader for truth and justice. He realised he had to level the playing field and if that meant fighting dirty, then so be it. He greased a few constabulary palms and it was amazing what doors opened up to him; sight of the occasional file or tape here, eavesdropping on an interview there. The public were his jury; he was just the conduit, the narrator who laid the evidence before them. His prey may never serve custodial sentences but their lives were not too pleasant after one of his exposés. If they felt aggrieved, they could try their luck with a lawsuit.

If there weren't sufficient cases to pay for his profligate lifestyle, he amused himself with his "Back in Time" articles. Finding the skeletons-in-closets of the rich and famous and at times the mundane and humdrum, all helped keep the bailiffs from the door. As it was, in several cases, he had been paid more to keep his composition out of the public domain than he would have earned by publishing.

He would sell his dossier to the interested party who would then do with it as they wished; one former Cabinet minister said he was planning to incorporate Whitaker's work into his memoirs. Strangely, to date it had never appeared, despite the gentleman's distinguished career being immortalised in print; probably an oversight.

In fact, if the hapless Hopsmith had been an MP instead of a headmaster, he could have listed at least part of the payment under research expenses. It was a jolly good job British taxpayers didn't know what their hard-earned money was funding.

By and large his journalistic articles were based on real life events; all he did was add a little polish and embellishment along the way. And my word how they sold! Just as well, as he had two ex-wives and five children to support. Thankfully, editors were queuing up to publish his work. One of the red tops even tried to tie him to an exclusive deal. Now why would he do that when every exposé eclipsed the previous one and he could increase his fee accordingly? The public had an insatiable curiosity when it came to crime or scandal. Damnation of the guilty, or potentially guilty, was the currency in which he dealt and it was making him a fortune. He wondered what the merciless childhood bullies and the teachers who turned a blind eye thought when they read one of his articles? Not quite "Pathetic Percy Podge" now, was he?

He contacted Keith at the office in Balham and the file he needed was to be couriered to him post-haste. He had some information from an online search but wanted to be completely sure of his facts. The information he'd compiled at the time would make very interesting bedtime reading.

He hadn't forgotten about Helen Bell-Martin-Anderson, or whatever the exasperating woman was now called but he could feel his body tingle at the prospect of revisiting an old unsolved case. What a delightful diversion this would be.

Who could possibly have imagined that both Helen and another resident of this sleepy little village in the middle of nowhere could be harbouring such secrets? Incredibly, while he was here, he could potentially kill two birds with one stone.

Unfortunately for Percival Lynton Whitaker, he would have done well to remember two things; firstly, recognition is a two way street and secondly, it is not only birds that can be killed with a single stone.

Chapter 3 – Making Waves

Helen Anderson had been bracing herself for the past few days, lest Percival Whitaker should manage to ambush her but his interest seemed to be waning. Since the arrival of a large package she had hardly seen him. He locked himself away and refused to allow anyone to enter, even the cleaning staff. He took his meals in his room and collected a fresh supply of beverage sachets from reception every day but, that apart, spoke to no one. Helen sincerely hoped his incessant beavering didn't relate to her but as she hadn't granted him an interview, it was difficult to see what information he could have gleaned which would result in this change of behaviour. Surely he had already done his homework so wouldn't have needed to have additional information sent to him? Maybe something even more salacious had taken precedence in his rancid mind?

Just as she started to feel a little more relaxed, another letter arrived.

This was intolerable! She decided she would talk to Gary. It seemed highly unlikely that the letters were connected to Percival Whitaker as he was the peremptory type. He used his size and overbearing manner to intimidate his target. He thrived on confrontation as it allowed him to analyse and sensationalise reactions and this filled several paragraphs in his execrable articles, not to mention his bellicose self-congratulatory monthly blogs in which he tantalised and teased his fans and tormented his victims.

Helen reasoned anonymous letters were the work of someone furtive and underhanded; someone who was not confident enough for a face-to-face encounter. The tone of this latest missive unsettled her more than the previous letters.

"You're evil personified and should be punished. Keep looking over your shoulder, Helen."

Before she talked herself out of it again, she reached for her phone. When she disconnected the call a couple of minutes later, she was pleasantly surprised. Gary hadn't dismissed her concerns out of hand, in fact he had told her he would meet her for a drink at the Blenny later and she should take the letters with her. Public place; he clearly didn't want to be alone with her. Nevertheless, things were looking up; now she just had to decide what to wear.

By six o'clock, Helen was settled into an armchair near the fireplace in the lounge bar of the Blenthorne Inn, sipping a vodka and tonic. It seemed Gary was actually quite pleased to see her.

From her position behind the bar, Lizzie was surveying the room, like a large eagle overseeing her eyrie. Helen looked suspiciously at the drink which Gary placed on the table before she tried it but common sense told her it was highly unlikely the proprietor of the pub had actually spiked it, no matter how much she would probably have relished doing so.

Gary had the letters spread before him on the table, Helen having already taken each from its envelope.

'Surely it's just the work of some crank; I hardly know why I didn't throw them away,' she said, as she studied his reaction.

'I'm very glad you didn't; things like this shouldn't be ignored. They've been arriving since shortly after you came to Blenthorne, you say?' he asked as he picked one up and examined it, having donned disposable gloves first.

Helen nodded. 'Isn't that a little over the top?' she asked when she saw him pull the small glove packet from his pocket.

'Probably, it's highly unlikely there are any discernible prints that would be of use forensically but at least they won't have to eliminate mine.' He smiled faintly.

That was a pleasant surprise. She wasn't actually sure he could do anything other than frown. Even when they were together in Devon briefly, he always seemed rather melancholy but maybe that enigmatic quality had added to the attraction. He was speaking to her again; she needed to play this for all it was worth.

'No dates on the letters. Maybe I should check the envelopes unless you're sure this is the correct order in which they arrived?' he looked at her intently.

'Oh absolutely without a doubt, the first one is crumpled as my instinctive reaction was to screw it up and chuck it in the bin. Then I thought maybe I should keep it just in case another arrived,' she paused, moving a little closer to her companion, crossing her legs and tucking an imaginary stray strand of hair behind her left ear before she continued;

'Shame this isn't the fifties, maybe a misaligned key on a typewriter would give us a clue as to the identity of the writer. As it is, the letters have been word-processed and could have come from anywhere. I saw a film once where the culprit was caught out by…'

'Still forensically traceable if we could find the device, even if the writer deleted the file,' interrupted Gary, clearly completely unimpressed by her recollection of an old movie. 'To do that though, we have to have some idea of who we're looking for. Without a doubt, we should pass these letters over to the police.'

'Can't you find out? I don't want to make it official. There would inevitably be all sorts of questions about Malching and I am trying so hard to put that all behind me. I mean, it must be someone local, mustn't it? I think *"leave here"* gives a clue, otherwise it would say *"leave Blenthorne"*. Also, if the sender wasn't here, why would they want me to leave? I think my presence must pose a threat to them, although I can't imagine who could possibly believe that, can you?'

'Why do you say "threat"?'

'I don't know; maybe not a threat then. Maybe I just make someone feel unsettled or uncomfortable; maybe they feel insecure in a relationship?' Would Gary pick up on the inference she wondered, not that she seriously thought it was Lizzie but it wouldn't hurt to plant that seed in his brain. His next question demonstrated he clearly hadn't made any such connection.

'Has there been any other contact? Have you been approached in any other way? Phone calls or items left at the hotel?'

'What sort of items?' asked Helen, looking vaguely alarmed.

'Anything out of the ordinary; something arriving that you didn't order?'

'Oh I see, I thought you meant like dead rodents thrown over my car bonnet or some such,' she said with a bit of a grimace as she drained the last of her drink.

'Now that would be pretty weird! You haven't, have you? Another?' he asked pleasantly, as he put the letters back into their envelopes and removed his gloves.

Helen smiled and shook her head at the first question and then acquiesced to the second as she passed her glass to her companion. 'Same again please; oh no, best not, I have ten hens arriving first thing tomorrow so make it an orange juice.'

She looked round as Gary went to the bar. Lizzie barely exchanged a word with him as she filled the glasses; why did he put up with her? He could get a job anywhere, plus he must have a pretty good pension, so he wasn't short of a bob or two. She looked around the room with casual interest.

She didn't recognise the dark haired woman sitting with her back to the window at the next table but the chap with her was a rather nice local farmer called Jack Barton. He must have noticed her glancing in his direction as he looked over and smiled. His lady friend was no doubt Mrs Barton; why was there always a wife? They seemed to be quite at home exchanging pleasantries with several of the locals.

It was Mario's night off from the hotel restaurant and he was sitting with his wife, Dawn, along with the strange woman from the post office. They made an unlikely threesome but seemed to have a shared enjoyment of crisps. One would have thought someone on Mario's salary could have stretched to a packet each; the cheapskate.

She noticed that Andrea Pearce and her employer Jono Johnson were also having a drink together. Helen wondered, not for the first time, if they were actually an item. Although if so, why did they bother to keep it quiet? She admonished herself; she was turning into Colleen Plumley, the museum curator. One busybody per village was mandatory but any more was positively an indulgence.

Think of the devil, there she was on the other side of the bar with her assistant, Tim Carney, proofreader, would-be poet and thriller writer. He hadn't been around the village much over the last couple of weeks, no doubt busy working on his latest manuscript. Presumably the literary world was thus far underwhelmed by his efforts; hence his need to supplement his income by working at the museum, though that couldn't pay much. He wasn't an unattractive young man, superficially at least; quite dark and athletic-looking, mid-thirties and roughly average height. Of course, being a pauper, he wasn't worth a second glance but some women found that appealing. Not her, perish the thought. She suspected his charms were probably lost on Colleen too. Gary's return interrupted her thoughts.

'I've just worked out what you meant when you said "ten hens". For a moment I thought Robin and Mark had decided to raise poultry but then I realised you were referring to a hen party,' he smiled wryly as he placed her drink on the table and sat down opposite her again.

Helen tugged the hem of her short black skirt in the direction of her knees as she laughed out loud, catching her breath slightly as she did so. Her body language was clearly not lost on Lizzie who gave her a frosty stare as she polished a glass which, given the amount of effort it apparently needed, must be totally filthy.

Helen started to relax, even enjoy herself a little. She let her guard down a smidgen and horror upon horrors, she overstepped the mark.

'If you're looking for poison pen candidates, maybe your partner would be a good place to start, she obviously dislikes me with a vengeance and I've no idea why,' she blurted out before she could stop herself.

'What? Of course she doesn't; she's the least judgemental person I've ever met and more to the point, she has no reason to dislike you,' said Gary dismissively.

'Maggie Blake, she's no better. I spoke to her in the street yesterday; she virtually blanked me! I mean at the end of the day, Gary, is Lizzie so insecure that she needs Maggie riding shotgun?' added Helen, with a small, ironic laugh.

It was supposed to be a light hearted throw away remark to deflect attention from her first faux pas but of course, as is usual when trying to make things better, she had just made the situation ten times worse. Any deeper and she'd need a ladder to get out of the hole she'd just dug.

Every muscle in Gary's body seemed to tense and he immediately stood up.

'I'll speak to an ex-colleague of mine regarding these letters without delay; is it okay for me to keep them?' He didn't wait for her to reply as he gathered the letters together.

Helen nodded. 'Gary, I'm sorry, I didn't mean…'

'Enjoy your drink and I hope your hen party doesn't cause too many problems,' he said tersely.

How could she have been so stupid! This had been her best opportunity to date and she'd blown it. Helen watched as Gary walked quickly towards the exit. She saw him hold the door open for the vicar and his wife, who were entering as he was leaving. She tried to resist the temptation to glance in Lizzie's direction but failed. Lizzie seemed deep in conversation with Andrea and Jono but Helen was sure she was aware of Gary's abrupt departure.

Hell and damnation! Weeks of preparation; shot to pieces in seconds. Her thoughts were interrupted as she became aware of a figure standing close behind her. She twisted slightly in her chair and saw the large and thoroughly unwelcome form of Percival Whitaker looming, his crumpled suit jacket flapping open and brushing her shoulder. So absorbed was she by her former companion, she hadn't noticed the repugnant man enter the bar.

'Dear lady, what a lovely surprise; can I get you another?' he asked, pointing at her glass, as he moved around studying his surroundings and no doubt gauging his audience.

'Thank you but I'm just leaving, Mr Whitaker,' said Helen hoping she kept any hint of panic out of her voice.

'Oh, just a few minutes of your time if you would be so kind; I promise I won't keep you long.' He was circling her table like a shark. Helen found herself hoping he might trip over the fireplace fender but he deftly sidestepped the obstacle.

'To be honest, your story, interesting though it undoubtedly is, has slipped down my list,' he announced loudly to the ceiling as he walked round and plonked himself down in the seat opposite her, placing his glass on the table.

'Really, have you found someone else to… pursue?' asked Helen in a measured tone.

'Let's just say I've made an amazing discovery since I've been here and I'm very much looking forward to the possibility of… now what shall we call it… how about "working together with a particular party"? Hark! Ears twitching, lips drying, the odd hand shaking; I do believe my words are resonating within these walls.' He paused to take a large gulp from his pint, as he allowed his gaze to travel around the bar; resting here, there and nowhere in particular.

Indistinct voices from the public bar drifted across a now almost silent lounge. Helen felt her silk blouse sticking to her back and wondered if she were the only person holding her breath.

'Coming to Blenthorne has indeed been fortuitous because the coincidences of life never cease to amaze me. Who would have thought our paths would converge again after all these years… but then why not? Everyone has to live somewhere and where better than a sleepy little place like this, if one wants to reinvent oneself? Anyway, I'm digressing. Basically, Helen, if we can't talk now, could you give me ten minutes, say sometime over the weekend? I promise I'll be sympathetic. No offence but currently I have other fish to fry.'

Helen almost dared to hope. Was he saying what she thought? Was he going to leave her alone if she granted him an interview and move on to ply his tawdry trade elsewhere?

'There really is nothing I can add to the information already in the public's possession,' declared Helen, aware that all eyes were on her as the gathered ensemble continued to watch the uncomfortable encounter.

'Come now, Helen; we both know that's not the case,' replied the journalist with a slight tilt of his freckled, slightly sweaty, balding pate.

She crossed her legs and twisted her body away from him as she finished her drink.

He drained his glass and stood up, breathing heavily. As he did so, he bent forward and whispered to her. The small smile she had allowed herself froze on her face as she stared straight ahead. To any observant onlooker it may have appeared she had suddenly seen an apparition.

Helen felt her whole body smart as a result of the comment dropped in her ear. She looked out of glazed eyes as she digested the words. Even after the hack had moved away from her table, she could still see his florid, blotchy face and smell his stale breath which had wafted around her like a miasma. She stood up unsteadily as she watched his large frame make its way towards the door. Hard to believe that earlier in the evening she had thought of Lizzie Lockwood as her nemesis.

*

After leaving Helen in the bar, Gary had contacted Detective Sergeant Ken Stokes to advise him about the anonymous letters. He was delighted when Ken invited him round for a shandy or two while Mrs S was at her exercise class.

Upon Gary's arrival, Ken wasted no time in reading the letters.

'Helen Anderson; how well do you know her?' asked Ken, as he leaned back in his armchair having just pulled the ring from his can of lager. 'Cheers, good to see you looking so well! Wouldn't hurt for you to put on a bit of weight though and make me feel a bit better. I keep telling Mrs S it's muscle but she insists it's cake,' he laughed as he patted his substantial midriff.

Gary smiled. 'You've been that shape ever since I've known you. To answer your question, I met Helen a few years ago; it was when Lizzie was inside. I travelled to Malchington Bay for Doug Maxwell's funeral. You remember Doug; he was a DS in Carlisle? I'm sure your paths must have crossed.'

'I knew him by sight but we never actually worked together as far as I can remember. Malchington Bay, now there's a place to avoid from what I read in the press at the time! You weren't there when the shit hit the fan over that nursing home business, were you?'

'Oh, I was there alright.' Gary went on to tell Ken briefly what he knew of Helen's involvement. 'She swore she was innocent,' he added.

'Did you believe her?'

'She was pretty convincing and I briefly got a bit too close to her but looking back I'm not sure my judgement was as clear as it should have been after Lizzie went to prison.' Gary paused; 'I was never happy about Lizzie's confession, but as you know, she wouldn't budge.'

'Has she ever talked about it since?'

Gary shook his head. 'I promised not to go there. It was a condition of our getting together; I have to respect that. But I will always firmly believe she was protecting her husband, Jim.'

'That's loyalty for you. I know there was a lot of doubt at the time regarding her culpability but what do you do in the face of a confession? Anyway, back to Helen; if I've got this correct, it appears she was caught up in whatever was going on in Malchington Bay and now she's receiving hate mail. On the face of it, she seems to be a victim twice over.'

'Basically, yes,' agreed Gary, nodding as he drained his shandy.

'Leave these with me, I'll get Gina to see what she can unearth,' said Ken, gesticulating towards the pile of letters, as he finished his can.

'Gina Williams? I thought she'd have been long gone; fast track wasn't she?' questioned Gary.

'Yes, until she cut one corner too many. She was lucky to stay in CID at all. As it is, looks like I'm stuck with her for the foreseeable future. I'm a calming influence apparently,' Ken chuckled, trying in vain to look modest.

'There's something else,' said Gary and went on to tell his friend of Helen's alarm at the arrival in the village of the investigative journalist, Percival Whitaker.

'Does he have anything on her?' asked Ken, looking at his companion shrewdly.

'I told her if she had been totally honest at the time, what more was there for him to discover by following her to Blenthorne? She still seemed very worried about it though.'

The two old friends chatted for another few minutes but Gary was mindful of the duration of Mrs Stokes' class and took his leave just prior to her return, thereby missing the interrogation regarding his relationship with the infamous Lizzie Lockwood.

Gary pondered Ken's words as he drove home. It did seem strange that Helen should attract so much ill-will. Moreover, the arrival of the journalist had apparently shaken her, yet Gary hadn't seen hide-nor-hair of him, so his investigations clearly hadn't stretched beyond a few gossipy conversations with the locals. Surely if he was hell bent on attempting to expose her in some way, he would be putting a bit more enthusiasm into his task?

Maybe the truth was simpler; she hadn't received the welcome she had hoped for in Blenthorne, so why not manufacture or manipulate events to grab his attention? Could it be that Helen had invited Percival Whitaker to the village? Was it also possible she had written the letters to herself?

*

The following morning, Gary's mobile phone rang just before seven o'clock. It was Helen. She was screeching hysterically; birds and rats, something about birds and rats. He tried to hide his irritation as he spoke in low measured tones in an attempt to calm her down. He told her he would come to the hotel in an hour or so.

'What on earth was all that about?' asked Lizzie as she rubbed the sleep from her eyes.

Gary explained briefly and said he would fill her in when he returned and suggested they could have brunch together if she wasn't tied up with her resettlement ladies at Hope Cottage.

'It's okay, you do what you have to and we'll catch up later. I'll want all the juicy details though!'

Gary showered, shaved and dressed, by which time Lizzie was downstairs and had made tea and toast. He promised to ring her when he was free and kissed her as he left the house. When he got to the hotel, Mark Stevens met him at the door.

'Helen's in a dreadful state and I'm not surprised, the poor lamb. Have you seen her car?'

'Her car, no, what's wrong with it? I couldn't really understand what she was saying over the phone,' said Gary slightly impatiently. 'Something about birds and rats, or was it rabbits?'

Mark ignored him. 'I wanted to call the police because although there's no actual damage that I can see, throwing all that stuff over someone's vehicle is just a wicked, cruel thing to do. Anyway, Helen seemed totally averse to the idea of making it official and I didn't want to upset her further by going behind her back. As it was, she said she'd rung you as soon as she discovered what had happened. Who would do a thing like that?'

'On the face of it, I've no idea, Mark. Where's Helen now?' asked Gary.

'In her room on the top floor at the back, next to the bathroom, she said to tell you to go up when you arrived.'

'I'll go and look at the car first and then I'll meet her in the lounge if that's okay with you, I don't suppose there are too many guests around at this time of day?' Gary was mindful not to be alone with Helen on her own territory; he'd made that mistake in Malching and he wasn't going to repeat it.

'Actually, we have hens all over the place, so best use the office,' suggested his host.

'Hens, yes of course the hen party. I remember Helen telling me they were arriving imminently.' Gary also remembered earlier in the same conversation with Helen when she had suggested she might find something unpleasant on her car. Now it had happened; the most amazing coincidence or…? He walked along the driveway towards the back of the building, his feet crunching on the gravel. He had a feeling that he was being watched from an upstairs window but resisted the temptation to look in that direction.

Helen's convertible was parked in the left hand corner of the carpark. It was facing the tall laurel hedge which surrounded that part of the property. On its windscreen was a white substance which looked like flour interspersed with streaks of yellow, probably egg. Strewn across the bonnet was a large amount of detritus; rotting food scraps and plastic along with a couple of rats and a vole in addition to two birds; a thrush and a blackbird if Gary was correct in his ornithological interpretation. There appeared to be no other damage visible. That was slightly strange in itself; the average vandal usually cannot help but add the odd scratch to a quality motor. He remembered from his days as a beat copper, one rather dim individual who etched his name into the nearside door; it didn't take too long to apprehend him.

Gary took out his mobile and messaged Ken Stokes. He received an almost immediate reply informing him that DC Gina Williams would be attending as soon as possible. Mark Stevens appeared from the direction of the back door.

'Isn't it awful? I've been telling Robin for ages we need CCTV covering this area. We have to move with the times. As I said to him last week, just because we haven't had any sort of problem yet, it doesn't mean we never will. If we had surveillance then we would know who the culprit was, wouldn't we? As it is, it could be anyone.'

As they walked back to the hotel reception, Gary thought the list of suspects could be narrowed considerably. In fact, it really came down to those present in the lounge bar when Helen had given him the anonymous letters. However, his money was on the lady herself. She would have had access to the food waste from the hotel and the smallholding next door had a never ending supply of dead birds that somehow managed to get under the fruit nets and then not find a way out. As for the rodents, living in such a rural area, a trap or two set with cheese or chocolate would always attract small, greedy vermin. Helen could easily have set up this scene, although clearly she couldn't quite bring herself to inflict any damage on her precious convertible.

He would shortly see what sort of performance she could produce as he made his way to the hotel office.

An hour later, he felt his suspicions were justified. He had neatly side stepped the lunge she had attempted and in fact avoided any physical contact, for which he congratulated himself. As he left, he arranged to see DC Williams back at the Blenny after she had interviewed Helen.

*

When they met up later at the pub, Gina greeted Gary like an old friend before they sat down at a small round table in the lounge bar. He didn't recall them being on such congenial terms from his days in the service but she was clearly working hard on her interpersonal skills.

'I've asked forensics to take a look at the convertible. We'll see what they come up with. As you said, doesn't look like there's any real damage and taken on its own, maybe just a prank but coupled with the letters that the DS passed to me this morning, it might take on a more sinister significance.'

Gary then outlined his theory regarding Helen.

Gina looked surprised. 'But why would she do that; attention seeking?'

'I don't think we should rule that out as a possibility. I think Helen Anderson has her own agenda. However, I could be wrong.'

Gina got to her feet, smiling. 'I'll be in touch in a day or two when we get some results back from the lab regarding the letters. Hopefully we can wrap this up quickly. I haven't been here for years you know, not even for a drink or a meal, strange really as it's a quaint little place.'

Little did either the retired police inspector or the detective constable realise but in a short while Gina Williams would be spending considerably more time in the vicinity than she could possibly have imagined.

Chapter 4 – A Serious Misjudgement

Percival Lynton Whitaker was feeling inordinately pleased with himself. After several days holed up in his hotel room, he'd granted himself a night off yesterday. Not in his wildest dreams had he imagined what fun he was going to have! Bumping into Helen was particularly fortuitous as it allowed him to stir things up a bit with the regulars at the pub. The delightful little delicacy he'd recently uncovered would be the tasty appetiser before the main course.

He had reeled her in beautifully; allowed her to think he was going to let her off the hook, which of course he was, for now. Then, as she dared to relax, he whispered a little snippet into her ear. It had just been a couple of words. Two tiny words and Helen's world had somersaulted. He knew he'd hit home from the way she blanched.

He pulled himself back to the here and now. First things first, as he had told Helen, he had other fish to fry and indeed that was partly true; his next catch would be hooked and hung out to dry and then in the fullness of time, it would be her turn to be dangling from his line. Goodness, he really was on form tonight; wasn't there a metaphor about a sprat to catch a mackerel? He really must include something along those lines in his next blog.

He climbed into bed thinking about the following day. He'd received a tantalising call early that morning which had necessitated some quick thinking on his part but years of practice had stood him in good stead and he now had a meeting arranged for the morrow. The agreed venue was a remote spot, suggesting the subject matter required complete privacy. Oh yes, he was going to enjoy this and who knew what might be elicited?

He went back to thinking about the subheading for his current exposé which he had been working on most of the day. He'd need to think of a title. Maybe it should be something like; *"The Leopard That Changed Its Spots"*. That would be good enough for now and it was certainly very apt. He pulled a tissue from the box provided on the bedside table and scribbled the words down.

He had everything he needed from the old material and had already wrapped the file carefully. He would take it to the post office first thing; no need to courier it back to Balham. After some cross-checking and a lot of internet research, his article was almost ready.

Now he had to turn his attention to the next day. He sighed with satisfaction as he gently drifted off into that pre-sleep state when reality becomes a floating pontoon for abstract ideas and random thoughts, blissfully unaware of the events awaiting him.

*

Earlier than usual the following morning, Percival Lynton Whitaker consumed a full English breakfast in his room. For once, he didn't return to the desk to sit at his laptop in front of the window, as had been his wont for several preceding days. Percival was old-school and although he was a touch-typist, he had been brought up in the days of manual typewriters so whilst he knew there was no need to thump, he couldn't help himself. If he were perfectly honest, he still missed his old portable; they had been together a long time, about forty years if memory served and the dear old thing didn't need a password to perform its function. He kept forgetting he couldn't just start typing on this beast and had lost count how many times he'd had to ask Keith to reset the damned thing. He had it written down now. Still took an age to "load" or "spool" or whatever the faffing-about was called. However, he had to grudgingly admit it did have advantages. After accessing information through the browser, thoughts flooded his brain and transformed themselves effortlessly into sentences as his fingers flew furiously across the keys in an attempt to keep pace. Today however, guests and staff alike would be spared his pounding.

Goodness, there was his phone ringing again. He really was "Percy Popular" all of a sudden! Of course he shouldn't be surprised as he'd liberally spread his contact details around, so clearly this was another worried party wanting to unburden themselves.

After a couple of minutes he disconnected the call. Through the mist, he could just make out the fells as he stood next to the desk by his window and smiled to himself. He needed to get a move on.

He quickly showered, shaved and put on a brushed cotton checked shirt with black sweatshirt and blue jeans. He hummed a little tune as the smug grin he'd allowed himself in the bathroom refused to budge from his face. He slipped on his new lightweight trainers which he'd bought specifically for the trip north. He decided this ensemble would be suitably casual gear to give the appearance of a planned walk.

He picked up his rucksack and stuffed his phone, laptop and the packaged file into it. After a quick look round, he believed he had all he needed and after opening the window to allow in some much needed fresh air, he swapped the *"Do Not Disturb"* for the *"Please Tidy Room"* sign on the handle, locking the door behind him. He hoped the residual smoke would dissipate in his absence. If not, he would no doubt be fined for contamination and also for disabling the alarm, if the staff realised what he'd done before he left.

Karen, the receptionist, appeared delighted to hear he was planning to walk for the day but expressed reservations that he was suitably attired for such an excursion due to weather conditions being unpredictable.

'You can get caught out at any time on the fells you know, because the weather just closes in on you so it can be sunny one minute then thick fog the next. Jeans really aren't a good idea, Mr Whitaker, as they absorb far too much moisture and get very heavy; you need something that will dry quickly and not hamper you. There is a very good outdoor clothing shop just along the road, so you could pop in there before you set off. They have all sorts of equipment as well. You'll definitely need a map, compass and whistle if nothing else. You can get walking boots next door,' she added, leaning over the desk and glancing at his trainers. 'Take some water and a few energy bars, just in case. Oh and please don't forget to enter your route in the book before you leave,' she pointed at the open book on the large mahogany table to the right of the foyer, which also bore a display of lilies under a mirror fixed to the wall.

Percival gave her one of his slightly condescending smiles. 'Never fear, I'm well prepared for what I'm about to do today. No doubt you'll be pleased I've vacated my room so it can be thoroughly cleaned prior to my return later.'

He paused as he walked towards the front door and looked back in the direction of the desk.

'I'll be back in time for dinner, make a reservation in the restaurant for me for eight o'clock, if you would be so kind.'

As he strode purposefully away, Helen Anderson walked up to the reception desk, almost as if she had been waiting for their guest to leave.

'What did he say to you, Karen? Did he mention where he's going?' she asked, seemingly nonchalantly.

'Walking, apparently; I told him he was ill-prepared. In fact, thinking about it, he would be better off going on one of the guided walks that Jono Johnson organises. Oh, and he didn't enter his destination into the walking book. He can't say he wasn't warned. I mean, he could get lost couldn't he, or have a fall?'

'With any luck,' said Helen quietly as she checked her watch and walked towards the office.

*

Roughly an hour later, Percival Lynton Whitaker also checked his watch. He had dispatched his package at the post office in the village via the veritable spinster behind the counter and had driven two and a half miles west. He had parked at the agreed meeting point but, so far at least, it appeared he was alone.

It was an overcast day with a hint of mist snaking down through the V-shape created between two fells. What was the difference between a fell and a mountain? He had no idea. Percival reached into the back seat for his outer garments. He climbed out of the car and noticed a distinct chill in the air; he wrapped his dark coloured woollen scarf tightly around his neck and then pulled on his green waxed jacket. The small carpark had a low drystone wall about three feet in height to the left side with the aptly named Dark Tarn beyond.

The rhythmic lapping of the water being agitated by the breeze was the only sound breaking the silence of the morning, save the occasional forlorn twitter of a passing bird. Percival did a complete turn and was disappointed to note he was still by himself. He walked slowly over and looked down into the water. He could see a shaky shadow cast by his reflection. He then suddenly realised that another shadow had joined his and was moving ever closer. He was surprised that anyone could have appeared so quickly and silently, seemingly out of nowhere.

He made to turn but didn't complete the manoeuvre. He felt a sudden sharp pain at the back of his head and realised in a flash that he had seriously misjudged the situation. This wasn't supposed to happen; he'd made a schoolboy error in allowing his back to be exposed. He was aware of putting his right hand up towards his head as the world started to wobble before his eyes and suddenly he seemed to be floating. Daylight became intermittent as confusion and darkness tried their best to claim him. He forced his eyes to stay open and just in front of him, could see Nanny levitating above the water; she looked quite cross as she admonished him.

'Percy L? Who's been a very foolish boy? There won't be any dippy egg soldiers for supper tonight.'

If he was aware of hitting the cold grey water a few seconds later, no sound emanated from his semi-conscious body.

Had anyone been watching, they would have seen a darkly clad, hooded figure wait for a moment by the water's edge and then walk quietly to the journalist's car to make a cursory search of the inside. The nimble figure then proceeded to remove the keys from the ignition and walk around to the rear of the vehicle. The boot opened moments later and gave up its contents in an instant. With the journalist's rucksack firmly on their back and the car keys replaced in the ignition, the darkly clad figure slipped silently away.

The sun made a sudden dramatic appearance as the clouds momentarily parted, painting a picture of tranquil serenity. The breeze was gently swirling as the birds started singing in earnest. The water had been displaced briefly as it swallowed its uninvited guest but quickly regained its former equipoise with little more than a brief gurgle. The only tangible reminder of human impingement on this scene of nature in all her glory was a family-sized saloon car. Of its driver, there was no sign.

*

Mario Sanchez, the maître d' at Fell View Hotel, looked at the single place setting near the window in the dining room. The time was nine fifteen; an hour and a quarter after the time for which Mr Whitaker had booked his table. The hotel restaurant remained busy; the hen party showed no sign of leaving anytime soon but they were ordering plenty of wine and not causing a nuisance to the other diners so no harm was being caused. He ran a tight ship and no rowdy behaviour would be tolerated. His tall and stately presence alone usually ensured this never happened. He discreetly left his post to go to reception to request a call to room number fifteen however, if Mr Whitaker was there, he failed to answer. Mario decided to leave the place setting for another half hour.

At nine forty-five he gave instructions for the table to be cleared and thereafter advised reception that Mr Whitaker would need to use the hotel's limited night-time room service, courtesy of the night porter, should he require sustenance upon his return.

He walked the short distance home at eleven forty-five and arrived at the rented cottage he shared with his wife, Dawn, ten minutes later. As he climbed into bed, after putting his suit jacket on a hanger and his trousers into the press, he remarked that modern technology should make it extremely easy for someone to cancel a dinner reservation, particularly one they had only made that morning. Dawn was undoubtedly awake but didn't seem to hear him; at least if she did, she chose not to respond.

*

Gary Carmichael walked towards the pub shortly after ten fifteen the following morning. It was a bright and pleasant day with a little autumnal breeze and only a few high clouds peering down on the village which always looked its best when bathed in sunshine.

He had just left Lockwood's after a productive meeting with Carl, the executive chef. In his earliest memory of the place, it had been an old barn, used for storage. Lizzie had renovated it several years previously and turned it into a fine dining restaurant. The meeting he had planned with Maggie was their regular monthly catch up. Most of the processes could be conducted electronically but Gary liked the hands-on approach. His mobile rang as he walked through the back door, after Maggie responded to his gentle tap.

His heart sank slightly when he saw the identity of the caller but answered the call nonetheless.

'Morning, Helen, how are you?' he tried to sound pleasant and upbeat.

'What? Um, I need a bit of advice actually. It's Whitaker the journalist; he went out yesterday morning but he didn't come back last evening.'

She went on to explain the exchange with the receptionist the previous morning.

'I mean, Karen did tell him how dangerous the fells can be if you're not properly prepared for the conditions. And she told him to leave his intended route plan in the book, which he didn't do, so he's only got himself to blame really and well, he just didn't come home. I checked his room this morning.

It was exactly as the cleaner left it yesterday. He's been out all night.'

'He may have stayed elsewhere; he wouldn't be the first walker to set off and fail to return to his original destination, particularly if he was as ill-prepared as you say. He probably ended up miles from here and booked into another hotel overnight,' suggested Gary. 'He'll most likely arrive in a taxi at any moment, looking a little shamefaced but none the worse for wear.'

'I hope you're right but I've tried his mobile and there's no reply. What shall I do? Robin and Mark have gone away for a few days; they left early this morning before we knew Whitaker was missing. What will they think if I've got a problem I can't deal with? What sort of impression will that make?'

Gary noted Helen's main concern was for her own reputation rather than the welfare of a hotel guest. Knowing how she felt about the chap, it wasn't too surprising. Also from what he knew of her, altruism wasn't high on her list of attributes.

'If you've had no luck getting through, I suppose you should report it. Obviously you have a duty of responsibility towards any guest staying with you. Give it until lunchtime and if he's not back, ring the police; not much use contacting the local mountain rescue team if no one knows where he was headed.'

'Yes, I know you're right, damn it! Why on earth did he have to come here?'

Gary listened politely for a couple more minutes until Maggie had made coffee and was clearly waiting for him.

She looked at him sharply as he returned his mobile to his jacket pocket. 'Don't tell me, I don't want to know; if it's anything to do with that woman it's bound to be some sort of catastrophe that only you can deal with. What did she want this time?'

'You just said you didn't want to know,' said Gary innocently, earning a glare from Maggie.

'Guest has gone missing; Percival Whitaker, the journalist.'

'Oh, the one that planned to write a piece on her? Now isn't that fortuitous? Before he can dish the dirt, he disappears. Why's she calling you? She should contact the police, or does she expect you to drop everything and go out and look for him?'

'I hardly think so. As you probably heard, I told her to report him missing if he's not back by lunchtime. Now, shall we get on?'

Maggie pulled the special face she reserved exclusively for Helen Anderson as she clicked onto the spreadsheet, of which Gary had an electronic copy on his laptop. After about twenty minutes they finished looking at the figures and talked about Maggie's idea for a special promotion for the following month. Gary turned down the offer of food and was about to make his way to the adventure holiday company when his phone rang again.

'Oh my word, she's really keeping you busy today. You should block her number.'

Gary ignored his companion as he rose from his seat and wandered over to the window before taking the call. 'Ken, hello, what can I do for you?' He listened intently for several minutes and asked a few questions. Afterwards he responded to Maggie's enquiring look.

'That was Ken Stokes, they've found Percival Whitaker,' said Gary looking at the floor and shaking his head as he returned to his seat.

'What did I tell you? That bloody woman making a mountain out of a molehill again! Where was he? Enjoying all the fuss, I expect!'

'As to where he was, I can tell you that; as to whether or not he enjoyed being centre of attention I fear that's highly unlikely,' he paused as Maggie looked at him expectantly.

'A couple of walkers parked their car by Dark Tarn at the bottom of Drew's Ridge. Before setting off towards the fell, they noticed something floating in the water. Ken said they were planning to ignore it but then noticed a hand protruding from a sleeve.'

Maggie put her hand over her mouth and she gasped. 'Oh Lord, no, the journalist?'

Gary nodded and was about to speak when Maggie interrupted him.

'Saints preserve us! Is he dead? Oh, he must be if he was found floating, I suppose,' she reasoned with herself logically.

'Yes, no signs of life when his body was retrieved,' replied Gary nodding his head.

'Had he fallen in?' asked Maggie optimistically.

'It would be nice to think so, wouldn't it? We'll have to wait for the post mortem results. If not, of course, then that adds a whole different dimension. I had better go and see if Helen's okay because the police will have told her by now,' Gary stood up to leave.

'Yes, that's a good idea. Go running round to the hotel to make sure she's not had an attack of the vapours. That won't send out the wrong signals, will it?' said Maggie sarcastically as she exhaled and threw her hands in the air.

'Robin and Mark have gone away for a few days, therefore as assistant manager, Helen will need support from a representative of the management company, which as I'm sure you're aware, is me.' Gary tried to keep the irritation out of his voice and chose not to make any eye contact with the disgruntled pub manager.

'Why did Ken Stokes phone you anyway?' asked Maggie rather petulantly.

'Because I spoke to him about the letters Helen had received and her worries about Percival Whitaker.'

He left a few minutes later after placating Maggie as best he could and rang Jono at the holiday company to postpone their meeting. He wondered with trepidation what sort of hysterical state Helen would be in when he arrived at the hotel.

When he walked across the forecourt at Fell View, he realised things had moved on apace. There were two marked police cars in the carpark and a dark saloon which Gary knew was allocated to CID. Gina Williams was in the foyer as he walked through the open entrance. He wondered rather absentmindedly, if she still lived exclusively with her cat.

He was about to approach her when Helen appeared from the direction of the office and flung herself at him before he could take evasive action. She sobbed uncontrollably for several seconds as he tried as diplomatically as possible to disentangle himself. He realised this would not be accomplished until he had somehow stemmed the tide of tears.

'Oh my God, Gary, he's been found dead; floating in a tarn a short distance from here. What will that mean for the hotel? There are police upstairs looking through his room, others are talking to the staff and they've already taken a statement from me. After what happened in Malching they're bound to think the worst.' She lowered her voice and glanced in the direction of DC Williams. 'The way that officer looked at me, so judgemental; I just wanted the ground to open up!'

'If you've stuck exclusively to the facts, such as what time you last saw Whitaker and what you knew of his movements, then I'm sure your answers satisfied her. Now we need to be practical,' Gary said firmly as he reached up and physically removed Helen's arms from around his neck, noting as he did so his polo shirt collar felt decidedly damp and found himself hoping her mascara was waterproof. 'I'm sure this situation can be contained and managed with a minimum of fuss and in the absence of Robin and Mark, I will liaise with the police team,' he said looking at her. There didn't appear to be any smudges around her eyes so hopefully his collar had survived the encounter.

'Will you? Oh, thank you! I've been terrified; I was just going to ring you but that woman has been interrogating me for what seems like hours. She wanted to know where I was yesterday! How can that be relevant? Why does it matter where I was? I mean, he fell in the water, didn't he?' she looked at Gary sharply despite the continued sobbing and eye dabbing.

'We won't know how he died until the post mortem results are available. Until then, the police will follow their normal lines of enquiry when dealing with an unexplained death.'

'Maybe he suffered a heart attack; he often seemed a bit short of breath. He drank far too much, smoked of course and never took any exercise. He's barely left his room for the last few days; do you know he disarmed the smoke alarm so that he could light up with impunity! That's what he thinks… thought… I was planning to charge him for a deep clean. Also, did you notice his florid complexion? Yes, it must have been natural causes; if it wasn't his heart then maybe some sort of sudden neurological dysfunction, even a vasovagal could have caused him to fall into the water and drown, right?' Helen looked hopefully at Gary.

'Possibly,' replied Gary non-committally, not wanting to admit he wasn't sure what a "vasovagal" was. 'As a matter of interest, where were you yesterday?'

'What? That's the thing, I wasn't here; I had some time off because I knew I would be running the place while the guys are away,' she said as she dabbed her eyes once more.

'That shouldn't be a problem should it? Presumably you weren't completely alone? Credit card transaction maybe or restaurant receipt? Anything like that will be sufficient to give you an alibi.'

Helen appeared to be about to speak when DC Gina Williams walked towards them, having just finished a conversation with the receptionist.

'I was going to ring you today,' said Gina dispensing with the formality of a greeting. Gary noted that Helen turned and quickly slipped towards the lounge as soon as Gina spoke.

'Just to let you know we had drawn a blank with those letters Helen Anderson received. Loads of smudged fingerprints and nothing of any use; paper standard size and quality, could be bought from anywhere. The envelopes had a local postmark so all we can say is that whoever's responsible for sending them comes from this area. Still, we have something more important to get our teeth into now. Suppose we need to keep an open mind as to whether the two things are connected.'

'Do you know what a "vasovagal" is?' asked Gary, hopefully.

'Um, my brother's a haematologist and I've heard him use the term because some people react to needles. I think it's some sort of faint, isn't it? Why do you ask?'

'Helen suggested that might be what happened to Whitaker.'

'Did she now; interesting but out of the question.'

'Ah! So not natural causes; an accident perhaps?' probed Gary, gently.

Gina shook her head. 'Not unless he managed to bash himself over the head with a solid object. No, someone smashed the base of his skull and he either fell or was pushed into the tarn sometime yesterday. It will be common knowledge tomorrow and the team are assembling as we speak but off the record today, I think we can safely say Percival Whitaker was murdered. The question is, why and by whom?'

Chapter 5 – A Motive for Murder

For the residents of Blenthorne it must have seemed like history repeating itself; police cars forming a cavalcade as they drove through the main street, just like the day, seven years ago, when they had come to arrest Lizzie Lockwood. Andrea Pearce hadn't been living in the area then but Jono had told her what a terrible event it was; particularly as no one believed Lizzie capable of murder, or whatever it was they charged her with, Andrea couldn't remember exactly. Of course, if Lizzie hadn't served a prison sentence, they would never have met. Then what would her life have been like? She tried not to think about being incarcerated but some memories seemed to stick no matter what, whilst other things "went in one ear and out the other", as her mother used to say! In fact, there was something from a few days ago that kept nagging away at her. She wondered if she should tell someone what she'd overheard. She would wait and see; on one hand, it might be totally insignificant, on the other, it might really put the cat among the pigeons but then again… maybe best not to get involved.

*

Ken Stokes looked in at the parish hall as he hitched up his trousers. The village didn't look much different to the last time he had been here, a birthday meal at Lockwood's for Mrs S, must be three years ago now; posh nosh came at a price so it wasn't a place to frequent often, not on his salary anyway. To think, at that stage he had been hoping to retire in the near future. However, Mrs S' insistence that they move house and increase their mortgage, coupled with the expense of having four growing daughters, had blown his plans out of the water. He winced slightly as he realised his metaphor was in particularly poor taste given the way the victim in this case had died.

He was clearly in the way of the tech team, standing as he was in the middle of the wooden floor of the draughty hall, as they set up their equipment. At least the pub did good food so being here for a few days wouldn't be too much of a hardship. He looked at his watch; time to go to the Blenny to meet up with Gary Carmichael for an informal chat. He hoped Lizzie Lockwood would be there too, as she knew the place inside out. Gary had said he'd ask if she was free. He wondered how well she knew Helen Anderson; no doubt he would find out soon.

He had looked at press reports of the Malchington Bay case when Gary contacted him regarding the letters Helen Anderson had received. Now a journalist who appeared to be interested in her was dead; coincidence or connection? He tucked his laptop under his arm and made his way in the direction of the pub. From what he remembered, the Blenny did a really succulent steak and ale pie and a pretty good ploughman's platter.

He had settled himself happily into a secluded table with a pot of tea and a mid-morning muffin when

Gary and Lizzie arrived. He looked up and smiled a greeting.

'What can I get you both?' he asked convivially, as he stood up.

Gary and Lizzie both shook their heads and sat down opposite Ken. 'We're fine for now,' said Gary, looking at his partner for confirmation. 'You've met Lizzie before, I'm sure?'

'Yes, I've attended a few police dinners over the years at the restaurant. How's that boy of yours, Lizzie? Mrs S raves about his mushroom and spinach ravioli every time we pass this way.' It never hindered an informal chat to ask after a loved one.

'He keeps in touch but he's working at a restaurant in France at the moment,' said Lizzie, wistfully. 'He and Faye split up a little while ago,' she added.

Of course, the approach didn't always work to his advantage. 'Ah!' he murmured. Clearly not a lot else he could say.

'Now, thank you both for taking time to see me; what I'm hoping for is a bit of background on our victim and also Helen Anderson.'

'Of course,' said Gary, affably. 'From what I recall, Percival Whitaker arrived a week ago on Wednesday.' He looked at Lizzie for confirmation and she nodded. 'His intention, he declared to anyone who would listen, was to find out as much as he could about Helen Anderson. He'd seen Helen's photo in a promotional piece the local paper had produced about the new hairdressing salon at Fell View Hotel, where she works. He wanted to get an interview with her prior to flogging an article to a tabloid or magazine.

'Anyway, she successfully dodged him for a few days and then his interest in her seemed to wane. At about the same time he suddenly took to locking himself in his room at the hotel and working fervently day and night.

'On Wednesday evening, exactly a week to the day after Whitaker's arrival, I arranged to meet Helen here in the bar to discuss the letters she had been receiving.'

Gary then went over his meeting with Helen.

'I left the bar at roughly six-fifty; Percival Whitaker arrived shortly after and spoke to Helen. Lizzie was working that evening, so she can fill you in on the next part.'

Lizzie nodded and picked up the tale. 'That's right, yes; the journalist came in and started talking to Helen. I didn't notice initially but then everyone sort of fell silent as he took centre stage. He was saying he had another story in mind, something that would take precedence over writing about events in Malchington Bay; "other fish to fry", as he put it. Then the strangest thing happened; just before he left, Whitaker whispered something to Helen which clearly shocked her to the core. So whatever he said, hit home. As to what it was, you would have to ask Helen herself.'

'I suspect she will only tell you what she wants you to know and if it's anything remotely incriminating, you won't get a straight answer,' added Gary, avoiding eye contact with Lizzie.

'I take it you don't trust her?' asked Ken, looking at Gary.

'Not entirely, no. It may be that I'm being unfair but as charming as she is, or can be, she's very… self-absorbed,' said Gary choosing his words carefully.

'Would it be worth me speaking to the pub manager, Maggie Blake, to get her take on the encounter?'

'I wouldn't think so because she was in the public bar, helping Bert. He's way past retirement age but he enjoys the routine of coming to work; he's an absolute institution around here and very good for business. The locals love him and tourists are fascinated when he launches into Cumbrian dialect; he hams it up disgracefully. I love him dearly, he's Maggie's dad and I couldn't have stayed in Blenthorne after Richard, my first husband, died if it hadn't been for them. I told Maggie about the interaction between the journalist and Helen Anderson later though; I think everyone present was talking about it. The whole thing was so odd,' said Lizzie, with a small shake of her head.

'So to summarise; our journalist came here to pursue a story about Helen, then inadvertently stumbled across another person whose story he must have believed would bring him an additional hefty payday,' said Ken as he drained his cup and added some more hot water to the teapot.

'Yes, agreed. So the questions have to be; who is it and what did Percival Whitaker know about them? Whatever information he had, was it sufficient to get him killed? Alternatively, did whatever he said to Helen make her so scared that she decided to silence him?' said Gary as he looked at his ex-colleague.

'You never lose it, Gary! Once a detective and all that; don't you miss it?'

'Sometimes, but I thoroughly enjoy looking after Lizzie's interests whilst she pursues other avenues; not least her rehab scheme at Hope Cottage.'

Ken felt he really ought to take the bait. 'Really? Sounds interesting, what's that all about, Lizzie?'

Lizzie outlined the aims of the rehabilitation project to Ken. On the face of it, he couldn't see that this had any bearing on the case but he listened politely. She then excused herself, as she had a meeting with one of the cottage residents and their resettlement mentor.

Gary stood up and smiled as she left, saying he'd be home for dinner. Then he settled down again and spoke in a measured tone.

'There's another thing, Ken; I'm not totally sure Helen's got an alibi for the time of Whitaker's death. She looked pretty rattled when I saw her at the hotel earlier, she told me she had had some time off that day but was vague as to where she'd been.'

'Do you think you could just drop me an email, Gary, if you've got time, outlining your take on the events in Malchington Bay; no idea if it's relevant but it will give me a bit more insight into the character of Helen Anderson. I've read the media stuff but you were there and you have a nose for what's important…'

Ken got distracted when his phone rang. After a couple of minutes, he disconnected the call. 'It seems we have had contact from a chap called Keith Howard, who worked as Percival Whitaker's assistant. He said he was asked by his boss to courier up a hard copy file pertaining to an old case a few days ago. Today, of course, he saw the breaking news report of his employer's death. Percival Whitaker was quite a celebrity in his own right, so the press will be descending en masse as we speak.'

'Did he say what the file contained?' asked Gary looking at Ken intently. 'Are you allowed to share the information with me?'

'Good grief, I think I can trust you after all this time; besides your experience will be invaluable. Not sure I remember the case too well, I'll need to do a bit of background but from what Gina just told me, it revolved around a girl by the name of Jane Macintyre. Wasn't there a strong suspicion that she killed her mother and half-siblings?' asked Ken, delving into the deep recesses of his memory.

'Jane Macintyre, now that's a name from the past; must be getting on for thirty years ago. From what I remember, she was questioned on suspicion of murder but nothing was proven. I was a fairly young and extremely enthusiastic police constable at the time and I remember taking quite an interest in the case, much to Cheryl's annoyance; she moaned I never did anything other than work, which I don't think was particularly fair.'

Ken shuddered slightly. He well remembered Gary's ex-wife. If she were a fruit, she would definitely have been a lemon that no amount of sugar could ever sweeten. He was pretty sure that "fair" wasn't a word with which she was familiar.

What was the time? His muffin had bridged the gap between breakfast and lunch but he was definitely getting peckish; maybe it was the aroma of a bacon bap wafting over from the next table. He realised that Gary was speaking again and turned his attention away from his stomach and silently told his brain to concentrate.

'I believe Jane and her mother lived in a village in Essex, can't remember the name offhand. They led a normal, quiet life, the mother worked part time in a local supermarket. By all accounts, Jane enjoyed arts subjects and sport. I think she had represented her primary school at swimming. She was described as a model pupil until she was about nine. Things changed around that time; she started rebelling against accepted norms and values. That coincided with her mother meeting and marrying Laurence, known as Larry, Borthwick. The family dynamic altered rapidly as her mother, Patrina, had three more children, two boys and a girl, within a short space of time. Larry was by all accounts quite a successful car dealer and the family became fairly affluent and enjoyed a comfortable lifestyle.

'I think the social worker's reports at the time suggested that Jane and her mother went from having a close relationship to constantly arguing with the suggestion that Larry wasn't exactly the ideal stepfather; no suggestion of any kind of physical or sexual abuse though. Jane had run away from home several times and was in care for a while before returning to live with the family. Her version of events was that she came home one day to find her mother and three half-siblings all dead. She was never charged; she explained away the blood on her clothing by saying she had tried to resuscitate each of them in turn. The killings were particularly brutal; each was stabbed so there was a lot of blood. The forensic team couldn't rule out her explanation for the transference of blood from the victims to her skin and clothing, so that rather shot a hole in any case against her.'

'Wasn't there a pet pooch that was also killed?' interjected Ken.

'Yes, something small, a dachshund, I think. There were various theories put forward at the time. Pat had lost her temper and committed suicide after killing her youngest children or maybe she had disturbed a burglar. Larry, whom it transpired had been having an affair, killed his wife and children to avoid an expensive settlement which might have cost him his company if they were to divorce. Some of his business dealings were apparently a little shady so maybe an associate bore a grudge. The neighbours attested to the fact that the dog always barked at strangers and they heard nothing on the day in question. Also, there was no sign of forced entry, which suggested the killer was at least known to the family, if not a part of it. However, to date no one has been prosecuted and the case presumably remains open.'

'So the case of the dog that didn't bark, eh?' said Ken.

Gary ignored him and continued;

'Larry believed Jane was responsible for the slaughter and severed all contact. In view of the stigma, social services moved her to another part of the country. As I say, it was about thirty years ago and she would have been a teenager at the time. That would make her about mid to late-forties now.'

'You can probably anticipate my next question, Gary. Who in the village fits the bill regarding age? If we cross reference the likely candidates with those who were in the pub at the time Percival Whitaker was sounding off about his next target, then we potentially have a shortlist!'

'We'll need to check with Lizzie; I wasn't actually here when he performed his party piece,' said Gary shaking his head.

At that moment, Lizzie appeared in the bar.

'Wouldn't you know it, the resettlement officer has tonsillitis! So my meeting was cancelled and I wondered if I could be of any help back here?'

'Indeed you can, Mrs L!' Ken said with enthusiasm. 'There's been a bit of a development in your absence and I'm sure Gary will fill you in on the details later, in confidence of course. Now please take a seat and let me get you a drink, then I want you to tell me exactly who was in the bar the night of the Whitaker incident, to the best of your recollection.'

'I'll get them.' Gary stood up and touched Lizzie gently on the shoulder. 'Usual? And do you fancy a sandwich? I suspect this could go on for a while.'

'Just an orange juice for me, thank you and I won't have anything to eat at the moment.' Gary walked to the bar to get the drinks and returned almost immediately.

'Why is it so important that I remember who was present the other night? Surely it's quite clear who did it? Wouldn't it make more sense to see where Helen was when Whitaker was killed?' said Lizzie, looking quizzically from one male companion to the other.

'Lizzie, Ken is just trying to establish the facts,' said Gary in a gentle conciliatory tone as he placed the glasses on the table.

'I'm sorry, Ken; it's just that Helen's been a magnet for trouble ever since she arrived. She rocked up one day, made a play for Gary then foisted herself on my good friends, Robin and Mark, at the hotel. Then we had poison-pen letters, followed by rubbish on her car and now a murder. I may be making a connection where none exists but before she came here we were all so happy; that is, I was happy,' Lizzie whispered the last, softly.

'Sweetheart, I know how you feel about Helen but if you can put that to one side for a moment, your insightfulness and recall are both going to be great assets in this case.' Gary put his hand on her knee as he smiled at her tenderly.

Ken waited a moment, feeling a little awkward. He nodded reassuringly. 'Now, Lizzie if you could just cast your mind back to that night…' he gently prompted.

Lizzie looked far from convinced that this approach was desirable or necessary but shrugged her shoulders and nodded.

'If I look from the bar I can probably tell you who was where. I didn't notice Mr Whitaker come in, so Mia must have served him. The next thing was Mia drawing my attention to the spectacle in front of the fireplace. The journalist was prancing around a bit, clearly enjoying himself, then he sat down at Helen's table, talking loudly so everyone could hear. As I told you earlier, all of a sudden he dropped his voice and leaned in really close. I don't know what he said but whatever it was, she froze on the spot; I'd never seen anything like it! I know I shouldn't say this, but I relished the idea of someone getting the better of her as she's not a kind person but I never thought she would actually kill Whitaker but he's dead isn't he…?'

'Lizzie, please!' said Gary with a note of reprimand in his voice.

'Sorry, I'll stick to the facts.' She shifted her position on her chair a little, inclining towards Ken.

'I know we had several tourists in that night but I don't suppose you will be interested in them, as for the most part they were just passing through. There was a party of four youngish men, I've seen them before, they travel up from Liverpool fairly regularly to walk the fells and all seem very nice. Well-spoken and polite; they usually spend a fair bit. Then there were three people in the far window seat, two ladies and a chap, all in their sixties I would say. I've not seen them before but they had a meal and said they were staying at a bed and breakfast in Rowendale, or it might have been Hallidale, just down the valley.

'As for the locals, there was Jono Johnson and Andrea; they usually have a drink or two at least a couple of times a week. They get on extremely well. I think in time they might get together but obviously after that terrible marriage, Andrea is cautious. Mind you, I would think Jono would be too if he knows how Andrea disposed of her husband!'

Ken listened politely to this potentially spurious information as from his long experience he knew that sometimes the smallest clue can deliver the greatest results.

'Really; what happened to Andrea's husband?' he asked encouragingly.

'She endured years of verbal and emotional abuse and then shot him with his own rifle. She suffered a head injury as a result of a car accident a few years previously, so I think there was a case for her to plead diminished responsibility or something but the fact that she admitted it was premeditated, well, that carried a custodial tariff. I met her in prison; she's very vulnerable even now and Helen is quite intolerant of her. In my book there's no excuse for that, just because Andrea's a little slow at times.'

Ken raised his eyebrows. 'Interesting, now can you remember who else was present, Lizzie?'

'The other side of the bar was Colleen Plumley and her assistant at the museum, Tim Carney. He hasn't been here long but seems like a nice young chap. Colleen is a bit of a character, smells slightly of mothballs but Tim seems to get on very well with her. Colleen and I are distantly related actually, going back to Victorian times. When I did my family tree, I found I had ancestors in this area, now isn't that a remarkable coincidence? A distant great aunt of mine was actually married to the owner of this place and she originated from Kent, as did I. Now you'll never believe her name; Elizabeth! Anyway, she worked for an MP and his family over at the large house in Rowendale. It was called Highfields House during her time but then it changed hands after an almighty scandal and was renamed Raven's Manor by the next owner. Of course I knew nothing of this when we came here; the Blenny was up for sale and Richard, my first husband, fell in love with it and the rest as they say, is history!'

Ken smiled and waited patiently.

'Lizzie, I think Ken would like you to stick to the relevant points regarding the other evening,' said Gary, gently.

'What? Of course, that's what I'm doing; more or less. Where was I? Oh yes, unlikely combinations; Hilary Cole the post mistress was having a drink with Dawn Sanchez and her husband, Mario, who was on a night off from the restaurant at Fell View. Hilary and Dawn are in the choir together and seem to have struck up a friendship. On the surface, I wouldn't have thought they had much in common, other than being about the same age. Hilary is quite a private person and lives quietly at home with her dog, whereas Dawn is very outgoing, flamboyant and colourful. They were discussing going for a spa day. Not sure Hilary even knew what Dawn was talking about. I think she's led quite a sheltered life and there's no family apparently. She told me once she was brought up by an elderly great aunt. She came to the village after the aunt died. She's always pleasant when I go into the post office but I wouldn't say I know much about her really.'

Ken smiled sanguinely. 'Maybe Dawn is just what Hilary needs; a vivacious friend to take her out of herself and show her there's a whole world out there.'

Lizzie looked doubtful. 'Dawn is a bit loud even for me. She did a few shifts at Fell View's restaurant when they were short of waiting staff. Her husband, Mario, is the maître d'. They've been here for about two years, I suppose. I did hear that she was an exotic dancer when she was young. He left his first wife when he met Dawn and they hooked up together; she's quite a bit younger than him. He must be about sixty and she's in her forties. Anyway, Mario picked her up on a few things one night and they ended up having a bit of a domestic in the middle of service. I mean, no one wants a floor show from the staff do they? He was mortified as he's a stickler for etiquette and high standards. So it was quietly decided that it would be better for all concerned if she didn't work there in future. She works part time at the hotel now as a chambermaid. That takes care of Mario, Dawn and Hilary, now who else was there?' She thought for a moment;

'Oh yes, Sally Barton and her husband, Jack, from the farm. Jack is another distant cousin. My aunt's stepdaughter married a Barton and they had ten children – ten! That's a bit of a tenuous connection but interesting nonetheless.'

Ken again smiled, hoping Lizzie would return to the matter in hand and was delighted that she picked up the thread where she'd left off without any prompting this time.

'So anyway, Sally and Jack were sitting quite near to Helen who was having a meeting with Gary about her poison pen letters; do you know she thought I'd sent them! I heard what she said about me being insecure and not liking her. I wanted to go over and tell her that I wouldn't waste the ink!' She stopped and looked at Gary with a slight hint of defiance.

'Sorry, I'm digressing; Sally and Jack. There's a bit of a tale there. Must be twenty five years ago, Jack was engaged to a local girl, Rachel something-or-other, who lived in Rowendale. Childhood sweethearts; in fact, Maggie can probably tell you more than me as they grew up together, although Jack's a bit older. Everyone was assuming it was only a matter of time before they got married. Jack goes off for some work experience in Somerset on the farm owned by a relative and when he comes back, he brings Sally with him. She was still a teenager, just a slip of a thing and he'd met her in a pub in Taunton. That was it, love at first sight. Poor Rachel, she left here brokenhearted. I heard she had married a plumber from Newcastle. I think that Mr and Mrs Vicar came in just as you left, Gary?'

Gary looked a little shell shocked by the long-running monologue but recovered himself.

'That's right; I held the door open for them,' confirmed Gary.

'Simeon and Gloria Humphries have lived here for donkey's years; he's the incumbent at our local church and a couple of others, incorporated into a single benefice. He's about my age and was in his early thirties when they first came to Blenthorne; I think she is about ten years his junior, although anyone could be forgiven for thinking they were a much older couple. When I first arrived here, I thought they were middle-aged. It was said that he was potentially destined for higher office, although I've often found his sermons a bit tedious. I believe it's usual for vicars to move on after six to eight years in a parish but in their case, Gloria got settled and Simeon seemed content with that.'

Lizzie paused for a sip of orange juice. 'Not sure what the diocese thinks about it but I don't suppose it's particularly easy to get priests in rural out-of-the-way places so maybe they're satisfied with the status quo. I believe the parish contribution is quite healthy. I know for a fact that several quite well off second home homeowners in the area give generously, as they appreciate living in a community with a thriving village centre and a functioning church. Not sure many ever attend services but they are on the electoral roll as members, so on paper at least everything looks good.'

Gary looked across and saw that a large group had just entered the pub; he excused himself and went to assist Mia behind the bar.

'Anyone else here, Lizzie, that you can think of?' asked Ken, hoping he still had her attention.

'Um, Mia's boyfriend, Connor Robson, was here but then that's quite normal. He props the bar up most nights if he's not working. In fact, Maggie had to have a word with him a few nights back when Percival Whitaker said something a bit cheeky to Mia. She wasn't worried; she can handle herself and an over-familiar punter is all part of the job.

Unfortunately, Connor took exception and told Whitaker to back off. Maggie gave him a free drink as the last thing we want is a poor social media review. You know what people are like with those online sites where they can say anything no matter how unjustified and that puts people off. It would me to be honest. Maggie was saying she and Carl were thinking of going to London for a long weekend, so I said best to check to see what other people think about the place before you book...'

Ken's attention waned at the thought of Maggie and Carl's weekend arrangements and his thoughts turned back to those present on the night of the Whitaker performance. He hoped his face didn't betray his lack of interest. After another ten minutes he thanked Lizzie and waved to Gary as he reluctantly left the pub with its promising aromas of tasty repasts. He looked at his watch, it was after twelve thirty. The SIO, Detective Chief Inspector Malcolm Cooper, was due to arrive at twelve forty-five for the first formal briefing.

Whilst he had been forced to pass on the prospect of further sustenance at the pub, Ken had plenty of food for thought and several lines of enquiry to follow up. Without knowing it, Lizzie Lockwood had been extremely helpful as in amongst the gossip he had elicited the fact that several of the women in the pub on the evening in question were the right age to be Jane Macintyre and moreover, all had come to the village in adulthood; Dawn Sanchez, Hilary Cole, Sally Barton and Gloria Humphries.

Yes, despite his rumbling stomach, it had been a good morning's work.

*

The team had assembled in the parish hall by the time DCI Malcolm Cooper arrived. He was slightly taller and younger than his sergeant and certainly less rotund. The two colleagues had worked together on many cases and their mutual respect and affinity was almost tangible.

Ken started the briefing by summarising his meeting with Gary Carmichael and Lizzie Lockwood. DC Gina Williams then told the team that she'd been advised a forensic search of the crime scene had uncovered nothing of value and, in particular, the victim's mobile phone hadn't been located. She had spoken to Karen, the receptionist at Fell View and established Percival Whitaker had a rucksack with him when he left the hotel the morning of his death and that no such item had been found so far. His laptop was also missing, as was the package in which he had placed so much value when it arrived for him by courier at the hotel recently. However, Gina said that she had checked at the post office and Hilary Cole had confirmed that Percival Whitaker had sent a parcel by recorded delivery to a London address. Gina had contacted Keith Howard at the journalist's office in Balham and he agreed to courier it straight back as soon as he received it, if it couldn't be intercepted at the postal sorting office. The forensic team had given her a tissue with some writing scribbled on it; *"The Leopard That Changed Its Spots"*. The cleaner had found it in Whitaker's bedroom once he'd vacated and decided against throwing it away, lest it meant something to him.

DCI Cooper left a discreet pause and spoke in his usual taciturn way.

'Okay, so despite having no material evidence from the area around Dark Tarn, we have several lines of enquiry with Jane Macintyre potentially being the most profitable. Is she here in Blenthorne and if so, what identity is she using now? Do any of the residents at Hope Cottage, Lizzie Lockwood's resettlement project, fit the age profile for Jane Macintyre? What did Percival Whitaker have on Jane? Was she in the pub the evening of the Whitaker/Anderson confrontation? If she did kill her family, could she also have killed him? We also need to look at Helen Anderson; what did Percival Whitaker say to her a couple of evenings before his death which shook her up so much? Was it enough to cause her to kill him; indeed, is she capable of murder?

'However, let's not forget Percival Whitaker has a past; he has upset a lot of people over many years, could there be someone else out there with a grudge against him? Let's look at Whitaker's recent work. The headmaster who killed himself; was there a family member looking for revenge? What about Whitaker's ex-wives or children? Was he providing for them adequately? Did any of them hate him enough to kill him? Unlikely, but we can't ignore the possibility. Right, I have to go and make a statement to the press who are mustering on the green.'

Why was it, Ken mused, that he never got the nice, straightforward open and shut cases? He looked at his watch. It was almost two o'clock and definitely time for a sandwich; then he would turn his attention to the complex business of trying to catch a killer.

Chapter 6 – The Truth about Malchington Bay

Lizzie Lockwood and Gary Carmichael dined early that evening. Lizzie had something on her mind which had been bothering her ever since Helen Anderson had shoehorned herself into their lives and her concerns were compounded earlier in the day as a result of the meeting with DS Ken Stokes. Whilst Gary had promised he would tell her what happened during his time in Devon, he had still failed to do so. She made up her mind to tackle the issue without further ado. Gary walked into the room and picked up the remote control before sitting down opposite Lizzie.

'Gary, please don't turn the television on, I need to talk to you.' She twisted her hands nervously. 'You know how I feel about honesty. I had precious little of it from Richard and even Jim towards the end,' she said, referring to her husbands in chronological order. 'I want our relationship to work but you really must be straight with me. Helen Anderson has inveigled herself into our lives like a cancer. You've changed the subject every time I've brought it up but I need to know what happened in Devon and why she thought she would be a welcome addition to your life here in Cumbria.'

The log burner glowed soothingly. It was rather too early in the season to need the central heating but a little chilly in the evenings and Lizzie loved the ambience the firelight created in the front room of the home she had bought when she returned to the village a couple of years ago. She gazed up as Gary moved across from one sofa to join her on the other.

'I know I've been avoiding the subject, I'm sorry. You were away at the time. Do you want a drink?'

'I wasn't "away", I was in prison, you can say the word and no, I don't want a drink, what I want is for you to stop prevaricating and tell me about Helen "I'm-such-a-victim" Anderson and what she meant, or means to you.'

'Lizzie, if I ever thought we would get together...'

'The past has no bearing on us, unless you choose to let it but I need to know,' she stated firmly.

'You're right, I've been an idiot; of course you do. It's a pretty shocking story and Helen turning up here out of the blue, sort of brought back all the stuff I'd buried,' said Gary, with an air of resignation.

Over the next hour, Gary Carmichael told Lizzie Lockwood of his time in Malchington Bay on the north coast of Devon.

'To put the whole thing in context and to explain how I met Helen Anderson, I need to fill you in on the background regarding my reason for being there in the first place.

'When I found out that my friend and ex-colleague, Doug Maxwell, had died, I decided to head down to Devon to attend his funeral. I had no idea of what I was getting into in "Malching" as the locals refer to it.'

Lizzie nodded as she tucked her legs up under her and gave Gary her full attention.

'Doug died as a result of a fall but had previously suffered a heart attack. I was planning to visit him a few weeks later in any case, as his wife, Sonja, thought a visit from an old friend might help with his rehab. As it was, when I went to Malching, it was for his funeral.'

'How long did you work with him?' Lizzie asked.

'It would have been about eight years or so I think, in Carlisle. They never had children and after he took his pension, he and Sonja moved to a bungalow in Devon. We always kept in touch after he retired but I'd never been down to see them – always meant to but never got round to it – you know how it goes.

'Funny thing was, when Sonja and I spoke briefly before the funeral, she said she wasn't expecting a particularly large turnout. I was surprised because they were both community-minded people and I was sure they would have thrown themselves into all sorts of local pastimes and activities.

'She was right though, there were very few people there; only about a dozen, at most, including relatives. That was the first time I met Helen. She was on the parish council with Doug.

'In addition, Doug played bowls and was the church's treasurer as well as being a warden. Yet oddly, his funeral was conducted by a celebrant at the crematorium. Sonja asked me to stay back after the wake. The tale she told me was surprising to say the least. I had known Doug for the best part of twenty years and I could hardly believe what I was hearing.

'It seemed some church funds had gone missing. An anonymous benefactor had donated a large sum of money, allegedly via Doug, but it had never reached its intended destination.'

'You mean it looked like he'd stolen it?' interrupted Lizzie, looking intrigued. 'You know, I think I will have a drink; let's open a bottle of dry white.'

Gary smiled and rose to go to the kitchen. He came back after a couple of minutes with two glasses in one hand, a dish of mixed nuts in the other and a chilled bottle tucked under his left arm. He put everything down on the coffee table and walked over to the window to draw the curtains before filling their glasses, returning to the sofa and continuing his tale. Lizzie had pulled the rug from the back of the sofa and draped it over her legs.

'Yes, the inference was that Doug had kept funds meant for the church. A short time later, some cash went missing from the bowls club, coinciding with Doug doing some decorating there. A hue and cry ensued, only for the money to be shoved through Doug's letterbox in an envelope marked "Bowls Club". Sonja was convinced he was being framed and asked me to stay for a few days to see if I could get to the bottom of what was going on. I agreed but told her I couldn't necessarily guarantee to deliver the outcome she wanted. She said she accepted that but needed closure. She kept thinking about the allegations and believed they were connected to his fatal fall.'

'What, she thought he had been pushed – murdered?' Lizzie looked surprised.

'No, she knew that couldn't be the case as there were other people around when he stumbled. She believed he had been so preoccupied with all that had happened that he absentmindedly missed his footing on uneven turf near the edge of the path. In short, she believed he had been hounded to his death by insinuation and rumour.

'In the time leading up to his death, most of his so-called friends deserted him, with the exception of Helen and a few others. He had undertaken gardening work and other odd jobs but after the allegations surfaced, he was sacked from virtually all of them. He resigned from the council and the church and no longer played bowls. When he died he was almost totally out on a limb.'

'Good Lord,' said Lizzie as she sipped her wine and automatically reached for a handful of nuts. 'Didn't he have an opportunity to clear his name when the allegations were made?'

'He had no starting point. The benefactor wouldn't allow the matter to be taken further. The vicar refused to tell anyone the identity of the donor, other than that a member of the congregation had come to the vestry after one Sunday service and mentioned a sum of money they believed had been paid into the redevelopment fund. Of course the vicar knew nothing of it. The rumours, the vicar insisted, must have been started by someone who overheard the conversation.'

'Hang on, how does this relate to Helen?' asked Lizzie.

'As I said, she had introduced herself to me at the funeral and it seemed she had distanced herself from the rumour mongering. Maybe that was why I felt a rapport with her.'

'Were you attracted to her?' asked Lizzie quietly.

'Yes, I suppose so at the time,' admitted Gary, studying his wine glass intently.

An uneasy silence followed. Lizzie felt a stab of jealousy but hoped her expression didn't betray her. She hastily changed the subject back to Doug's dilemma. 'So no one had any idea, other than the vicar, who the benefactor was?'

'No, in spite of the impact on Doug, the vicar would only say he had to respect her request for anonymity, even though he disagreed with it.'

'You said "her", so they knew it was a woman?' questioned Lizzie.

'To be honest it was an educated guess on my part as, at the risk of being labelled sexist, I believe most donations tend to come from women.'

'Wouldn't the commission that oversees charitable donations get involved if a theft had taken place?' asked Lizzie as she drained her glass and reached for a refill.

'Exactly, yes and I think Doug would have welcomed their intervention to give him the opportunity to clear his name. As it was, things remained in limbo and the innuendo and rumours abounded to the point he became a social pariah.'

'Did you discover the lady's identity?'

'Yes, I had an advantage because I could look at things objectively. During my brief stay in Malching, I got to know a few of the locals, in particular a very enigmatic elderly lady by the name of Zlata Bocharova, originally from the Ukraine but exiled to England just before the Second World War with her mother and brother, her father being an outspoken critic of the Soviet regime. She'd had a successful career as a model in the fifties and had then moved into fashion design and retail, working for several major houses in Paris and Rome as well as London. Suffice it to say, she made a lot of money and clearly had an impact on the society pages at the time. The lounge and dining room of her London home were featured in one of those glossy magazines which were so popular before people had access to the world through their computer screens.'

'How the other half live!' said Lizzie with a sigh. Gary smiled at her and carried on with his tale.

'Zlata had employed Doug as the gardener at her property near Wesley Wood on the outskirts of Malching. I met her at the funeral, along with Helen. When I thought about it afterwards, I believed the anonymous benefactor had to be someone who was cash rich. Zlata would fit the bill, trading down from a large house a few months previously and buying a penthouse apartment overlooking Malching harbour. She would have had a significant amount of capital, so I went to see her and asked her outright. She admitted as much, bless her; she thought she was protecting Doug by not taking the matter any further and clearly cared about him and Sonja very much.'

'So she hadn't started the rumours?' asked Lizzie, becoming more intrigued by the minute.

'No, she was the soul of discretion. I only knew her briefly but I liked her a lot; she was full of grace and charm. This is going to sound really silly and politically very incorrect but she was a real lady.'

'She certainly made a strong impression on you. I take it you tried to get her to go to the police; after all, she must have had an audit trail?'

'I asked her about that and she told me she had used an intermediary. She had apparently seen the documents but had handed them back to her "trusted friend". When I asked her why she hadn't spoken to her friend when the allegations first surfaced, she said she had, repeatedly and been told on each occasion it was highly likely to be a banking error which would take time to rectify. Then Doug had died and she hadn't been sure how to proceed after that.'

'Was it Helen?' interjected Lizzie sharply.

'She wouldn't say. I tried to persuade her of the need to restore Doug's good name, in memory at least. I pointed out that if this intermediary had nothing to hide, they would surely be prepared to show me the same paperwork they had shown her. In the end, she said she would think about it and contact me. That was the last time I spoke to her.'

'Why, what happened?'

'The next morning when I went down for breakfast, the hotel owner told me there had been a fire during the night in Zlata's apartment; her neighbour raised the alarm but it was too late to save her. When I returned to my room, I checked my emails and there was one from Zlata telling me she had mulled over my request to name her confidant and asking me to visit her in the morning. I firmly believe she was going to tell me who it was. Tantalisingly, she also said there was another potentially more serious matter about which she would like my advice.'

'So you believe she was killed before she could talk to you?'

'At that stage I couldn't be certain she was killed, but it was one heck of a coincidence if not, so I decided to speak to the police. You see, there was a small incident at the funeral. Zlata had dropped the butt of her cigarette into a bin when we were milling around outside just before setting off for the wake. The contents of the bin caught alight and it was the quick thinking of the local GP, Jeremy Sampson, who saved the day by grabbing a vase of roses and emptying the water into the bin. Shortly after, an attendant arrived with a fire extinguisher but by then the doctor had dealt with the situation. I couldn't help thinking that the incident had possibly given someone an idea of how to dispose of Zlata. She was known to be careless with cigarettes so maybe a fire at her home could be made to look like an accident.'

'Did the local police team agree with you?'

Gary nodded. 'They set up an investigation prior to the Fire and Rescue Service report being published. It was subsequently established that an accelerant had been found in the bedroom rubbish bin, butane, in fact. A neighbour heard Zlata's doorbell ring during the evening so it was clear someone had gone to see her. Despite a media appeal, no one came forward to admit to being there.'

'The post mortem revealed Zlata had nearly three times the normal dose of benzodiazepines in her system. Officially, the cause of death was smoke inhalation and asphyxia. She was a habitual drinker, she would probably say just socially but she offered me spirits before lunchtime on the day I went to see her. She had consumed a large amount of alcohol before she died but even so, the idea she would mistakenly take her sleeping tablets three times was pretty hard to believe. I had probably been seen going to her flat so who knew what she might have been telling me? I think she was murdered to prevent her from talking to me further.'

'Did the police accept there was a link between this lady's death and the allegations against Doug Maxwell?'

'Most certainly; I gave them my take on a possible motive for killing Zlata and enquiries into Doug's friends and acquaintances ran parallel with the investigation into her death. I had asked Sonja if she could think of anything unusual in Doug's behaviour or anything he said around the time the allegations started. The only unexplained thing as far as she could remember, was a sheet of paper she'd found when clearing out his study and luckily she'd kept it. When she gave it to me, it contained a list of times, dates and the initials "EC".'

''What did "EC" stand for?'

'The best Sonja could come up with was Zlata's friend, Edith Crofter. Edith had a son, Henry, an ex-mariner who had retired from the merchant navy and lived in Spain for a while before returning home to care for his dementing mother. He was secretary of the cricket club and played bowls with Doug. However the dates listed were after her death the previous year, so it seemed we had drawn a blank there. The only other thing Sonja mentioned was that the first date on the list coincided with Doug doing some decorating at the GP surgery.

'As that was the only piece of information I had to work with, I started there and looked at the surgery website. I suddenly realised the answer was staring me in the face. "EC" was not Edith Crofter; it was Epilepsy Clinic. The dates of the clinics coincided with the dates Doug had on his list. To cut a long story short, I found out, with the help of the police, the doctor was setting up appointments and claiming for several fictitious epileptic patients. Now if Doug found this out when he was decorating at the surgery, surely that could be a motive for the doctor to discredit him.'

'What would be the point in claiming for fictitious patients? Do GPs get paid for individual patients on their list?'

'Yes, but it's a piffling amount. No, the significance was the fact these non-existent patients were given an epileptic diagnosis which allowed Dr Sampson to prescribe barbiturates for them. These he then sold through dealers as a very lucrative side-line. In fact, I nearly caught him one day. Sonja had told me that Doug was particularly concerned about the war memorial so I went up to Wesley Wood to see the place for myself. She thought he was worried about the state of the footpaths and the amount of litter. I think it was more likely that he had found out what the doctor was doing and where he was conducting his business.'

'So I can see why he would need fictitious patients but why would they be given appointments?'

'If patients were to be prescribed epilepsy medication, there had to be a coded entry on the GP computer system, after which they needed regular specialist monitoring. If they hadn't been allocated appointments, discrepancies would have been picked up. To an auditor, the surgery would appear to have a lot of epileptic patients whose conditions were not being managed through regular face-to-face consultations; hence the need for a dedicated clinic once a month with some non-existent patients mixed in with the real ones. He then created fictitious consultation entries with general monitoring information. He made up whole backgrounds for some of them, really rather inventive; must have taken him ages.

'Sonja was very helpful regarding all the procedural stuff; she wasn't retiring age when they moved to Malching so she'd worked at another surgery in the town.'

'Didn't the doctor's staff notice that a high proportion of the patients didn't turn up?'

'He worked as a sole practitioner and handled a lot of admin processes himself. He registered fictitious patients so they would be allocated NHS numbers. He gave his receptionist Tuesday afternoons off if there was to be a clinic that day and after putting the answerphone on, took emergency calls himself. He made the appointments and saw the patients in and out. The genuine epileptic patients on his list attested to this. Whilst they thought it a bit strange, no one really bothered to ask why.'

'Why didn't Doug go to the police?'

'I think he would have done when he felt he had enough evidence. However, before that happened he was overwhelmed by snowballing spurious gossip which clearly took precedence over all else. He wanted to clear his name but didn't know how.'

'Yes, I can see that; if he had made allegations against a respected local GP with his own reputation in tatters, who would believe him? What a terrible mess, not only for him but for his widow,' said Lizzie thoughtfully.

Gary nodded in agreement.

'But I don't see how Helen fits in? I remember the headlines but I didn't know about the prescription fraud; I don't think that was mentioned in the press reports, was it?' asked Lizzie. As fascinated as she was by the tragic tale of Doug Maxwell, her main focus remained Gary's connection to Helen Anderson.

Gary shook his head. 'No, Folly End Farm, the nursing home, stole the headlines; I don't think Doug knew about that. Once I started to look at the doctor, I realised that was where the real story lay. The prescription angle was just a side-line for him.

'In a nutshell, he was doing away with residents at the nursing home and charging roughly forty percent of each victim's estate to hasten their demise – thereby leaving their relatives with at least some of their inheritance.'

Lizzie shook her head in disbelief. 'Yes, shocking! Ordinary people were actually paying the doctor to dispose of their loved ones. It's outrageous that such a thing could happen.'

Gary remained silent and nodded solemnly.

'So was Helen complicit?' asked Lizzie, hopefully.

'Helen was the nursing home matron,' Gary replied. 'After I got to know her superficially, she invited me for lunch and then subsequently dinner. I suppose I hoped to gain some information that might help me understand what happened during Doug's last weeks, as Sonja was too close to be objective.'

Lizzie's gaze intensified. She felt her chest tighten.

'Inadvertently, or maybe by design, Helen told me quite a lot about herself. She's a senior nurse with many years' experience. I found out later that she and Jeremy Sampson had worked together at a neurological centre in Sussex some years previously but of course I didn't know that at the time. He went into General Practice and she went on to manage a residential home near Eastbourne. She moved to Malching to work at a purpose built centre on the site of an old farm, hence the name. The place was amazing, all the trappings of a five star hotel. She had a pretty good life there, her own self-contained apartment on the first floor and an excellent salary, so what possessed her to get involved in the doctor's hellish scheme is anyone's guess. She said he coerced her into turning a blind eye and after the first one of course, she was in too deep to get out without incriminating herself.'

'How did he kill without raising suspicion? I don't think that was mentioned in the papers.'

'He used live bacteria, which can cause sepsis in vulnerable people. I'm told this can be done by injecting contaminated liquid, say water from a pond, directly into the blood stream. He refused to co-operate with the investigation but each resident who died over the previous year had the same cause of death on their certificate, usually coupled with one or more chronic conditions. The fact remained it was the common denominator. Five in one year was rather too much of a coincidence, the police agreed and when they started to dig, a couple of the victims' relatives owned up to their part in the scandal.

'In most cases they needed money and saw their inheritances being swallowed up in nursing home fees. I believe they uncovered thirteen deaths in all. In the past there had been larger gaps between them but for some reason, Dr Jeremy Sampson got greedy, not sure if it was for the money or just power. He certainly didn't have a lavish lifestyle. Anyway, we'll never know as he died in prison less than a year after he was sentenced. He always maintained that the entire plan was Helen's brainchild and he was a pawn, albeit a greedy one.'

'Do you think there is any truth in what he said? Was that why Percival Whitaker was pursuing her; had he uncovered more information than had come to light at the time? It would fit in well with his "Reasonable

Doubt?" denouncements,' observed Lizzie shrewdly, barely able to keep the glee out of her voice.

'I suspect that's why Whitaker wanted to interview her. As to whether Jeremy Sampson was telling the truth, I'm still not sure. Is Helen capable of colluding in murder? I don't know, but it's possible. Could she kill outright? I really have no idea. Maybe, if she felt she was cornered.' Gary placed his glass on the coffee table.

'She asked me to be a character witness should the need arise but as it was, there was insufficient evidence to charge her,' he added grimly.

Lizzie nodded; then another thought came to her. 'Why did you first think something was wrong at the home?'

'It came down to the note Sonja found. She thought it related to a person,' said Gary, looking relieved to be on safer ground. 'The main candidate for "EC" was Edith Crofter, so in the first instance, I sought out her son, Henry. Whilst I soon realised the initials didn't relate to Edith, I continued spending time with Henry. He seemed like a nice chap and we had a couple of meals with a few games of darts in the local pub. He told me he'd sold up abroad to come home to look after his mother.

'Not being able to break the habit of a lifetime, I decided to have a look at his background. From the briefest of internet searches I found that he had been declared bankrupt as a result of a property venture in Spain. He had creditors chasing him as well as angry clients. So he'd lied about that; was it embarrassment or something more sinister? I started to wonder what else he might be lying about. That led me to take a closer look at the nursing home where Edith was living at the time of her death. It wasn't cheap. What if her cottage needed to be sold to pay her fees? There seemed to be little else wrong with her, save the dementia so it's possible she could have lived for years. If the cottage was sold, Henry would be homeless with his inheritance haemorrhaging at an alarming rate.

'As the whole scandal was exposed, it turned out that was the case. Amazingly, the owner of the hotel in which I was staying was also involved. Her father owned half the business and with all his savings practically gone, it was going to have to be sold to cover his fees, so she colluded with her understanding GP to speed up the process. I don't think she was wicked, just desperate. Do you know, she offered me a job looking after her hotel should she serve a jail sentence!'

'You weren't tempted then?' asked Lizzie, with a wry smile.

'Good God, no; Malching looked tranquil and serene on the surface but under the cosy exterior was lurking a poisonous nest full of vipers.'

'It sounds like it, if the vipers caused the death of an innocent man,' observed Lizzie ruefully.

'No, actually I don't think they did. You see, there was a bit more to it than Sonja told me originally. As I said at the beginning, I explained when I agreed to look into the matter that she might not like what I found out and of course that turned out to be the case.'

'What, there's more? Good heavens, Gary, you could write a book.'

Gary smiled. 'I went to see Sonja just prior to coming home. She said pretty much the same thing to me as you've just done. The people of Malching hounded her husband to his death. Firstly his coronary and then his fall from the coastal path. However, the truth behind Doug Maxwell's death was much simpler than that.'

'Was it? Nothing you've told me so far has sounded very simple,' remarked Lizzie wistfully.

'I felt all along that Doug was a level-headed, sensible chap and moreover, an outstanding police officer. I've seen in him a tight spot many a time and it never fazed him. If he was out of his depth he would have turned to someone he trusted to help him clear his name. What he wouldn't do is roll over and let events overwhelm him.

'The truth was much closer to home. What was the thing he cared most about in life? What was the thing he couldn't bear to lose? What mattered more than his reputation and his status within the community? It had to be Sonja.'

'What'd she done? Was she going to leave him?' asked Lizzie quietly.

'That's what he feared. It transpired she'd been having an affair with Henry Crofter for months. I suspected something was amiss when I questioned Henry and also Sonja about something Helen had said to me. Apparently Doug lost his temper with Henry during a bowls game. When I asked them, Henry and Sonja said it was due to the pressure he was under and both separately described the incident as a "storm in a tea cup". It was bound to happen occasionally in view of the way he was being treated by all and sundry.

'However that wasn't true. Helen told me the altercation happened several weeks prior to the church scandal and there were no rumours circulating at that time. Helen had no reason to lie about the date, so what was it that Doug and Henry had really disagreed about?

'Coupled with that, I subsequently saw Sonja and Henry together on the cliff path when I was visiting Helen. They were clearly visible from her bedroom window on the first floor of Folly End. They were obviously having quite a heated conversation and from the body language, it looked like more than just an exchange between acquaintances. I put it to her and she admitted it; she and Henry had been involved for nearly a year.'

The reference to the bedroom hadn't gone unnoticed by Lizzie but she managed to quash the burning desire to get side-tracked and demand additional information on the subject. She told herself Gary was probably fixing a curtain rail.

The supercharged atmosphere and emotional tension seemed to be sucking the oxygen out of the room. Lizzie's heart was thumping and she had to wait until she could trust herself to speak without her voice quivering.

'No! Goodness, what a terrible burden to live with,' she said evenly, quietly pleased with her restraint and dignity. A thought suddenly struck her;

'Did they ever find out who killed the elderly lady, Zlata Bocharova? Could that have been Helen?'

'Suspicion rested heavily on Jeremy Sampson. He was her GP and he prescribed her medication. She had never married but had obviously been a very attractive lady in her day and I suspect enjoyed the company of men. I suppose those traits remain. She thought of Dr Sampson as an honest friend, albeit not an admirer as she was a good twenty five years older than him but she trusted him unreservedly. I strongly suspect it was he who supposedly acted as an intermediary to facilitate her donation via Doug to the church restoration fund. As it was, he probably just kept the money. Unfortunately, the police have never been able to find any trace of it. The case remains open on file. There wasn't anything really to connect Helen to Zlata's death other than she was someone whom Zlata trusted and would have had no hesitation in admitting to her flat.'

'When you say "there wasn't anything really to connect Helen to Zlata's death" you sound a little doubtful?'

'I have nothing concrete but there was "another potentially more serious matter" about which Zlata wanted my opinion. I never got to the bottom of that. The only small link I can make to Helen would be that Zlata was a friend of Edith Crofter and may have had suspicions over her death but it was never more than a vague feeling. It could explain why Helen would want Zlata out of the way.'

'The whole thing's incredible and presumably, without your intervention, none of it would ever have come to light.'

'It would have done eventually as Jeremy Sampson's insatiable greed or megalomania seemed to be increasing. A second general practitioner is required to sign every death certificate, so I've no doubt a connection would have been made before long.'

'I suppose you just wanted to forget the whole thing when you returned to Cumbria?'

'Absolutely right, yes; being back to normality felt so good, I had no desire to dredge it up again. That's why it was an unpleasant surprise, shock even, when Helen turned up here. I wanted no reminders of Malching.'

'Understandable,' said Lizzie with feeling. 'And Helen and you?'

'I got too close for a while and had a very brief relationship with her. It was foolish and something I wanted to put behind me as soon as I left there. When you came home and after Jim... um, here we are today.'

Lizzie nodded gently. 'Thank you,' she said simply. 'I needed to hear that.'

'I'm sorry, Lizzie; I should have been more open about the whole thing. I don't know why I was so reticent, particularly when you've given me every opportunity to talk about it. I told Helen a little while ago that you're the least judgemental person I have ever met and I meant it. It's crazy because if it was something work-related we'd have thrashed it out ages ago. I'm just useless when it comes to emotional stuff.'

'It's a learning curve for us both and let's be honest, I'm not great at sharing either; about Jim and things, you know…'

Gary nodded.

Lizzie stretched out her legs from her curled position on the sofa and stood up. 'I think that's quite enough to chew over for one evening. Are you coming to bed?'

'Ken asked me for an email jotting down roughly what I've just told you, so I'll do that first.'

*

Gary was pleased to have got the whole Malchington Bay episode out into the open. Lizzie persuading him to talk about it had lifted the cloud that had been hanging over him since Helen's arrival.

Lighter of heart, Gary rattled off a missive to his former colleague. He found himself turning back the clock to his days in the service as his last paragraph made its way onto the screen.

"The question has to be, did Helen kill Percival Whitaker? Or was it Jane Macintyre, whom we know he was also pursuing? I think it's a fair assumption that one or other is the killer, but which?"

Chapter 7 – Spadework

The following morning, Ken skim read the email from Gary outlining the events in Malchington Bay. He decided to look at it properly later in the day; it might be relevant, time would tell.

Each member of the five strong police team in the parish hall had a clearly defined role in the enquiry into the death of Percival Whitaker. Leaving Helen Anderson to one side, background checks were being carried out on anyone who could conceivably be Jane Macintyre. As their pasts were already a matter of record, Andrea Pearce and the residents at Hope Cottage had already been ruled out.

Gina Williams told the team that the Macintyre file was winging its way back to them and it should arrive by lunchtime. The case was still classified as an open investigation so she had also requested the official documents.

'Boss, we have several candidates who could possibly be Jane. Colleen Plumley is out of the frame as she's a bit older, as is Lizzie Lockwood. Maggie Blake was born here, so that's pretty unequivocal in spite of the fact she's potentially the right age.'

'Right, while you are all getting on with digging, I'm going to have a chat with Helen Anderson to see what it was Percival Whitaker told her that shook her up so much in the pub on the night he was grandstanding; too early to dismiss her as a suspect,' said Ken over his shoulder. 'We'll see if I get a straight answer, however from what I've been told by Gary Carmichael, I think that may be a long shot.'

Ken made his way to the hotel and asked to see Helen. He was shown to a seat in the lounge and offered coffee. He declined and opened his laptop to read Gary's email in more detail. After ten minutes, he returned to the desk to remind the receptionist he was still waiting to see Helen Anderson and if it really wasn't convenient, she could meet him at the police station in Carlisle later in the day. Miraculously, she appeared within thirty seconds.

'I'm so sorry to keep you waiting, Sergeant Stokes. There's so much to do and it's all falling to me in the absence of the proprietors.'

'Is it really? I thought Gary Carmichael was overseeing the management of the place while your employers are away? Mrs Lockwood has a financial interest, so if you really are struggling, I suggest you give one of them a ring.' Ken tried his best not to look too smug.

'Indeed, yes but they're busy themselves, of course, and I wouldn't want them to think I couldn't cope. Now, what can I do for you? Has no one offered you tea or coffee; how remiss. I'll get some immediately.' She turned to leave the lounge.

Ken stopped her in her tracks. 'No, thank you; let's just get on with it, shall we?'

For the most part, Ken Stokes was an amiable chap who was happy to play the part of the congenial rotund detective. However, just occasionally, if he was suffering from a nasty attack of dyspepsia or being particularly irritated or obstructed by the attitude of a recalcitrant interviewee, he abandoned that persona. To be fair it might not just be Helen, it could be the fact that Mrs S had advised him tersely in a text message that her mother had arrived and was in situ for the following few days.

Helen nodded briefly and sat down in an armchair opposite the detective.

'I expect you are aware by now that Percival Whitaker's death was not a natural one; I understand from several people that a couple of nights before his death, he approached you in the Blenthorne Inn. I'd be grateful if you could give me the gist of that conversation please, in your own time.'

'Goodness, to be honest, Sergeant Stokes, he took me by surprise as I wasn't expecting to see him. I'd just had a meeting with Gary Carmichael regarding the hateful letters I've been receiving and as you can imagine, that alone had been extremely distressing. Gary seemed to attach quite a lot of importance to the letters, as whilst their tone wasn't exactly threatening, it was unsettling. It took a while for me to admit I was worried but Gary said he would help me by speaking to a colleague, which may have been you? Once it was out in the open, I had an amazing feeling of relief, like a weight had been lifted. Of course, that lasted no more than a few seconds as no sooner had Gary left than Mr Whitaker appeared.

'He'd been trying to corner me ever since he arrived. I'm sure you know of his profession; he calls himself an investigative journalist but he's a muckraker. If he hasn't got a story, he makes one up. I strongly suspect that was what he was going to do in my case. I don't know if you are aware but I was peripherally involved with the terrible business in Devon at Folly End Farm a few years ago.'

'From what I understand, your involvement was a little more than that, wasn't it?'

Helen looked a little startled.

'I was completely innocent of any wrongdoing; no charges were ever brought,' said Helen tersely.

'Indeed. You were telling me about your encounter with Percival Whitaker at the pub just prior to his death?'

'Yes, but I wanted to give you some background information so that you can understand my state of mind at the time. I was definitely emotional because you see, I'd just upset Gary. I made some careless throwaway remark about Lizzie. You're a man, can you see the attraction? I would have said her money but Gary's not that kind of person. Maybe that's why I…' her voice petered out.

Ken said nothing, his face inscrutable as the silence hung between them.

'Anyway, I was just scolding myself for being so insensitive and there he was, Whitaker, looming over me. He strutted around my table for a while and then sat down opposite me. He spoke quite loudly, addressing the ceiling mainly. He was aware that other people were around but he didn't care. When I thought about it afterwards, it was like a theatrical performance; an actor showing off in front of their audience.

'He basically told me that his interest in me was on hold for the time being as he had another victim in his sights or as he put it; "other fish to fry". I took that to mean he had somehow stumbled across some sort of salacious information about someone else that lived in Blenthorne.'

'Did he tell you that specifically?' asked Ken, looking at Helen intently.

'No, that's not his style but he alluded to it,' said Helen grimly.

'So anyone in the bar could have heard what he was saying?' asserted Ken.

'Oh yes, without the slightest difficulty. He is, or rather was, an imposing figure, both large in frame and character. Whilst everyone ostensibly appeared to be in their own small groups or couples, what he was saying couldn't have been lost on any of them.'

'Now, you told my Detective Constable that you couldn't remember where you were on the day Percival Whitaker died. Have you recalled anything that might be of help?'

'I didn't exactly say that; I told DC Williams that I had some time off as I knew I'd be working flat out for the following few days while the proprietors of the hotel were on holiday. I have a lovely convertible which I barely get time to drive. She's my pride and joy and it was very relaxing just to point her nose out of the carpark and drive around the area.'

'And no one saw you?' asked Ken.

'No, my petrol tank was nearly full and I don't eat lunch. I avoid the touristy areas because the real beauty of the lakes and fells is to find remote areas, off the beaten track. The silence and stillness are awe-inspiring. You should try it sometime; it would do wonders for your stress levels. I did a round trip of about thirty miles, stopping off here and there. Unfortunately for the purposes of an alibi, I can offer you nothing, save to say that of course had I known I needed to, I would have made jolly sure I got myself noticed.'

'Must have been pretty upsetting the day after your encounter with Mr Whitaker to get up and find rubbish strewn all over your car,' said Ken, looking at Helen steadily.

'Oh my word yes, my baby covered in detritus! Only the night before, Gary asked me if anything untoward had transpired in addition to the letters and I was able to say no; then the following day that happened. It was a great shock.'

'I saw the photographs. No actual structural damage though, no scratches or dents so at least whoever did it had a bit of respect for a fine piece of machinery.'

'I suppose that's one way of looking at it. At the time I was not only shocked but very angry, however that was prior to this terrible business. It does rather put things into perspective, doesn't it? What's a few nasty letters and a bit of rubbish compared to a death? You don't think they are connected, do you? I'm not in any danger?'

'In my experience, people who do things in a furtive or clandestine manner are highly unlikely to resort to physical violence but we will be keeping an eye on the place and you can ring at any time if you're worried,' he paused and then added;

'I think that about covers everything for now. Thank you for your candour, Ms Anderson and for your time.' Ken got up from his seat and picked up his laptop.

Helen appeared to visibly relax as she too rose and, with a small smile, extended her hand. 'No problem at all, Sergeant Stokes; I only hope I've been of some help,' she added, sweetly.

After shaking hands, Ken started towards the door then turned back as if thinking of something at the last moment.

'Oh yes, one more thing, several people have mentioned that just before he left, Percival Whitaker whispered something to you. What was it he said?'

A full five seconds passed before Helen spoke. Her voice sounded a little shaky and her smile fixed.

'Whispered something? Oh really, goodness me how very strange! No, you know, I don't believe I even remember the incident to which you're referring. As I've already explained, my emotions were running high prior to my encounter with him.'

'Ah okay, don't suppose it's important. If anything does spring to mind, just give me a call or drop in at the parish hall. If I'm not there, any of the team will take a message.' Ken handed Helen a business card containing his contact details.

Ken left the hotel and walked back towards the hall. Something was bothering him. Percival Whitaker was a large man; maybe he was barking up totally the wrong tree. Could Helen Anderson, who was quite slight of frame or indeed Jane Macintyre, about whose physique he knew nothing, have had the strength to overpower someone of the journalist's size?

He needed to speak to Gina urgently.

It was a pleasant, warm autumnal day with a slight breeze from the west. The tranquil community scene belied the fact that among their number most likely lurked a murderer. Ken quickened his pace as that uncomfortable thought refused to leave him.

*

He got back to the hall just as Gina Williams was about to leave to attend the post mortem. He shared his concerns with her and she nodded in agreement.

'Yes, that was bothering me slightly. We know our victim was a hefty unit, so would Helen or potentially Jane be strong enough or tall enough to bash him across the skull, causing him to fall into the tarn? I'll see what the pathologist thinks and let you know,' said Gina as she climbed into her car.

'Oh, one more thing before you go, does Helen Anderson strike you as the kind of person who would enjoy a day of splendid isolation, communing with nature at various tranquil locations around the fells?'

She shook her head. 'Not unless any of them had a designer shoe department attached.'

'Ah, as I thought; thank you, Gina,' Ken smiled at his colleague.

So Helen couldn't remember what Percival Whitaker had said to her two nights prior to his death, even though it dumbfounded her at the time and she had no alibi for the day in question. She was definitely still in the frame, although clearly she wasn't Jane Macintyre, even from beyond this life, Percival Whitaker had told them that. How fitting it would have been if she were.

He was pulled out of his daydream by a motorcycle courier handing him a package for which he had to sign. He opened one end slightly and peered in, yes, a black loose leaf file marked "Jane Macintyre".

He looked at his watch. He would peruse the contents over lunch. Whilst it wasn't strictly protocol to discuss an ongoing case with an ex-officer, Gary Carmichael had an interest in the original enquiry so it would be worth finding out if the dossier triggered a memory and it was possible he could add something insightful. They had always worked well together and Gary was the soul of discretion. A few minutes later, after a quick phone call, he was on his way along the main street and across the green to Lizzie and Gary's home where he was reliably informed a cheese and tomato sandwich was waiting for him. He fervently hoped there would be more than decaf coffee on offer; what he really needed was a large mug of fully-leaded.

*

The two friends had finished lunch and were sitting outside in the secluded garden with its high hedges to make the most of the day, which had come as a pleasant surprise after the chill of the previous evening. The folder was several inches thick with typed notes, photographs and some diagrams of the house in which Jane's family were slain. Ken placed it on the patio table in front of them.

'We'll have the official investigation documents later today but for now we can make use of this. Larry wasn't at home and had a solid alibi. Jane had two half-brothers, Dale was five and Marcus four at the time of their deaths. It would appear they were killed in the room which they shared at the top of the three storey Victorian house. Their sister, Amy was two. She and her mother were downstairs in the kitchen. The dog was found in the hallway. The detailed photos of blood trails and broken crockery suggest Pat Borthwick may have put up a fight.'

'Best not to ask how our deceased journalist friend got hold of these!' remarked Gary wistfully, as he flicked through the photographs.

'Indeed. An obliging contact who wanted the truth to come out with no thought of monetary reward, I'm sure,' replied Ken as he shook his head, a small knowing smile playing round his lips.

There were several photographs of the family together in happier times. Jane only appeared in one distance shot.

'From what I can see, she looks just like any other teenage girl, long dark hair and slim figure, wearing what looks like a track suit. Of course, she may have filled out now; women tend to do that in their forties and they don't shift it after that.'

Gary almost spat out his coffee. 'Crikey, Ken! You're very lucky that Lizzie's at Hope Cottage!'

Ken looked a little shamefaced.

'This must be the children with their dad. Yes, it's written on the back; *"Larry with Dale, Marcus and Amy – Christmas 1980 – new bikes all round"*. No sign of Jane in the picture so presumably no bike for her. Again, how did Whitaker get hold of this?' Ken said with a small sigh.

'He was resourceful, that's what made him stand out and brought so much success. In a way that was his problem, I think. Each case had to be bigger than the previous one, more sensational, until he finally uncovered something for which someone was prepared to kill. At least, we assume that's the motive. If Jane was resentful enough to kill her family for perceived injustices, let's say, not getting a bike when her siblings got them, then the intervening years may not have ameliorated her reasoning. If she killed in the past then maybe she's killed again now,' said Gary, grimly.

Ken confided his concerns to Gary regarding a woman being physically strong enough to have killed the journalist. 'Is it Jane's modus operandi? I mean if we take it as read that she killed her family, she used a knife last time.'

'The proximity of the water may have helped. He was battered over the head, I believe?' asked Gary, to which Ken responded with a nod. 'Anyone of either sex striking a glancing blow might have caused their victim to lose their footing. After that, toppling over into very cold water fully clothed in a semi-conscious state; yes, it's reasonable to assume he wouldn't be able to get himself out. The pathologist will determine whether he died from the blow, drowned or conceivably had a heart attack as a result of shock. Maybe Jane took a knife with her but once she was there, she improvised; less evidence to get rid of. If she had stabbed him and lobbed the knife into the water, it would have been discovered in a search of Dark Tarn. The other alternative is, of course, that the murder was impulsive rather than pre-planned, so the killer used what was to hand. More coffee?'

'You see, that's why you made DI and I will always remain a DS,' observed Ken sanguinely as he proffered his empty mug.

Gary smiled as he went into the kitchen and returned a short time later with refills.

'Actually, I've just thought of something; wasn't there a suggestion that Jane was running with a rough crowd? Mostly older than her; I think there was a boyfriend who had done time for assault. That was one of the reasons social services agreed with her mother and stepfather that she should go into care for a while, to try to break the connection. She had been caught stealing from local shops and I think there had been a few other instances of anti-social behaviour. I'm sure she had a juvenile record. It should have been wiped but knowing how tenacious our journalist was, I'm sure he would have managed to unearth a paper trail.'

Ken flipped through the papers in the file. 'Oh yes, here we are. Good God, you have the memory of an elephant.'

'Wonder what happened to the boyfriend? Of course, he may have been involved; it wouldn't have been easy for a teenage girl to kill her mother and siblings without any of them being able to escape or at least raise the alarm. Although it was evening, so the boys were probably asleep. I think Amy had chickenpox, which explained why she was downstairs with her mother.'

'You're right again, damn it! It says here a bottle of some sort of moisturising lotion was found near the bodies in the kitchen, suggesting Pat was about to apply some to Amy's spots when they were disturbed.'

'Lots of photos of the blood splatter pattern by the look of it,' said Gary, picking up a relevant photograph.

'Wasn't there a vague suggestion that Pat could have killed the children then herself?'

'There was some talk of depression or low mood but nothing concrete. Presumably the investigating team had access to her medical records, so if she'd been receiving counselling or was on medication, they would have known and no doubt the media would have unearthed something. It was nothing more than hearsay from what I remember. Also, would she have smashed the crockery if she'd done it herself? I don't buy that. I think the husband was a bit of a wide boy, so that must have been hard to live with at times,' commented Gary.

Ken was studying the crime scene photographs again. 'It appears that two wounds were found on each of the children's bodies. One entry wound to the upper torso, in the boys' cases, both penetrating the right ventricle of the heart and then one to the left side of the neck; severing the carotid artery. Amy's wounds looked almost identical to her brothers. A sharp, thin kitchen knife was found at the scene and identified by Larry Borthwick as belonging to the family. Pat had three stab wounds; one to her neck, one to her chest and one to the abdomen. Of course, if she did kill herself, the angle of her entry wounds would be different; none of the wounds look tentative, so I agree with you, she couldn't have done it. The killer was sensible to leave the weapon behind because they didn't then have to dispose of it. I don't know what knives we have in our kitchen – do you?'

'Me? No. Although if it was part of a set and there was a gap in the knife block, I suppose that would be obvious. No prints I assume, that would have been too much to hope for.'

'No prints and not much about the boyfriend. He seems to have been called Nick Smith. That's helpful, shouldn't have too much difficulty in finding someone after almost thirty years with a name like that,' Ken said ironically.

'Maybe that's it! Whitaker had discovered something recently about Nick. Maybe he's our suspect rather than Jane?' pondered Gary.

'Certainly, I think it would be helpful if we could find him, if only for elimination purposes,' Ken pulled out his notebook and scribbled for a moment. 'Is there anyone in the vicinity who would fit the profile? Nick would be older than Jane, say five to ten years. Arrived in adulthood, now in his late-forties to mid-fifties and more importantly, was present in the bar when Whitaker was showing off.'

'I'd left, so that rules me out! No, the only people that fit the age profile are Jack Barton and Simeon Humphries. Jack was born here and his people have been established in the area since early Victorian times. In fact, Lizzie gave you chapter and verse on the Barton family.'

'Yes, how could I forget?' commented Ken, with an ironic smile.

'That just leaves the vicar. Highly unlikely, however stranger things have happened. He might have seen the light and taken the cloth. Married his secondary school girlfriend, Jane Macintyre, and lived a blameless existence in Blenthorne for the last quarter of a century or so,' Gary said, draining his mug and replacing it on the patio table.

'Wouldn't that be something; somehow identifying Nick and inadvertently finding Jane? Only flaw with that theory is that Whitaker definitely said he had turned his attention to another person, not people,' sighed Ken, looking perplexed.

'I don't wish to be pedantic but I think what he actually said was, he had "other fish to fry". Of course the plural of "fish" is in fact "fish".'

'You, pedantic? Never!' exclaimed Ken with a grin.

Gary ignored the interruption. 'Definitely worth looking at them I would say. I'd actually hate to think that we might be on the right track as I quite like them in a strange way. They're quirky but every community needs diverse characters,' Gary smiled gently.

'You're right of course; we do need to look at them closely. As for Laurence Borthwick, didn't he pass away a few years later? Some sort of water sport accident? I know it made the papers at the time. In spite of the suggestion he was having an affair when his family were killed, I don't believe he ever remarried,' said Ken, sifting through the remains of the document. 'No, nothing more about him in here; could be something on the laptop, I suppose, but we have no idea where that is.' He closed the file. 'This has been really useful, thank you for your insight. I knew you would be able to help me put some meat on the bones of this case.'

'No problem, nice to be a distance from it if I'm honest, because that business with Doug Maxwell in Malching was far too close to home; you got my email?'

Ken nodded. 'It made very interesting reading; loads of detail that never made the news. I didn't realise how instrumental you were in exposing the whole scandal.'

'I was actually terrified I would find something incriminating against Doug but thankfully I was able to help clear his name.'

'If you're as perceptive in this case, we'll have it closed by this time tomorrow!'

Ken suddenly remembered the note found by the journalist's bed and mentioned it to his friend.

'It looks like he scribbled it down on a tissue so he wouldn't forget it; any ideas?'

'Um; *"The Leopard That Changed Its Spots"*, presumably some sort of metaphor,' suggested Gary as he wrote the words down. 'I'll let you know if I think of anything.'

After a few minutes small talk, the two friends parted company with Gary going off to the restaurant and Ken going back to the hall to filter some of his thoughts and give the team a few more angles to pursue. All in all, he was very pleased with his progress over the last couple of hours and the lunchtime repast hadn't been too shabby either.

*

Shortly after Ken had sat down at his desk, Gina Williams returned from Percival Whitaker's post mortem. She sat down opposite Ken and he looked enquiringly in her direction.

'Pathologist has some tox tests to run, obviously, but preliminary findings are interesting.' She consulted her notebook. 'Percival Whitaker was a fifty seven year old male who was one hundred and eighty five centimetres tall, that's six feet one inch, as you like to say, "in old money" and he weighed one hundred and ten kilogrammes, which converts to seventeen stone four pounds, making him clinically obese. The pathologist said the deceased had several pre-existing chronic conditions. From the medications found in his bathroom, he was taking,' she turned the page and continued reading; 'an anti-hypertensive in the form of an ACE inhibitor for high blood pressure, a statin for cholesterol, a beta-blocker for a cardiac arrhythmia, that's an irregular heartbeat in everyday language and a sulphonylurea for type II diabetes. He was also on tablets for a benign prostate condition, which I'm reliably informed is something which affects some men as they get older.

'Basically, he should have been looking after himself diet-wise and watching what he was drinking, although it looks like he was doing neither.'

She smiled at a colleague who had brought her a cup of coffee before returning her attention to her notebook.

'Now we get to the nitty-gritty. The way the pathologist described it, the brain floats happily in the skull until something disturbs it. In our victim's case, he received a blunt trauma basilar skull injury from a solid object, such as a rock or large stone. This led to both coup and contracoup damage. The sudden impact made the under-surface of the brain slide dramatically in the skull base, the temporal and frontal poles jammed against the sphenoid ridge and frontal bones respectively and contusion would have occurred thereafter. Basically, he was whacked on the back of the head making his brain thrash around, resulting in extensive bruising at the front.

'This can lead to death but not in his case. Clearly it was sufficient for Whitaker to lose his balance and thereafter he either fell or was pushed into the tarn. Once there, his age and physical condition played their parts and he died from asphyxia caused by water inhalation. So he was clearly alive when he went in and then drowned; it's unlikely he was conscious but not outside the bounds of possibility. He entered the water approximately twenty four hours before he was discovered. Pathologist confirmed, in his opinion, the blow could have been delivered by someone of either sex, even a child if they were tall enough. From what we've found out about him, he was a ruthless character but that's a pretty grim way to go.'

'Yes, particularly if his assailant knew he wasn't dead. If that's the case, we are dealing with a sadistic and cruel individual. Just like the one that killed Jane Macintyre's family.'

'Looks that way and to think, they are living here in this quiet village in full sight of everyone, their true identity obscured. Glad we aren't staying here!'

He had to concede Gina had a point; if the killer knew the police were hot on their trail, who knows what they might be capable of?

Chapter 8 – Peeling the Layers

The following day, Lizzie Lockwood had just finished a short meeting with Carl Blake, the executive chef at Lockwood's, and the resettlement officer to check how one of her Hope Cottage residents was getting on working in the kitchen. She had been very pleased to discover that all was running smoothly. She also needed to see how another of her charges was faring at the hotel but would wait until Robin and Mark were back as she had no wish to see any more of Helen Anderson than was completely necessary. She found herself gravitating to the graveyard, where her ancestor and namesake, Elizabeth Tester was buried. Presumably the first Lizzie had come to love the area and people as much as she herself did.

She absentmindedly started fiddling with her watchstrap. Gary's explosive revelations about Malchington Bay were still fresh in her mind, as was the identity of Jane Macintyre. Also, if she were totally honest, she was extremely irritated there was another suspect, other than Helen Anderson, in the Whitaker case.

The more Lizzie thought about Jane, the more she felt sorry for her. Gary had filled her in on the outline of the case in strict confidence; Lizzie had no idea why he needed to emphasise that, anyone would think he thought her a gossip. As it was, she hadn't even told Maggie.

Jane had clearly had a pretty dysfunctional childhood regardless of whether or not she was guilty of any crime. Lizzie was determined to keep an open mind. The problem was that she kept wondering which of her neighbours fitted the Macintyre profile.

She sat down on the bench, pulling her olive green fleece tightly around her and looked out towards the hills in the distance. Her view was obscured slightly by a light autumnal mist that had descended during the last hour or so. The churchyard was quiet, apart from a little birdsong and a growing collection of fallen leaves blowing around on the gravel path.

She started thinking about Sally Barton; could she be Jane? Lizzie had known her ever since she moved to Blenthorne all that time ago. Sally was in the pub the night of the journalist's performance. She and Jack had met in the mid-eighties. She always chatted happily to Lizzie when they bumped into each other, she had never mentioned her family and certainly, if she had any, they didn't visit.

Hilary Cole was there too, having a drink with Dawn and Mario. She wasn't a serious contender, surely? Whilst she could conceivably be the right age to be Jane Macintyre, logistically, she couldn't have killed Percival Whitaker as she was at the post office all day and many in the village would attest to that. That left Dawn Sanchez and Gloria Humphries. Dawn was a colourful character and Gloria quite the reverse. Her thoughts were interrupted suddenly by one of the ladies in question appearing, as if by magic.

'Can I join you, Lizzie; do you mind?' said the slim dark-haired woman.

'Hello, Dawn; of course not, it's nice to see you.' said Lizzie, moving along the bench a little to make room for Dawn to sit down.

'Hope I'm not intruding. I have a confession to make; I asked Maggie where you might be as you weren't answering your phone and she said she thought you could be here.'

'She knows me too well! What can I do for you?' asked Lizzie, suddenly intrigued.

Dawn didn't reply immediately. She took a piece of chewing gum out of her mouth and looked around, clearly wondering what to do with it. Lizzie pulled a tissue from the pocket of her fleece and handed it to Dawn, who took it and wrapped her gum up before manoeuvring it into the pocket of her tight blue jeans.

'Ta. Filthy habit but at least it stops me smoking! The thing is; the police want to speak to me tomorrow morning. I'm a bit worried about it because I don't know why they've picked on me. I know you've had dealings with them and I'm sorry to bring that up but I need some advice. You always seem so confident, I couldn't think who else to turn to.'

Lizzie felt quite flattered. 'I'm sure they haven't singled you out, they'll be speaking to all the locals eventually.'

'I didn't even know the bloke that was killed,' said Dawn with a sharp intake of breath.

'Did you ask the officer who contacted you why they wanted to speak to you now?'

'No, can you find out for me?' asked Dawn, looking pleadingly at Lizzie.

'I'm not sure how. I know Ken Stokes of course but he wouldn't be obliged to justify the team's reasoning to me or anyone else. Gary told me off for telling the police how to do their job when they first arrived, because I said they need look no further than Helen Anderson.

'Just answer the questions honestly and don't leave anything out because you don't think it's relevant. Is there something in particular that's bothering you?' Lizzie asked gently, hoping she wasn't being too direct.

She waited patiently whilst Dawn twiddled a strand of her straight shoulder length hair. When it became clear she wasn't going to be drawn out, Lizzie tried again;

'Before he died, did Percival Whitaker ask you to meet him?'

'What? No, of course not, why would he? I've told you, I didn't know the bloke; that is; I don't think I ever met him …' she replied uncertainly.

'Maybe not but that doesn't mean he didn't think he knew you, or knew *of* you.'

'I came to ask for your help and now I feel like I'm being grilled,' Dawn crossed her legs away from Lizzie and folded her arms across her chest in a defensive posture.

'Maybe it would be best if you wait and talk to the police tomorrow, Dawn.' Lizzie gambled that reminding Dawn of tomorrow's interview would bring her worries back to the forefront of her mind and encourage her to stay. She was delighted when the younger woman remained seated.

Lizzie found herself wondering how tall Dawn was; average height for a woman, possibly a bit above and agile-looking. She could have whacked the journalist over the head and pushed him into the water.

'The thing is, Lizzie, I've got baggage. Nothing really bad but I worked as a… hostess… I suppose you could call it, for a while, after my ankle gave out and made it difficult for me to dance; did you know I used to be a dancer?'

Lizzie nodded. 'Yes, I was going to try to get you to audition for the Blenthorne Brigade when we next have a pantomime; would you be interested? If your ankle isn't up to actually dancing, then maybe you could be our choreographer?' She fervently hoped a small bit of flattery might distract Dawn, sufficient for her to open up further.

'Really, you want me to join your group?' Dawn flashed a beaming smile at Lizzie. 'It'd be okay at amateur level; it's just doing it every day, I couldn't hack it any longer. I know on the telly it looks like they get on well and they have lovely clothes, amazing hairdos and makeup but in reality, it's ever so competitive and catty and I'm not just talking about the women!'

'We have the odd prima donna in our group too but leaving Maggie aside, I think we're a pretty happy and friendly bunch,' remarked Lizzie, tongue-in-cheek.

'Honestly, it's been years but I'll think about it.' Dawn looked a little flushed as she smiled again at Lizzie, completely missing the attempted joke at Maggie's expense.

'Thanks, Dawn. You were saying you worked as a hostess?' prompted Lizzie encouragingly.

'Yeah, some of the people I associated with were a bit dodgy; I never asked too many questions when I was young and if men wanted to spend money on me... but ignorance is no defence, is it?' she paused, flicking a large chunk of hair from the left side of her head, revealing a huge silver looped earring at the bottom of her lobe and a stud higher up. 'One thing leads to another though. I thought as I got older and lost my looks, I'd end up turning tricks on street corners or off my head on smack... you know what I mean, so I used the contacts I had and got a job in a bookies.

'I suppose what I'm saying is; I'm worried that the police will think Whitaker found out and that would be a motive for me to top him. You see, Mario doesn't know about it, at least, not all of it. He'd go mad; when I met him he was married to someone else and she was a right piece of work, running up debts, having affairs – you name it, she did it. I suppose I tried to portray myself as completely the opposite of her, when actually I was very similar, just younger. I was in debt too and Mario was kind to me. I don't want to lose him; no one's ever been there for me the way he has. I've been totally faithful to him since we've been together; I haven't looked at another man. Okay, I may have looked, but never any actual hanky-panky, in spite of being chatted up more than once. In fact, you know that group from Liverpool, there's one that...'

Lizzie smiled, wondering if she should encourage Dawn to talk about her potential extra-marital opportunities but decided it would likely just be a distraction from her main focus.

'You're an attractive lady, Dawn,' Lizzie interjected, 'so I'm not totally surprised but to be brutally honest,

I hardly think Percival Whitaker was going to expose your past for the purposes of discrediting you in the eyes of your husband. It wouldn't be juicy enough for him, unless there's anything you left out?' Lizzie paused as Dawn shook her head slowly. 'I believe he was interested in scandal on a far larger scale than a young single lady leading the high life or flirting a bit, even after she's married!'

Dawn appeared to relax. 'You really think it wasn't me he was interested in? Only, when he started spouting off in the pub that night, I thought he was speaking directly to me.'

Lizzie decided she liked playing detective and changed tack a little.

'As a matter of interest, several people have reported that Percival Whitaker said something to Helen Anderson which clearly made her very uncomfortable. Were you close enough to hear what it was?' Lizzie looked intently at Dawn.

'No I wasn't. I was sitting with Mario and Hilary from the post office, we were chatting and gradually the whole pub fell silent as Whitaker warmed to his theme, as you probably noticed. I think we were all a little embarrassed but at the same time gripped by his performance and Helen's reaction. It was a bit like people who can't help but look at the aftermath of a car crash so that they can recoil in horror. You get my drift?'

Lizzie nodded; suddenly realising there was more depth to Dawn that she had previously imagined.

'Interesting that you've struck up a friendship with Hilary Cole, I've known her for years, of course, but only superficially; I wouldn't say we're close, what about you?'

'That's difficult to judge,' replied Dawn. 'I like her, she's totally different to anyone I've ever met. I know people think we're chalk and cheese and maybe we are but we got chatting when we were singing in the choir and she's actually quite funny when you peel away the layers. We snicker at Gloria Humphries as she takes herself so seriously; the silly woman can't make any eye contact, so we're never sure who she's speaking to. Hilary's nowhere near as stuck up as people think.'

'I suppose I've tended to see her as someone who's always in the background, on the periphery of the community. That makes me sound pretty shallow, doesn't it?' Lizzie felt quite shocked by her own revelation.

'Not at all. I think Hilary's to blame; she pushes people away. She doesn't like anyone to get close to her as she's worried about people thinking she's a nuisance. From what she's told me, I think her parents were very strict but she loved her aunt very much.'

'Yes, I know she lived with an aunt. Did her parents die?' asked Lizzie, picking up on the point, further horrified that she was spending hours of time helping ex-offenders but had hitherto barely bothered about a near neighbour.

'Now you come to mention it, I'm not sure. I sort of assumed her parents had died but I can't remember her actually telling me that, why?'

'If her parents died when she was young, that would be one thing. If, on the other hand, they abandoned her to the care of an aunt, maybe she felt rejected and that would explain her difficulty in getting close to people.'

'Oh yes, I can see that. I think she mentioned that she had been born in Scotland, do you want me to ask her about her parents?'

'No, don't risk damaging your relationship with her if she's touchy on the subject. On a positive note, you seem to have brought her out of her shell.'

'I don't know about that but life is too short to ignore people who maybe just need a friend, isn't it?' said Dawn, disarmingly. She looked at her watch; 'I must go.'

Lizzie felt further ashamed that she had pigeonholed the woman beside her as an airhead.

'It's been lovely to chat with you, Dawn. We really must get together for coffee or a proper drink sometime soon, how does that sound?'

Dawn smiled and nodded as she rose to her feet and said goodbye.

Lizzie would pass on the information she had gleaned and hoped it would eliminate Dawn from the police enquiries, although she wasn't totally convinced that her new friend had been completely candid with her at every level.

In addition to the confidences she had elicited from Dawn Sanchez, she had another valuable piece of information. Dawn had said that when Percival Whitaker was holding audience in the lounge bar of the pub shortly before his death, she had thought he was speaking directly to her with his "other fish to fry" comment. What if she hadn't been alone in that assumption, particularly if someone else had something of far greater magnitude to hide?

*

After an early dinner with Gary and a quick debrief regarding Dawn Sanchez, about which Gary promised to apprise Ken, Lizzie made her way to the pub for the evening shift. Maggie was having the night off and whilst it should be quiet, she didn't like leaving Mia on her own. Andrea was always willing to lend a hand but she tired easily, especially after a day at work.

When she got there, the lounge was pretty dead; just Colleen Plumley, her assistant Tim Carney, and Connor Robson, Mia's boyfriend, standing at the bar.

Connor was a strange chap, somewhat monosyllabic and it was difficult to see what the attraction was. Mia was outgoing and always ready to exchange a bit of banter with the customers. Connor on the other hand was introverted; sullen, even. He was a few years older than Mia, so his reticence couldn't be attributed to the awkwardness of youth. He worked as premises manager at the local primary school in Rowendale; in addition, he did a few night shifts as a porter at the hotel and a bit of gym work. Lizzie didn't think he had grown up locally; his accent would certainly suggest he was from further afield. She didn't normally have problems chatting to people and had tried to talk to him several times but found it tough going, so had given up. All she did subsequently was pass the time of day. As was usual, in acknowledgement of her greeting, Connor allowed himself a half smile and buried his head in his pint once more. No doubt Colleen would make up for any gaps in the conversation. However, before she had the chance to impart any pearls of wisdom, Mia spoke.

'Oh, by the way, Lizzie, my mum said if things stay quiet this evening, could you pop upstairs to see her. I think she has something that she wants to speak to you about.'

It seemed to be her day for confidences, she thought ironically. As it wasn't busy in the bar, Lizzie told Mia she would go up there and then.

Mia nodded and smiled as she bent her head towards Connor to hear something he had said, clearly for her ears only.

Lizzie walked quickly up the familiar staircase. The flat at the Blenny held many memories. So much had happened here over the years, Richard and then Jim… She pulled herself out of her reminiscences as she knocked on the door of the flat. Andrea called out a cheery greeting and Lizzie entered the hallway.

'Lizzie, thank you for coming up; I hope I'm not wasting your time,' she said a little hesitantly as she appeared from the living room.

Lizzie wished Andrea wouldn't be so self-deprecating.

'You could never do that, Andrea. Mia has everything under control downstairs so I thought I'd come up to the flat while it's quiet. What did you want to see me about?'

'Tea and cake – I've been baking! Or would you prefer coffee?' Before waiting for Lizzie's answer, Andrea turned and walked quickly back through the door to the main living space, one end of which was given over to a kitchen area.

Lizzie was mindful of Andrea's difficulties. It seemed traits that were already present took on even more significance after a brain injury. She liked to look after people and if it put her at ease to do so, then it was easier to acquiesce than to decline. Good thing Lizzie hadn't had a sweet course with dinner.

'That sounds wonderful, Andrea,' she said, following her through the door. 'The thought of one of your cakes would be too much for anyone to resist but I'll take a smallish slice, so that there's some left for people to enjoy tomorrow. I'll have tea with it, if I may.'

Andrea smiled at the floor as she twisted her hands in front of her. It appeared she already had the tray ready as she reappeared from the kitchen area within a minute; a conjecture which she confirmed upon returning to the lounge.

'Just had to boil the kettle again as I wasn't sure what time you'd come up.'

They sat down on the familiar sofas.

Lizzie had a bite of cake and a sip of tea. 'Oh my word; how delicious is that sponge? If you ever get fed up with working with Jono, I'm sure Maggie would offer you a job baking for the Blenny.' She paused for a moment then added, 'Mia said you wanted to talk to me.'

Andrea smiled hesitantly. 'You're very kind, Lizzie.'

Lizzie waited but when Andrea failed to elucidate further, she prompted her friend.

'So… what did you want to talk to me about?'

'Oh gosh yes, sorry. I just wondered if I could ask your advice, really. I don't mean to be a busybody but it's Helen Anderson. I didn't say anything before as I don't want to make trouble for her, honestly.'

'You would never make trouble for anyone, Andrea.'

Again Andrea looked at her hands tightly clasped in her lap.

'What do you want to tell me about Helen?' Lizzie prodded gently.

'Oh yes, sorry… it was the evening Mr Whitaker was here. He came in when I was having a drink with Jono, bless him, he's so kind, Jono that is. Anyway, just as Gary left with a bundle of papers after talking to Helen, Mr Whitaker arrived. He didn't sit down immediately just paced around a bit, pretending to talk to Helen but actually just showing off. He was being unkind but dressing it up with smarm and smiles. Then he took the chair opposite her. Nasty man, I felt sorry for her in a way. She's been quite nice to me recently, so I can't judge her too harshly. It's just that Maggie dislikes her with a vengeance so I don't want to upset her.'

'Well no, all of us do that at our peril. So go on; you were telling me what transpired the night Percival Whitaker came to the pub and spoke to Helen?' Lizzie coaxed encouragingly.

'Oh yes, so I was! To be honest, I thought he was going to create a scene and I hate that, as you know. Any form of confrontation makes me hyperventilate and I know that's bad for me so I try to avoid it. Jono suggested we leave as he sensed I was beginning to panic but I said I would go and powder my nose and it might all blow over by the time I returned. So, I went to the loo and when I was coming back, I think that was the moment Mr Whitaker was dropping his bombshell.

'I was just passing Helen's table near the fireplace when I noticed a tissue on the floor. Maggie hates rubbish being left around but she was in the other bar, so I bent down to pick it up. That coincided with Mr Whitaker leaning forward and whispering something to Helen. I particularly took notice as he was that close, I thought he was going to kiss her but he didn't, obviously.'

Lizzie waited as Andrea blinked rapidly.

'Did you hear what he said?' She asked after a moment when Andrea failed to volunteer the information.

'Oh yes, but it didn't make any sense and it wasn't anything nasty. It was just a name; "Trevor Gill".

That's all he said, not "remember Trevor Gill" or "Trevor Gill sends his regards" or anything, just the name. I wasn't going to say anything as it wasn't like he was threatening her. What do you think it means?'

'I don't know. I can only assume Trevor Gill is someone from the past whom Helen would rather have not been reminded of. I'll speak to Gary and he can let Ken Stokes know, as it might be relevant.'

'I don't want to cause Helen any anxiety; I'm not a vindictive person.'

'You've only told me what you overheard, Andrea. Ken might want to speak to you but all you need to do is tell him exactly what you've told me.'

'Alright, if you think it's worth bothering him.'

'There are several lines of enquiry being followed up at the moment, I think and every piece of information offered by witnesses will help with the overall picture. I expect Ken will give you a ring, if that's okay?'

Andrea looked relieved. 'Oh yes, that would be fine. Thank you, Lizzie, you're so kind. I knew you'd know the right thing to do.'

Lizzie smiled at her timid companion as she got up and left to go back to the bar.

Lizzie wondered who Trevor Gill might be as she walked slowly down the stairs. She would ask Gary if it was someone from Malchington Bay. On the other hand, maybe it was someone from Helen's earlier life. Ken would put one of the team on to it, no doubt. Every minute it seemed more and more possibilities were opening up.

She was certainly getting entangled in this case; maybe she'd missed her vocation. She smiled to herself as she walked through the office into the bar area towards a waiting customer.

*

After Lizzie had gone, Andrea cleared away the tea tray. She hugged her cup closely. She loved Lizzie so much; almost as much as she loved Gary. She was sure the whole village was just waiting for her and Jono to announce they were an item. He was a lovely man and clearly thought the world of her but when your heart has already been taken, there's nothing you can do about it. Of course, Gary would never think of her in that way and she didn't really want him to. He belonged to Lizzie and she was indebted to Lizzie for her kindness after she came to Blenthorne. No, she was happy with the status quo. That's what Helen Anderson had threatened. She believed she could muscle her way in and replace Lizzie. That was unthinkable.

Andrea didn't regret what she'd done; sometimes the end justified the means. Served her right, she sat there playing the persecuted victim the evening she had given Gary the letters and made the suggestion herself that vermin might be thrown over her car. So she'd got what she wanted, hadn't she?

Andrea just hoped the police wouldn't find out about her; surely they had far too much to think about now?

Anyway, she had told Lizzie what she'd heard Mr Whitaker say to Helen. She said she wasn't vindictive but wouldn't it be just wonderful if Helen Anderson was implicated in murder? She replaced the cup on the tray and took it into the kitchen, pulled on her rubber gloves and ran the hot water tap.

*

'First Dawn Sanchez confides in Lizzie and now Andrea Pearce! Is your good lady charging a consultancy fee?' laughed Ken the following morning when Gary rang him with the information from Andrea.

'Frankly, I think she's enjoying herself. However, now we have another angle; who is Trevor Gill and how does he fit into Helen's life? He's not from Malching, as far as I know.'

'Maybe you could ask Helen about him; I got precisely nowhere when I tried to question her but if anyone can elicit anything, it's you. Go and talk to her, Gary, and see what you can discover about our friend, Trevor. You might catch her off guard.'

After a little persuasion, Gary agreed to assist Ken. He did facetiously ask if he could also be considered for a consultancy fee, causing his former colleague to snort so loudly he made himself cough.

Ken said he would contact Andrea later in the day. Before hanging up, he made a cheeky request of Gary.

'I'll have to speak to Lizzie first and get back to you.' Gary replied non-committally, as he replaced his mobile in his pocket.

*

Armed with his brief, Gary set off later that morning to see Helen Anderson at the hotel. On the surface, all appeared to be back to normal with guests leaving the front entrance, clearly equipped for walking. Helen was in the reception area when he arrived.

'Gary, this is a pleasant surprise! Do come through to the office; can I get you a drink?'

Gary shook his head as he followed Helen away from the public space.

Instead of sitting behind the desk, Helen sat on the sofa and patted the space next to her. Gary instead opted for the upright chair that faced the desk, turning it around to face her. The dynamics of the situation had played into his hands superbly. Helen's choice meant his seating position was higher, allowing him to look down at her; thus giving him a psychological advantage. First point to him, he thought with an inward smile.

He saw from the look on her face that she immediately realised she had made a tactical error but clearly there was little she could do about it.

'I've just called round to check all is okay here. Detective Sergeant Stokes said you were rather overwhelmed after the discovery of Percival Whitaker's body.'

Safe ground; she seemed to relax a little.

'I was rather fraught at the time with the police everywhere but now they've decamped to the parish hall. Since they searched Whitaker's room and interviewed the staff, they've pretty much left us alone, so on the surface, I think we have things running as normal. I'll let you know if there's anything I need help with.'

'I just heard two guests commenting on what a pleasant hotel it is and how welcome they had been made to feel as they left for the day,' lied Gary smoothly.

'Really; that's terrific news. Thank you so much for passing it on. I do hope the guys think I've done a reasonable job when they return.'

'No doubt about it Helen, the hotel couldn't be in better hands.'

Helen crossed her legs and smoothed her already immaculate hair with her left hand as she smiled.

Gary decided he had buttered her up sufficiently.

'One more thing while I'm here; just a heads up before the police ask you about it. I've heard via the grapevine that there was a witness to Percival Whitaker's parting shot to you in the pub the other night. Probably of no importance but just in case it jogs your memory, apparently it was a name; "Trevor Gill" does that mean anything?'

Helen stared wide-eyed at Gary for several moments. He had seen her use this stalling device before.

'You know, that evening is such a blur in my mind, with all that's happened since, I really couldn't begin to think about one small incident. If I looked blank or surprised or whatever has been suggested, I suspect it was because I had no idea to whom he was referring. Let me think... I knew a Trevor Gilham once, maybe that was it? He was an old boyfriend from my pre-university days. If Whitaker had been digging, I suppose he may have unearthed dear old Trevor but there would be nothing newsworthy in that. We had a few dates, did what teenagers usually do and spilt up. End of. Does that help at all?'

'You see that's the thing, until all the bits are put together, we have no way of knowing what will help and what's irrelevant. Okay for me to pass this to Ken Stokes and the team?'

'You just said it was a heads up! Be honest, Gary. You really think I killed Whitaker? Bludgeoned him to death because he had unearthed someone I haven't seen since I was eighteen?'

'No, Helen I don't think anything at the moment. I really hope you aren't involved and moreover I hope what you've just told me is the truth as these things have a way of coming back to bite.'

Gary felt slightly irritated that Helen had handled the situation so well. As to whether this Trevor Gill or Gilham was relevant, time would tell but for now he could think of no reason to prolong their conversation.

As he left, after declining her offer to stay for lunch, he rang Ken Stokes to report back. Sadly, he had little cause for self-congratulation.

'Helen's clearly still in the frame,' replied Ken.

Gary had to admit Ken had a point. If Jane Macintyre hadn't killed Percival Whitaker then it was looking more and more likely that Helen Anderson had.

Little did either of them realise as they finished their conversation that the investigation was going to take an unexpected turn in the very near future.

Chapter 9 – Evasion and Discussion

Ken put the phone down after his conversation with Gary regarding, among other things, Helen Anderson's mystery boyfriend, Trevor Gill. There were a few other aspects of the case he wanted to talk through with him but as he had just wangled an invitation to stay, as a result of the cheeky favour he had asked Gary the previous day, there would be plenty of time for that. He had been home the previous night and listened to his mother-in-law pontificating on every subject under the sun, from human rights legislation to bankers' bonuses. Suddenly his fear of being slain in his bed if he stayed in Blenthorne was outweighed by his overwhelming desire to get as far away as possible.

Just after he sent Gary Carmichael to the hotel to see Helen, he had interviewed Dawn Sanchez at the hall. She had more or less repeated what she had told Lizzie in the churchyard. Her story checked out up to a point. She appeared on the radar from the age of twenty two but prior to that, she didn't seem to exist. She had tried to explain this away by suggesting she had moved from place to place as a child as her family were travellers. Somehow it didn't ring quite true. The travelling community was tight-knit, people didn't often leave, particularly not at that age; most girls were married as teenagers, from what he understood. Also, travellers chose to move around but that didn't mean they could completely slip through the system. Added to that, Lizzie had apparently been unconvinced Dawn had told her everything.

Definitely a question mark there and he had set Gina on to it. If there was any dirt, Gina would dig it out.

Ken studied the report in front of him. The team had looked at Sally Barton's early life in detail. It hadn't been difficult to trace her background. She had been in local authority care as a child and later began a job in Somerset where she met her future husband, Jack. No evidence of a name change prior to her marriage and records of her early life had no gaps.

A storm erupted when Jack had returned home with Sally in tow. His long term girlfriend was a local lass whom everyone liked. She knew nothing of his relationship until Jack came back and broke the news to her. She didn't take it well. She threw a brick at the windscreen and scratched the side of his car with a screwdriver. Made quite a scene on several separate occasions with the drama being played out in front of the whole village but when it became clear Jack wasn't going to change his mind, she left, cursing the couple and hoping to bring fire and brimstone down on them and their offspring for all eternity. They had a few problems for a while with many in the community thinking Jack had behaved badly but time passes and people forgive, although many older residents clearly hadn't forgotten, as their testimonies to the team confirmed.

The couple appeared to be happy and their union had produced two children, so clearly their rocky start hadn't had any lasting effect. Try as he might, Ken couldn't think of a connection, however tenuous, to the present case. He was confident Sally could be eliminated from further enquiries.

He yawned; good gracious, he was tired! After listening to his mother-in-law's diatribe on the state of the nation, she had turned her attention to his oldest daughter who had taken to "living in sin", having just moved in with her boyfriend. He had told Mrs S this morning that this case was going to be complicated and rather than arriving home late and leaving early, thereby disturbing the household, it would be best for them all if he stayed in Blenthorne for the next few days, ideally to coincide with the departure of her mother, but he refrained from adding that, as some things were best left unsaid.

He had packed a bag and placed it in the boot of his car after Gary had messaged him to confirm Lizzie was happy for him to stay.

He had a wander around the village to clear his head before the conference call update with his team and the DCI. The village hadn't changed much over the years. The shops managed to keep going with support from the community and the tourists who flocked to the area in the better weather. There seemed to be a goodly supply of Europeans this year he noticed, as well as Americans and a coachload of Japanese holidaymakers. As long as they spent their converted euros, dollars and yen, he was sure they would continue to be welcome. He looked at the post office which was joined to the local shop. He wondered again about Hilary Cole. Of course she couldn't be the killer; she was in plain sight the day of the murder, so he wasn't sure why she kept coming into his head.

For the sake of thoroughness, they would look at her background prior to her coming to Blenthorne.

He realised the tall, lean form of the vicar was approaching him, smiling thinly. He wondered why he always felt the irrational desire to run away at such times. After all, he needed to look closely at Mrs Vicar and maybe even the vicar himself if the somewhat wild speculation he and Gary had indulged in, regarding the identity of the couple, was to be given credence. Could they be Jane Macintyre and Nick Smith respectively?

'Detective Sergeant Stokes, it's nice to see you, we've met at the Blenthorne Inn in days gone by, I believe,' said the vicar, extending his hand. Ken shook it and nodded in agreement.

'This is a bad business; how is the investigation progressing or are you unable to tell me?' the clergyman asked in a semi-conspiratorial tone.

'I think it's fair to say we are following some very productive lines of enquiry. Actually, it's quite fortuitous that we've bumped into each other, as I was hoping to have a word with you and your wife soon; maybe we could get something in the diary now.'

'Really, I'm not sure what we can tell you? Mr Whitaker was many things, I believe, but a church attender he was not; at least, not since he came here.'

'No, I understand that. I've been told he spent most of his time working in his room on an old story that had resurfaced since he arrived in Blenthorne. There are two things, actually; you and your wife were present in the pub when Percival Whitaker spoke to Helen Anderson, I believe? I would like to get your take on that exchange. I would also appreciate some background detail, Reverend, regarding yourself and your good lady.'

The merest flicker of something passed across the vicar's face. Was it alarm? The reverend recovered his composure in an instant. Had Ken imagined it? He couldn't be sure.

'Goodness that sounds intriguing, I'm not at all sure we can tell you anything of interest. We call at the inn occasionally just to keep in touch with the wider community and of course we witnessed the encounter between Mr Whitaker and Ms Anderson. There's no doubt it was rather uncomfortable to watch but then they both left and we enjoyed a convivial drink in the company of a few villagers before retiring.'

If the vicar hoped the detective would be satisfied, he was disabused of that notion immediately.

'It's purely routine, nothing to worry about. Could I come to see you this afternoon do you think, about two thirty? And maybe Mrs...' ever since Lizzie had referred to them as Mr and Mrs Vicar, he thought of them as such and now couldn't remember their surname.

'Gloria,' said the vicar, clearly trying to be helpful.

It didn't help.

'Yes indeed, if I could have a word with her afterwards maybe, say three o'clock?'

'I'll speak to her, Sergeant, but I have a tutorial in the Keswick area this afternoon. I'm leading a group of aspiring clergy on a discussion regarding multi-culturalism. They are a plucky bunch but some take themselves a little too seriously at times and the earnest discussions can drag on a bit, even for me. However, we need to attract people into the profession and hopefully I'm doing my small bit in that regard. I'll be with them from two until after six, I'm afraid.'

'Tomorrow then, at a time to suit you?' Ken persisted.

'Tomorrow um... I might be able to give you half an hour; I'll ring you if I may.'

Ken proffered his card.

'Do you happen to know if Mrs... your wife is free this afternoon or early evening? May I call her?'

'I… yes, by all means but I'm afraid I am not party to her movements. She's usually engaged in some form of pastoral duty. She takes her role within the community very seriously.' He wrote down a contact number on the back of a till receipt that he found in his pocket and passed it to the policeman.

'Much obliged, Reverend; I'll contact you in the morning if I may, you can always come to the parish hall if it's not convenient for me to visit the vicarage but we do need to get together as soon as possible as the investigation needs to keep moving forward.'

Ken hoped he had made it clear that his request wasn't optional. They made their farewells and parted company. Was it his imagination or had the vicar been a little evasive?

Humphries, of course, that was their surname – shame he couldn't have remembered that five minutes ago.

*

As he walked back to the hall, Ken attempted to ring the vicarage but got the answerphone. He left a message for Mrs Humphries and asked if he could pop round at two thirty for half an hour or so. Upon his return, he and the team spent the next hour discussing the results of their morning endeavours and he rang Andrea Pearce, who confirmed her conversation with Lizzie Lockwood regarding Trevor Gill. Just before lunch, the team participated in a conference call with the officer in charge, DCI Cooper.

After a sandwich, two mugs of tea and a small bar of chocolate, Ken made his way to the vicarage. Although he hadn't received a reply to his answerphone message he decided to try his luck on the off chance that Mrs Vicar would be at home. She wasn't.

Undeterred, he decided to visit the museum which was run by Colleen Plumley and her assistant, Tim Carney. He understood from Lizzie that Colleen and Percival Whitaker had become quite cosy on several occasions prior to his self-imposed exile. He would be interested to hear what he and Colleen had talked about. He knew that Lizzie Lockwood was somehow related to Colleen and he rang to ask if she were free to give him a bit more background information. Rather irritatingly, she said she would meet him at the museum. He decided it couldn't do any harm and he had rather foisted himself upon her as a house guest.

As Ken drew up in the carpark, he saw Lizzie Lockwood's car. She got out as he approached and they chatted amiably as they walked up the drive to the entrance. Lizzie's background synopsis on Colleen was thorough and informative and Ken suddenly appreciated why she was such a tour de force among the local community. Coining a phrase his old superintendent often used, there were clearly "no flies on her". He found himself thinking how much more objective she was now, compared to when he had interviewed her in the pub. On that occasion her comments were clearly prejudiced by her intense dislike of Helen Anderson.

As it was, by the time they arrived at the entrance, Ken knew that the museum was situated on the north side of the Barton farm. The farm had been much larger in bygone days but now it appeared that several outbuildings had been converted into offices, some of which were rented out and other units which were currently unoccupied. The land on which the museum stood once accommodated livestock but the cattle were now outnumbered by sheep that didn't need such large enclosures and so two of the former cowsheds now formed the main part of the museum.

Colleen had run the establishment by herself in the early days. However, its popularity and her decision to serve refreshments meant that she needed help. She had employed casual staff originally but realising some of her artefacts were quite valuable, decided she needed someone who not only had an understanding of their worth but was able to clean and display them appropriately and, moreover, talk to the visitors in a knowledgeable way.

It had been mutually beneficial when Tim Carney arrived in response to her discreet advertisement in a suitable journal. Plans had been drawn up and were now underway for the museum building to be enlarged. The original intention of displaying family treasures had now been extended to encompass items of cultural or historical interest from all parts of their corner of Cumbria. The current facilities were proving inadequate on busy days. Twice in the last month they had had to close temporarily on health and safety grounds as they struggled to cope with ever-growing visitor numbers. Lizzie believed that Colleen was not overtly avaricious but it did gall her to have to turn away paying customers. They were particularly popular on cold or wet days for obvious reasons. They opened their doors three full days and two half days per week, which gave them some time for inventory, renovation, cleaning and displaying of treasures.

Lizzie felt Colleen was in her element, not only was she doing something she loved but she and Tim had formed a strong working relationship which spilled over into their personal lives. In fact, Tim had even taken up lodgings with Colleen.

As they entered the building Tim was standing behind the reception desk and he smiled a greeting.

'Sir, Madam; two is it? Oh sorry, Lizzie I didn't recognise you for a moment.'

'Hi, Tim; we're here to see Colleen, she's expecting us,' said Lizzie. 'Tim Carney, this is Detective Sergeant Ken Stokes.'

Ken looked at the youngish chap in front of him. His hair was fine in texture and flopped over his forehead. He was sporting the usual designer stubble, favoured by the young.

'It's a pleasure to meet you, Detective Sergeant. I'll let Colleen know you're here.' He gave the police officer a firm handshake before picking up the phone and speaking to his employer.

'And you, Tim; have you been in the area long?' asked Ken.

'To be honest, it seems like ages because I fit in so well, I feel as if it's always been my home. I love it; the place and the people. I haven't felt like this before and that's the truth. I never venture far from the village; I don't need to because I have almost everything I want from life in Blenthorne. Colleen has been marvellous, not only giving me this job but a place to stay. I can't imagine leaving now. In the small amount of spare time I have, Colleen encourages me to indulge my passion for writing; she's so supportive. I haven't been published yet but I live in hope. As it happens, I've been working on the manuscript of a new thriller and I'm sending off some sample chapters today; so fingers crossed!'

'I'm sure she's equally pleased to have found you, Tim,' said Lizzie pleasantly, clearly resisting any temptation to encourage Tim to talk about his literary endeavours.

At that moment Colleen Plumley appeared from a side door, leading from the workroom.

'I'm sorry to keep you waiting folks; hello, Lizzie.' She leaned forward and planted a kiss firmly on Lizzie's left cheek. 'I've just taken delivery of some pottery which originated from this area many years ago and I have to decide how best to clean it up without damaging it. Come through this way. Oh, and I've had a look at the plans you gave me showing the Blenny when it was a coaching inn, I'd like to display them if it's alright with you?'

'Yes, of course you can, no point leaving them laying around in a dusty old drawer in the office at the pub is there?'

'I can't believe your old drawers are dusty, my dear,' murmured Colleen wryly, before directing them through the workroom to the office space beyond.

It was all rather ramshackle and untidy with boxes, both wooden and cardboard, on almost every surface. The chairs facing the desk had seen better days; one looked mock Georgian with arms and a saggy looking seat and the other, a slightly less worse-for-wear Edwardian dining chair. A modern swivel chair with threadbare upholstery was positioned behind the desk. The office had a faintly musty smell. Three walls were solid and the fourth was made from plywood. The extension would be accessed from this point, Colleen explained and there was to be much larger dedicated office accommodation in the new part of the building.

'Of course, to some extent we are victims of our own success, aren't we, Tim?' said Colleen to her assistant who was hovering by the door. Colleen approached the chair behind the desk and eased herself in. Actually, Ken observed, she didn't so much sit down in a controlled manner by bending her knees, as concertina in the middle. She then put her trust not only in gravity but also the integrity of the chair, making a sort of "oof" sound as she landed. Once settled, she put her hands on the small free space in front of her on the desk and looked expectantly at her guests.

Ken decided she was possibly more than a little eccentric. She was less than average height with a stocky build and clad in dark green trousers with a large blue tartan pattern. The material was clearly sturdy but even so, stretched across her midriff with difficulty. Her pink blouse was tucked in at the waist and had rather grubby long sleeves which were buttoned at the cuffs. Her glasses were suspended on a chain around her neck and sat on her ample chest. Her hair was predominantly grey and cut in a short bob, pushed away from her face by a wide tortoiseshell coloured hairband.

Tim nodded, smiled and appeared to be about to speak but instead turned and left the room in response to the shrill sound of the handheld reception bell.

'Really from the moment we opened our doors, people flocked to us. To start with, it was mainly locals; some being supportive and some out of good old plain curiosity. Subsequently though we've attracted people from all over the world. This year we have an entry in an area tourist guidebook and we didn't even have to pay for it! Jono Johnson said he would put us in touch with his website designer but to be honest I'm not sure we need it; still, apparently everyone has to have one these days. The more popular we become, the more donations we receive. I really think we may have to consider taking on more staff but then of course the overheads start to mount up. In many ways it's nice just being the two of us and, in addition, we have a couple of ladies who take care of refreshments in the busier periods.'

'Tim was telling us he likes it here but do I take it he hasn't been with you long?' asked Ken conversationally, pulling his notebook from his pocket. 'Do you mind if I jot down a few things, just to jog my memory later?'

'Of course you can, my love. Tim's been with me for almost a year now; I can't believe the difference he's made. He doesn't mind what he turns his hands to you know, he's so eager and he has a real creative eye for displaying our treasures to their best advantage. We're here from eight thirty each day until practically seven o'clock in the evening, even if we're not open to the public. Sometimes I have to insist he leaves me to finish off by myself or he would miss his choir practice; he's a tenor, I believe, but usually plays the piano. To be honest, it's him or poor Hilary Cole who is technically correct but has no flair, whereas Tim is apparently a touch player; as if I know what I'm talking about, don't have a musical bone in my body! Anyhow, if we've had a particularly tiring day, we sometimes treat ourselves to dinner at the pub but of course recently he's been tied up with writing his new book so I've been dependent on my own company of an evening,' she smiled and inclined her head towards Lizzie.

'And we very much appreciate your patronage, Colleen. Speaking of the pub, I noticed that you struck up a bit of a friendship with Percival Whitaker. I suppose if Tim's been busy, it was nice to find someone else for a drink and a chat?'

Momentarily, Ken felt like a spare part at his own interview, with Lizzie leading the conversation with seamless ease.

'Yes, I thought that would be the reason the police wanted to see me,' said Colleen shrewdly, directing her gaze at Ken.

'I wouldn't say a "friendship" exactly. He clearly wanted to pump the Blenny regulars for information. I think it's well known in the village that I'm not only interested in artefacts and collectables but I'm also a conversationalist. I enjoy getting to know people and finding out what makes them tick, not in a malicious way, at least I hope that's not how I'm perceived, though we all enjoy a juicy piece of gossip from time to time and anyone that tells you otherwise is being less than honest. With the possible exception of Andrea Pearce, there wasn't a person present in the pub that wasn't transfixed when Percival Whitaker teased Helen Anderson.'

Ken couldn't help but think there was probably more than a bit of truth in what she said.

'You could have heard a pin drop, so whatever he said, shocked her deeply,' finished Colleen.

'Why do you say "teased", Colleen?' enquired Ken, 'in what way did Percival Whitaker tease Helen?'

'Because he pranced around like a cat toying with a mouse; he let her think she'd got away and he'd lost interest in her, only to sit down and metaphorically squash her with his giant paw. That's what she looked like after he said whatever it was just before he left, a small mouse who'd been left in a trap for later.'

Ken was letting this image ingrain itself for a while as he glanced at Lizzie, who also remained silent. However, Colleen was now in full flow.

'I quite liked Percival and as I said earlier, I knew what he wanted from me. I gave him snippets of information; at my age, men aren't exactly queuing up to buy me drinks. With the possible exception of Tim, of course, but that's different... we're housemates!'

Lizzie and Ken both smiled.

'What did he want to know in particular, Colleen?' asked Ken as he adjusted his position on possibly the most uncomfortable chair he had ever had the misfortune to sit. He didn't like to fidget too much as he feared being deposited on the floor if the seat gave up the ghost completely.

'To start with, it was all about Helen; what did I know about her past, what did people in the village make of her, was she well liked, that sort of thing. Clearly she wasn't liked by some, Maggie Blake in particular but then I don't need to tell you that, Lizzie, do I? She's very protective of you and so is Andrea Pearce but in a less direct way. I told Percival that. Also, I did mention you had more reason than most to feel uncomfortable about her presence in Blenthorne,' Colleen looked directly at Lizzie.

Lizzie flushed a little, nodded almost imperceptibly but didn't speak. Ken felt slightly sorry for her but then reasoned if she hadn't gate-crashed his interview she wouldn't have heard Colleen's comment.

'The general consensus was that Helen wasn't a small community sort of person. She has a past as I'm sure you both know and I suppose she came here to get her life back together. There's nothing wrong with that. However, I couldn't see her staying for long. Particularly if there was nothing or no one to keep her here...' she let her voice trail off as she looked pointedly at Lizzie who had taken to studying the floor with intent.

'I think she quite likes the couple from the hotel though and they certainly seem to appreciate her management skills, so maybe I'm wrong, perhaps she plans to remain for a while longer yet.'

She stopped and smiled at them.

'You said "to start with, it was all about Helen". Did that change after a while?' Ken asked, flipping back the pages in his notebook.

'I can't put my finger on it exactly but thinking about it, I'd say yes. Percival suddenly asked if I knew the name... um... Jane someone or other but it meant nothing to me. Originally, I thought he meant had I heard of her in connection with Helen Anderson and maybe she was someone from Helen's past. When I asked him who she was and why he was interested in her, he said it wasn't important, it was just a name he'd heard in passing. Then he changed the subject and started asking me about the museum's popularity and if Tim and I ever got a day off! After that of course he took to staying in his room and we didn't have any more cosy conversations.

'When I thought about it a bit more, I came to believe he had begun a new investigation into an entirely different person. I think his conversation with Helen a couple of nights before he died confirmed my theory. I never saw him again. I'm sorry he's dead. I know he was a thorn in the side of many but for some, particularly the relatives of victims of unsolved crimes, he was a beacon of truth and moral justice.'

'Also I suppose those with nothing to hide could just sit back and enjoy reading the results of his investigations for their own entertainment,' speculated Ken contemplatively.

'Ah yes, lovey, but how many of us truly have nothing to hide?'

*

They left Colleen shortly afterwards and waved goodbye to Tim Carney who was admitting three visitors whom, if he had to hazard a guess, were probably from Middle America.

'Perceptive sort of woman,' observed Ken.

'Yes, that's apparent from talking to her and she's definitely a character; a bit of a sticky beak, as she admitted herself but shrewd in the extreme. Clearly Percival Whitaker thought he was playing her and she knew exactly what he was about from the start but she didn't mind in the least because she's a... what did she call herself... a "conversationalist", what a wonderful description,' smiled Lizzie.

'I think she confirmed more or less what we already knew regarding Percival Whitaker. Right, I'm off to see if Mrs Vicar is home yet. What's her name? I remembered it earlier and now it's gone again,' Ken asked as he walked towards his car.

'Humphries, Gloria Humphries. She wasn't home you say? That's strange. Unless it's choir night she's always in. Spends most days cleaning her house and ironing Simeon's shirts, I believe; not that there's anything wrong in that, obviously, if it makes her happy.'

'I tried her about two thirty and there was no answer. Her husband gave me to believe that she was out and about all the time with pastoral duties.'

'What, Gloria? Hardly! Oh, she wouldn't turn anyone away from the vicarage if they went there for help but she's not exactly the type to be visiting the sick and needy. Maybe she just didn't hear the doorbell. Do you want me to come with you? She keeps herself to herself pretty much. I know her as well as anyone, maybe she'll relax a bit if I'm there. Not trying to muscle in, Ken, obviously.'

'No, of course not, perish the thought!'

Lizzie had the good grace to blush for the second time that afternoon before they got into their respective vehicles and drove to the vicarage. After parking and alighting from their cars, Lizzie knocked on the front door. She was joined by Ken as they waited for an answer. When none was forthcoming, Lizzie pulled out her mobile phone and searched her contacts. She pressed a number and they both waited. It went straight to voicemail.

'She's not answering her mobile. They always allow the answerphone to pick up the landline and then ring back as they feel appropriate, so no point even trying that. I hope she's okay. I'll try Si – don't ask, it's what he likes to be called. If he can't take the call, I can leave him a message saying we're concerned about Gloria.'

After another few minutes of standing outside the vicarage and having left a message for the vicar, they moved off down the path.

Ken looked around just before he climbed into his car. It might have been his imagination but he was almost sure he saw the net curtain move in the window of the bedroom to the right of the building.

'What is it?' asked Lizzie, seeing her companion looking at the building with interest.

'Not sure but if I'm right, I suspect Gloria Humphries is in there and has been watching us from an upstairs window. No, don't look up. Now why would she do that, do you think? In my experience, people only avoid the police when they're afraid or have something to hide.'

Little did either of them realise but what Gloria had to hide was more significant than they could possibly imagine.

Chapter 10 – Flight in the Night

Upon returning to the hall at around five o'clock, Ken found Gina sitting at her desk, keen to impart her latest information.

'Toxicology report is through.' Gina stood up and handed Ken a fax. 'I've just finished reading it. Results confirm compliance with the intake of regulated prescription drugs.'

Ken nodded. 'Ah. The pathologist highlights cirrhosis of the liver, cardiomegaly of the heart and atherosclerosis of the arteries. Full of big words as usual but I think we get the gist!'

'Those bits are clarified if you read on; in layman's terms, his liver was scarred, his heart was enlarged and his arteries were clogged with fatty deposits.' Gina pointed towards the bottom of the fax. 'Looking at the concluding paragraph, the pathologist confirms the deceased's lifestyle choices and possibly his genetic predisposition meant he wouldn't have had much chance of getting out of the water without assistance after the bash over the head.' She sat back down in her chair still facing her colleague and added, 'I wonder if his assailant stayed around to make sure, or if they trusted to luck?'

'Maybe they had enough medical knowledge to realise from his general appearance and demeanour that his surviving the blow would be well-nigh impossible.' Ken had Helen Anderson in mind as he articulated this thought. Then he remembered that Lizzie Lockwood too had trained as a nurse… no, surely not? There was nothing for the journalist to find out about her past that wasn't already in the public domain, was there? Should he be staying under her roof? He suddenly thought of his mother-in-law; no contest.

'Have we got anywhere with Hilary Cole?' he asked, quickly changing direction. 'I know logistically she couldn't have done it but even so…'

Gina spun her chair around to face the desk and leaning forward, started to tap her laptop keyboard.

'We're still looking into her. She was born in Scotland to Presbyterian parents and the family later moved to Northern Ireland, her father being a minister. She then came to England at the age of fifteen and went to live with a great aunt; as yet, we don't know why. The aunt died, leaving Hilary on her own a few years later. She worked for a high street bank then a building society. She moved here in her twenties and when a vacancy arose, became the post mistress. She lives on the north side of the village with her collie dog in a small cottage which she owns outright, presumably bought with the proceeds of her aunt's estate but we're still checking that out. Don't think there is any way she can be Jane Macintyre though, no significant gaps in her life and as you say, she couldn't have done it as she has a cast iron alibi for the day in question.' Gina paused and then continued;

'Now Dawn Sanchez on the other hand, has no traceable past. She has attempted to explain this away, as you know, by suggesting her family were travellers but couldn't give any more detail as to their names and possible current locations. I'm wondering if we're actually looking in the wrong place.'

'Go on?' Ken looked at his colleague with keen interest.

'What if she's an illegal? Came into the country in the back of a lorry? Commonplace now but it wasn't completely unknown thirty odd years ago,' said Gina, looking hopefully at her senior colleague.

'Now that is an interesting possibility. Go and see her. Ask her outright. Explain to her that if she did enter the country illegally there are ways out of the situation, particularly after all this time. She'd probably be entitled to stay here as the wife of a European national, regardless of any right to remain for which she would potentially qualify. She may just be panicking through ignorance, if that's the case. Either way, it seems like we're running out of candidates to be Jane, doesn't it. What if we're barking up the wrong tree entirely?' Ken shook his head as he looked at the detective constable.

'Whitaker starts working on the Macintyre case and then he turns up dead. Surely that's just too much of a coincidence, isn't it?' averred Gina, logically.

'Maybe, but we can't become so focused upon Macintyre that we ignore Anderson. That said, something is bothering me; Gloria Humphries is avoiding us and we need to know why. Delegate her to the team as a matter of priority. Usual background stuff; where she was born, her parents, schools, anything and everything we can turn up. Then you can go and see Dawn and put your theory to her to see how she reacts. I'll try to pin the vicar down in the morning. Oh, and Gina? Good work so far.' Ken, whilst often irritated by his junior colleague, was an advocate of praise where it was due and the illegal entry angle was something he hadn't thought of.

However when morning came, pinning down the vicar was easier said than done.

*

The dawn of a new day saw Gary Carmichael pouring out breakfast cereal and boiling the kettle for tea. Ken appeared in the kitchen, wearing sensible blue slippers and a warm looking deep red fleece dressing gown, which gaped slightly around his stomach.

'Morning, Ken, what are your plans today?' asked Gary, not at all sure Ken's current state of attire would be fully appreciated by Lizzie, should she appear.

'The vicar and his wife have to be our top priority. As I said to Gina yesterday, we are running out of Macintyre candidates.'

Before he could say anything more, his dressing gown pocket started to rumble. He took out his mobile and listened briefly.

'Damn and blast! They've done a runner! Can you credit it? That, I most certainly didn't expect!'

'Who have, surely not Si and Gloria?' asked Gary incredulously.

'The very same; neighbour reports hearing them drive off late yesterday evening. Gina stayed over at the hotel last night as she worked late. She was jogging before breakfast.' Ken pulled a face. 'Noticed the vicar's car wasn't in the drive and thought it strange. Saw a neighbour putting out her rubbish bin and asked if she'd noticed anything unusual. She told Gina that her terrier started barking just before bedtime. She looked out of the window and saw them packing up the car; their external light was on for about half an hour, she estimated. Gina's put out an alert so we'll see if that elicits any results. I don't know, maybe I should have seen this coming. Must let the DCI know.' He took his cereal and made for one of the kitchen stools, phone pressed to his ear.

Gary picked up the two mugs of tea and took them over to where his ex-colleague was sitting.

'Is he coming to Blenthorne?' asked Gary, when Ken disconnected the call.

'Thankfully not, he has a community meeting this morning and then some sort of team building for senior officers later in the day. As you know, there's not much actual policing at his level anymore; it's all diplomacy and politics. Still, at least he's in the loop, such as it is. He just grunted when I told him.'

'You said maybe you should have seen it coming but I don't see how. You hardly know the vicar and his wife. I've known them for years and had no idea they had anything to hide. Of course, that's assuming their departure is due to this case and it may not be; there could be another explanation. Though I grant you, the timing does look highly suspicious. In fact, I can't remember them ever taking as much as a holiday before. If he has annual leave from his church duties, he normally just potters round the village.'

'What do you know about them, Gary?'

'I don't know as much as Lizzie, obviously. Oh speak of the devil!'

Lizzie appeared in the kitchen doorway wearing a fluffy cream coloured dressing gown. 'What have I missed?' she enquired as she walked towards the teapot, briefly glancing in Ken's direction and averting her gaze immediately.

'It appears the vicar and Gloria have packed up and fled. Ken was asking how much we know about them.'

'Left the village, good gracious, surely not? You know, funnily enough, I've been thinking about that since yesterday when Gloria wouldn't answer the door, Ken. I realised I know remarkably little. They call into the pub for a drink once a month or so to try to keep in touch with non-church-going villagers, which never hurts when looking for donations. They're a sort of institution here; vaguely comical and a little over zealous but highly principled and totally dedicated to the calling. At least he is and she's slavishly dedicated to him. She sees her role as that of devoted wife and I'm sure the idea of a career of her own would have been abhorrent.'

'Are there any children?' asked Ken as he shovelled his cereal in as quickly as possible.

'No; Gloria doesn't strike me as the maternal type. She doesn't get involved with Sunday school or youth activities in any way. They've always held confirmation classes at the vicarage for teenagers; my son, Alex, attended but I don't think he enjoyed them. Gloria used to appear half way through the session with a large glass of milk and a small plain biscuit for each for the candidates. I think most of the village see the couple as being a bit eccentric but harmless. They are rather penny pinching though. There was an instance years ago when Si thought the congregation should have a whip round to pay for his washing machine to be repaired. I'm sure Maggie remembers that but I don't suppose it has much bearing on their disappearance. Presumably you're checking the ports?'

'Yes, Gina got on to that immediately. They may have gone to Liverpool to head for Ireland or the Isle of Man. Alternatively, maybe they've driven further south with the intention of taking a ferry to Europe. If they packed the car up, then I don't suppose they're flying anywhere; unless they intend to put some stuff into storage, in which case they could be on a flight headed anywhere. I don't think they planned this in advance. It looks like a classic knee jerk flight in the night to me.'

'Umm, you're right I'm sure. Shouldn't be too much of a problem to get a search warrant issued in the circumstances,' observed Gary as he collected the discarded cereal bowls. 'Toast with marmalade or jam?'

Ken grinned; 'Go on then, one of each. Yes, we do need to take a look round the vicarage; not sure what we'll find but definitely worth a search of the premises. If she is Jane Macintyre, just maybe she's left something behind that will prove it.'

*

Gary had a meeting with Jono Johnson at the adventure holiday company arranged for nine o'clock so he kissed Lizzie goodbye and parted company with Ken at the front door, arranging to meet up for dinner.

He arrived at the company office a few minutes to nine and Jono answered his knock immediately. The office was open plan and situated upstairs over the outdoor clothing retailers. There were two windows in the office, both facing the same way, from which it was possible to see the length of the main village street. This gave a clear vantage point, affording views of the village green and at the far end, a glimpse of the Blenny. He pulled himself out of his thoughts and concentrated on Jono, who was telling him how healthy the business was looking.

Jono suggested he should sit at Andrea's desk to look at the latest website homepage. He logged Gary into the system and then apologised as the phone was ringing. In spite of Jono's clear acumen for information technology, they still used a generic password which took him straight to Andrea's desktop. In view of her still fairly fragile health, Andrea didn't start work until ten thirty each day and only stayed after four if they were particularly busy. As things were normally quiet first thing, Jono was happy to manage alone. He clearly had a prospective new client on the line and had launched effortlessly into his sales pitch.

Gary didn't like to look at the website until Jono was free to go through it with him. He idly glanced at the icons on the desktop. One in particular caught his attention. He knew he probably shouldn't, but he opened the file before he had time to talk himself out of it. What he saw made his world momentarily turn upside down.

After a few minutes, Jono had finished his call and was clearly buzzing from the possibilities raised by a prospective new corporate client. Because of this, he was probably unaware that Gary wasn't as fulsome in praise for the latest presentation of his marketing ideas as he might have expected. For his part, Gary was distracted and didn't hear most of what Jono was telling him. His first thought, his only thought, was to go to the Blenny. He had no idea how he was going to handle the situation but handle it he must. He made the appropriate noises, praising Jono for his clear forward thinking strategy and made good his escape.

As he left Jono to make his way along the village street, his heart was thumping in his chest. It was amazing to think how it could be possible to believe he knew someone only to find he hardly knew them at all.

*

Andrea was getting ready for work in the master bedroom of the flat she shared with Mia, although Mia had recently taken to staying over at Connor's place. As a mother, she was still trying to adjust to that. He was nice enough but there was just something about him, something controlling. He reminded Andrea of her late husband. She had no evidence on which to base this feeling as Connor was never anything but politeness itself. She had tried to bring up her concerns with Mia but was brushed aside. If only she had listened to her own mother; a small wave of unease washed over her. Stuart had started out as the ideal partner; kind, caring, everything she thought she wanted. It took a while for her to realise her mother had been right; beneath the surface he was a bully. She'd planned his death so carefully; payback for the years of sadistic cruelty and humiliation. She liked to plan. She stopped herself going over it all again. He was out of their lives now. He would never hurt her or Mia again.

It looked like it was going to be an overcast sort of day with low cloud and a heavy atmosphere. She preferred it when it was brighter as it lifted her mood. She liked to hear the birds sing and feel the warmth of the sun on her shoulders as she walked to the job she loved. It would take less than five minutes to get there and as usual she had been up before seven. She put on one of her light grey trouser suits which she had bought to wear at work from spring through to late autumn. Lizzie had taken her to Carlisle just before she started her job and what a day they'd had, lunching in an Italian restaurant and trying on all manner of clothes. She didn't remember when she'd had so much fun.

She brushed her still slightly damp, short, mid-brown hair with the odd speck of grey and chose drop pearl earrings. She was just putting the second one in place when she heard her phone ping. She checked it to find a message from Mia who was downstairs getting the pub ready for action and was surprised to find that Gary was on his way up to see her. She wondered what he wanted.

She would have to tell him she could only give him a few minutes as she didn't want to be late for work. She got anxious if she was late. She couldn't put that down to her head injury, she had felt like that for as long as she could remember. In fact, she had been put on medication when she was at school. Anxiety made the palms of her hands sweat and her heart rate increase. Gary would understand that she couldn't be late. They could always meet up another time if there was something he particularly needed to talk to her about.

She wore a little makeup and had applied it after she got dressed so she was confident that she looked reasonably presentable.

She heard a knock on the door and went to open it immediately. Gary looked grave as he entered the flat. Oh dear. What was he going to say to her? She didn't have to wait long for her answer.

After he had left, she rang Jono to say she didn't feel well and would it be okay if she didn't come into work until after lunch? He had replied that she could take the whole day off and then see how she felt tomorrow.

How she felt tomorrow! Oh my goodness, if he only knew.

She made herself a cup of drinking chocolate, pulled out her earrings and took off her suit. She hung it back in the wardrobe and replaced it with a floppy jumper and leggings. She put the radio on softly and sat down on the sofa while Gary's words played over in her mind and her emotions caused her stomach to churn. Tears forced their way from her eyes and tumbled down her cheeks. She wiped them with a tissue which she then twisted between her fingers as she chewed her bottom lip. What had she done?

He had sat on the sofa opposite her after declining a drink or piece of sponge. He always had at least a drink so she knew there was something amiss. Also, his demeanour suggested it wasn't a social call.

'I'll come straight to the point, Andrea,' he had said. 'I've just been to the office and I saw a file on your computer. Is there anything you would like to tell me?'

She had panicked immediately. He was a trained police officer, albeit retired but he would have picked up on the vibe even if he had been a country bobby. Not that they existed anymore. She remembered the village in Sussex near their holiday caravan park. They had a village policeman who lived in a cottage with the station office attached and he used to ride around on his bike. It had been a quaint little place with woods and a lovely waterfall; now what was it called? She couldn't remember off hand, not that it mattered now.

'I'm sorry, Gary, I don't understand,' she had stammered.

'You had a file on your laptop entitled "Anderson". To my knowledge, the company has no clients by that name, either corporate or individual.

'You're a very thorough and meticulous person, Andrea, and when I opened the file, there were all the letters you had sent to Helen listed in chronological order and indeed one to Percival Whitaker, which presumably is why he came here. I just need to know why? I would have said you were one of the kindest, most caring people I've ever met. I can't tell you how much respect I had for you. You have coped with adversity and misfortune in a way that can only be admired by all that come in contact with you. So why would you send malicious and threatening letters to someone you barely know? Or are you going to tell me you didn't send them? Someone else must have used your terminal; Jono maybe?'

'No, it wasn't Jono, it was me,' she had replied defiantly, sitting up straight and looking him in the eye. 'I wrote the letters and sent them to Helen and I wrote the note to Mr Whitaker but he never guessed it came from me; he never even so much as spoke to me after he arrived.'

Gary had shaken his head and looked at her sadly.

'Why on earth would you do something so cruel?' he asked, looking at her incredulously, like he didn't really know her.

'When Helen first came here, I asked her how I could be of assistance and she treated me like I was an imbecile. She changed I grant you that, once she realised she couldn't just turn up and expect you to fall at her feet, though she was working on it. You were upset by her arrival, I don't know why unless she had some sort of hold over you. That's what Maggie thought. For a little while it seemed she would keep her distance but then little by little, she ingratiated herself with the owners of the hotel and I saw what she was up to. I was in the pub one night you were having a drink with her. In time it would have been dinner and then what? No, I couldn't allow that to happen. She's a scheming, unscrupulous, rapacious woman.'

'She may well be all those things but I can't see why you would take it upon yourself to try to frighten her off? Even if she is as bad as you believe, with respect, I can't see how that involves you?' he had looked at her with a piercing stare. She had never seen him look like that before or heard the edge of steel in his voice.

She couldn't tell him the whole truth but she told him a large part of it.

'Lizzie,' she said, disarmingly.

Gary had seemed taken aback. He paused and swallowed deeply.

'What about Lizzie?' he had asked quietly, the steel was gone.

'Lizzie is the most wonderful person in the world and I love her. Oh, not romantically, you understand, but in a deeply indebted way. She gave me a second chance after all that happened with Stuart. I served a prison sentence for killing him as you know and without Lizzie giving me the opportunity of a new life here when I was released, there is no doubt I would be dead now. Yes, honestly. I couldn't envisage any future until she gave me one, she is a true friend and that word is bandied about now with little thought. I mean you only have to look at social media, don't you? Who really has a hundred friends, two hundred or more… totally ludicrous! What I feel for her is deep, unconditional gratitude, friendship and love, the result being I would do anything for her. We were all getting on so happily then along came that woman, Helen Anderson. She thought she could take you away, take Lizzie's place; you may not think that was her game but trust me it was! I wasn't going to let that happen. You and Lizzie belong together. So I put a plan together and executed it.' Her chin jutted out defiantly as she felt her cheeks flush.

He had looked moved, deeply moved and he didn't speak for what seemed like minutes, in reality, it might have been ten seconds.

'Don't you think I'm capable of making my own decisions and protecting my relationship with Lizzie?' he asked quietly, with sadness in his eyes.

'Not when it comes to a woman like that, no. Maggie agreed with me,' she had added in the hope of some small amount of validation.

'What? Maggie was in on it?' Gary had suddenly looked up at her in utter confusion and disbelief.

'No, well not really, but she did say something ought to be done about the situation. I didn't tell her I was doing something; I wanted to though.' She had paused and wrung her hands again, her knuckles white from the pressure she exerted.

'Then, of course, Helen was sitting in the bar with you the night of the Percival Whitaker incident and I realised I had miscalculated. Far from driving her away, it had given her an excuse to get closer to you. Then I heard her say she hadn't had any nasty experiences like dead vermin thrown on her car, so I decided to arrange that along with some kitchen waste, oh and eggs and flour for good measure. I had to act immediately because Mia was staying with Connor that night, so I wouldn't have to explain why I was going out at four in the morning if she heard me. I hoped the gesture might scare Helen away but clearly it didn't.'

'I suppose at least you didn't cause any criminal damage to the car.'

'No, of course not; it's probably quite valuable, isn't it? That wouldn't have been right at all.'

She waited and then asked the question that had been eating her up.

'Now that you know, what will you do? Will I go back to prison?'

'You've committed a criminal offence, Andrea,' the steel had returned.

'Yes, but you see, Helen…'

'I'm not just talking about Helen,' Gary had interrupted. 'That's the problem when you set in place a course of action, you can't necessarily control the chain of events that follow. You were instrumental in bringing Percival Whitaker to Blenthorne and now he's dead.'

'I know and I'm very sorry about that, honestly but I'm out on licence since Stuart…' she had stopped mid-sentence.

'What do you want me to say?' his gaze shamed her to the core. She hadn't replied.

Gary had left a short time after and so that was the end of that. He would report her to the police. Her licence would be revoked because she had violated the terms of her parole. However, at least she hadn't broken down completely and told him how she felt about him. He would have been gobsmacked at that revelation. He said he respected her and admired her. Those were detached sentiments. One can respect and admire someone they don't know personally. At least she had retained a bit of dignity, a small crumb of comfort and sometimes that was all one had left.

She picked up her hot chocolate and the bottle containing the painkillers she took for her migraines. It was a funny old world, she thought, as she tipped out a handful of tablets and looked at them sadly, before tossing them into her mouth, sipping her drink and swallowing. She coughed a few times but finished both the contents of the bottle and her chocolate drink. She wondered if she should leave a note but to say what? "Sorry, my darling Mia, I couldn't face up to the consequences of my recent actions. Because of me, a man is dead." No, that is a sin she would take to her grave. Mia didn't deserve to have the burden of knowing just what a wicked woman her mother truly was.

She went to the bathroom as she was worried she may become incontinent once she was unconscious; she had heard that people involuntarily open their bladder and bowels at such times and she would hate to make a mess for anyone else to have to clean up, how terribly embarrassing.

After that, she returned to the lounge and stretched out on the sofa. There was no way she could face going back to prison. Not now, after she had had this lovely life here in Blenthorne with Mia and Jono. Bless his heart; he had been so kind to her. If only she could have felt something other than gratitude for him. She waited for sleep and ultimately death to relieve her of a life she felt she could no longer live because of a future she couldn't bear to face.

As her mind drifted to a place of soft light and gentle warmth, a thought suddenly came to her. Oh my word; yes of course, that was it... the village policeman... her memory which so often failed her, had suddenly delivered a gem, yet she would never be able to tell anyone. No one would ever know now... yes indeed, it was a funny old world.

*

While Gary was with Andrea Pearce, Ken and the police team were searching the vicarage. The furniture was serviceable, if a little shabby in places. The couple clearly weren't bothered about style but the lounge in particular was a comfortable space in which to relax. The carpet was patterned and had seen better days but the rug in front of the hearth was soft with a rich deep pile. There were mounds of magazines and books scattered around the place, a discarded puzzle on a small table by the wall and an open sewing box with a partly embroidered cushion cover spread over a wide selection of silks. There were two leather armchairs with worn arms and both had a good view of the television set. It was a scene of domesticity found in almost every home in the land. There were the usual assortment of knick-knacks around but something was distinctly missing.

'There aren't any photographs. I mean, everyone has a few, even me, though to be fair they are mainly of my cat,' conceded Gina. 'But every Christmas I get given new ones of my nieces and nephews in their school uniforms. None of that here, is there?'

'I was just thinking the same thing. Even if they have little in the way of family, you would think they would have a wedding photo somewhere. Check to see if the team have found any in the bedroom, maybe they keep one by their bed,' suggested Ken.

'Nope,' said Gina as she came back down the stairs. 'Looks like they've taken most of their clothes, both wardrobes are pretty bare in the main bedroom. Funny thing though, we know they don't have children but one of the other bedrooms is kitted out as a child's room. I wonder why?'

'A nursery you mean?' questioned Ken.

'No, not that I know much about children but I would say it's more a pre-teen bedroom. There's quite a lot of blue, so at the risk of stereotyping, it's probably been designed for a boy but there's no sign of occupancy.'

'Check to see if they did have a child at some stage. While you're on that, see if there's a marriage certificate on file. We might find some personal papers here but if they've got stuff to hide then they've probably taken anything incriminating with them. I would, in their situation.'

Ken's phone rang and he turned and walked out of the room to take the call. After a couple of minutes he returned to an expectant Gina.

'Now that is a turn up! That was the DCI. We've been warned off. No more enquiries into the Reverend Simeon and Mrs Gloria Humphries. Apparently he's heard from on high and we have to take his word for it that Gloria is categorically not Jane Macintyre and leave well alone.

'If she isn't Jane Macintyre, then why did they take off like that? They must have something to hide, that's not normal behaviour,' said Gina, articulating what Ken was thinking.

'Exactly; he's a dedicated man of the church, for him to flee the parish to which he's been devoted for over a quarter of a century, it must be something of magnitude. I wonder what?'

Luckily for Ken, he wouldn't have to wait long to have his curiosity satisfied.

Chapter 11 – Questions and Explanations

Gary left the flat above the Blenny and made his way to the churchyard. He needed a bit of time to go over the events of the morning. Andrea had admitted she had sent letters of a threatening nature to Helen Anderson in an attempt to intimidate her into leaving the area. That qualified as harassment. Whilst her explanation was perhaps reasonable from her perspective, that couldn't excuse what she'd done and yet…

He sat down on the bench and hoped for some sort of divine intervention as to what he should do. He knew what he ought to do, but could he? Andrea said she had done it for Lizzie. She had looked at him so disarmingly; he was totally nonplussed. However misguided, she was fundamentally a decent person. She would plead guilty when charged and would undoubtedly return to prison. Unless he could persuade Helen not to press charges but then he would be indebted to her and he didn't want that. What he really needed was some advice from the vicar and therein lay another tale.

He was still undecided as to his course of action when a familiar voice called to him.

'What are you doing here in my favourite spot?'

'Oh, Lizzie; I needed some time out to think, actually. You won't believe what's just happened.'

He spent the following few minutes telling Lizzie of his conversation with Andrea.

'Oh my word, that's incredible. Bless her dear, kind heart. Gary, you can't tell anyone.'

'I have to! I don't like it any more than you but whichever way you look at it, she's committed criminal acts; the letters to Helen and then the car. More importantly, Whitaker would still be alive if she hadn't written to him. Lizzie, there's no choice.'

'You say that but…' Lizzie broke off in midsentence as her phone rang. She looked at it, stood up and walked towards the church as she answered it.

'Who was that?' Gary asked Lizzie when she returned to join him on the bench.

'Oh, just one of my ladies in a bit of a two-and-eight over something her resettlement officer said. I need to get over to Hope Cottage, sorry.'

*

Lizzie replaced her mobile in her pocket, kissed Gary and returned home as quickly as she could. She hated lying to him but she'd had no choice. She left again after freshening up. She had a three hour journey ahead and her curiosity was compelling her to make all possible haste.

As she drove, she contemplated the phone conversation she had just had. It had nothing to do with any of her Hope Cottage residents, the caller had been Reverend Simeon. He told her that he and Gloria had not left the country but were in hiding over the Scottish border. They wanted to talk to her in person before making any decisions. He assured Lizzie they'd broken no laws and begged her to place her trust in someone she had known for years and agree to a meeting.

Lizzie put her reservations behind her. An hour into her journey, she sent Gary a text apologising profusely for lying and telling him of her intended destination just in case anything should happen. She thought she was probably being melodramatic but she couldn't forget that a man had lost his life in the last few days and that currently Mr and Mrs Vicar were the prime suspects, not least because they had upped sticks and run.

She had the directions Simeon had given her and crossed into Scotland. The weather was closing in and it had started to rain. She wondered what it could be that had spooked Si and Gloria so much that they had felt their only option was to flee. Why not come to her in the village rather than ask her to meet them at a cottage near Flencham, which apparently was a small hamlet fifteen miles from Dumfries.

After reaching Flencham, Lizzie took the lane on the right, half a mile further on to the north east as instructed. In fact, it was more of a single lane dirt track with the occasional passing place. The rain was getting heavier and with it had descended a thick mist. She checked in vain for a phone signal. She started to become slightly uneasy and was seriously wondering whether she should bail out but admonished herself for being pathetic, she'd faced worse than this in her life. She thought back to her husbands, Richard and then Jim, her parents, all the people she had lost… she told herself to stop being such a wimp. She stopped the car for a moment to regain her self-control. She started the engine again after a couple of minutes and continued along the track. Around the next bend, her destination came into view.

It was a small stone cottage with a long sloping roof which almost reached the ground on the left. It had the tiniest of windows at ground level on that side. It looked like the other side had two storeys, so possibly a couple of bedrooms upstairs. She parked on the grass verge and ran to the porch. Simeon Humphries had clearly heard the car and opened the door before Lizzie could knock.

'Come on in out of that filthy weather, my dear girl. Thank you for making this journey; you really are a true friend.' Simeon Humphries then did something that took Lizzie completely by surprise; he hugged her.

Clever, thought Lizzie. Identify and reinforce the relationship immediately.

'Let me take your coat. Did you have any difficulty finding us? Now you must have some refreshment. I've made sandwiches and the kettle has just boiled as I was going to make Gloria a cup of tea.'

Simeon showed Lizzie into a small sitting room from a door off the hallway. The door on the other side presumably led to the kitchen which logic dictated must have a sloping roof. The sitting room was sparsely furnished. It had a two seater sofa and an armchair; the pattern of which had long since faded and it all looked a dull rust colour. A brown and orange rag rug was spread out over an elderly pale linoleum-covered floor in front of an open, unlit fireplace. A two-bar electric heater stood to the right of the fireplace, presumably because that was as far as the cord would stretch from the electrical socket. Other than that, there was a coffee table in front of the sofa and an occasional table in the left corner of the room, on which stood a small lamp with a dusty orange shade.

'Where is Gloria?' asked Lizzie after she had responded to her host's greeting.

'She's upstairs. I'll be honest with you, she wasn't completely sure that ringing you was a good idea. She felt we should cut all our ties with the past and start afresh but as I explained, running may not be the answer and that's really why I wanted to speak to you in person. We've both known and respected you for years; I would go so far as to say you're the closest to a friend Gloria has ever made. Neither of us ever believed that you committed the crime for which you served a prison sentence. You're a selfless person, Lizzie, and we admire you, however misguided you were when you confessed to manslaughter.'

Lizzie had long ago decided the best way to deal with questions regarding her incarceration and the events that led to it, was to remain silent.

Simeon disappeared briefly and came back with a large tray which he placed on the coffee table. 'Now, would you like tuna and cucumber or ham and mustard?' he asked, as he removed a tea towel covering a plate of sandwiches. 'I want to tell you our story and then be advised by your counsel as to our future plans. Shall I pour the tea?'

Lizzie nodded as she sat down in the armchair and breathed a sigh of relief. She again berated herself for entertaining the idea that these two kindly folk would want to harm her. She helped herself to a plate.

'Ham and mustard, to start with anyway; looks like you've made enough for an army!'

'Yes, it is strange isn't it; preparing food is so mundane yet somehow so calming. It's a basic human instinct to want to feed people. That's how I met Gloria actually; she was working in a café. I found myself buying cups of coffee three times a day before I could pluck up the courage to make conversation with her. I was a rather awkward, inexperienced curate in a London suburb in those days.'

'Oh, I see,' smiled Lizzie, not really sure how she was supposed to respond to this information and whether or not it was relevant to their current situation.

'How did you know of this place, Si?'

Simeon sat down on the sofa. 'I own it. My grandmother lived here most of her life. I inherited it upon her death; of course, it's all very well and fine during my working life, my accommodation is provided but it's very difficult for a member of the clergy to get a foot on the property ladder afterwards; should they so desire. So I kept this place as an investment. I'm not sure it's worth a great deal as there isn't much in the way of local amenities, however it's something for our retirement. We came here last night to give ourselves some breathing space.' He paused and then asked; 'What's happening at home?'

'The investigation into the death of the journalist is continuing. The police have a particular lead they are pursuing and I expect they'll find the identity of the killer in the end, they usually do.'

'No doubt our departure raised some eyebrows,' commented Simeon, looking at Lizzie intently.

'You could say that, particularly as Ken Stokes wanted to talk to Gloria yesterday. Simeon, does the name Jane Macintyre mean anything to you?' Lizzie hoped the directness of the question may elicit an unprepared response.

Simeon Humphries barely blinked. 'No, I'm afraid not, who is she? Does she have something to do with the murder?'

'It's possible. Percival Whitaker was investigating the circumstances of her family's death roughly thirty years ago. There was a suggestion that she was somehow involved. It seems likely that the night he visited the Blenny and spoke to Helen Anderson, Jane Macintyre was present. She realised from what he was saying loudly to Helen that he knew of her identity and it's at least possible that she silenced him. That's why the police need to speak to Gloria, to eliminate her from their enquiries. Now taking off as you did last night, I'm afraid it looks like an admission of guilt,' she paused, hoping Simeon would say something. When he remained silent, Lizzie continued;

'Of course, Jane might not be the killer but until the police have spoken to her, she will remain the prime suspect. Si, why not go up and get Gloria.'

'I'm sorry to disappoint you, Lizzie, but I'm not Jane Macintyre,' said a timid voice from the hall.

Gloria appeared in the doorway, her gaze fixed on Lizzie. She looked small and frail and was wearing a large black cardigan, the sleeves of which covered most of her hands; the events of the last few hours had clearly taken their toll. Her fists were clenched, gripping the cuffs as her arms hung limply by her sides. Her nondescript hair was scraped back in a ponytail with wisps dangling around her face and there were large dark circles around her eyes.

'Gloria, it's so good to see you! We've been very worried. Come and sit down. If you're not Jane then please explain what all this is about.'

Simeon rose and stepped towards his wife but she put her hand up. 'No Si, she's right. I need to explain. I've lived with this for years and whilst I've loved being Gloria Humphries, I'm going to have to be honest. I've spent most of my adult life burying the past but that's the thing about a secret, isn't it; it haunts you, wherever you go and whatever you do. I've never really been free; it's always there in the background. I thought I was safe in Blenthorne. I kept myself tidy and quiet but always supported Si in his ministry. Then out of the blue, along came Percival Whitaker; I knew it was me he was talking to in the pub that night when he said I'd gone there to "reinvent" myself. I'd adopted a new identity years ago, so I suppose that's what he meant. It's not fair, I was so young. I didn't know, I swear I didn't, until it was too late and by then I had a child whom I had to protect.'

Gloria sat down on the sofa next to her husband and he gripped her hand.

'My dear, would you like some tea and a sandwich?' he asked solicitously.

'Maybe later but for now I just want to get this burden off my chest,' she smiled weakly at him as she shook her head.

Lizzie waited for Gloria to tell her story in her own time. She helped herself to another sandwich after Simeon caught her eye and motioned towards the plate.

'Lizzie, have you ever heard the name Jason Carpenter?' asked Gloria.

'Um, the name rings a bit of a bell, but I can't quite… oh, wait a minute, didn't he kill his wife and dispose of her body? And wasn't there some sort of underworld connection?'

'That's right. Do you remember any more of the story?' she asked softly.

'Yes, there was a girl he was living with who um, let me think; her name was Christine… something. Oh my God,' Lizzie dropped the half eaten sandwich onto her plate as she stared at Gloria in disbelief. Completely forgetting it was really rather inappropriate to use such a term in front of an ordained priest.

'Are you Christine?' Lizzie felt her voice quiver as she continued to look at the vicar's wife in disbelief.

'Christine Townshend. Yes. I'm Christine. I lived with Jason after his wife left him; at least that's what he told me. It was only after I'd been with him for the best part of two years and we'd had a child together that I found out that his wife, Candice hadn't left him at all, she was buried in the garden.'

It sounded so matter of fact the way Gloria… Christine… put it. Maybe if she'd lived with the knowledge for so long, she had become desensitised.

'We met when I was sixteen and he was twenty four. He was a labourer working on a building project at my school. He used to talk to me when I arrived at school and so I'd hang around at the end of the day when I was supposed to be in the library doing my homework and we would go to the local café together. I knew he was married, he told me fairly early on but it didn't matter because we were just friends. I didn't have many and it was the first time anyone had ever really taken any notice of me.

'My parents were in their forties when I was born and we never had a television set, so when everyone was talking about the soaps, I was always on the outside looking in. I used to stand on the edge of a group smiling, hoping someone would ask me to join them. They never did. At home we read books and had a grandfather clock that ticked loudly in the parlour. That was usually the only sound from after tea until bedtime; that awful clock, ticking my life away. When we went on holiday we stayed in a bed and breakfast place on the coast about twenty miles from home; the same one for a week every year. We sat on the beach during the day and if it rained, we sat in a shelter on the promenade until it stopped. It was a pretty dreary existence so meeting Jason was the most amazing thing ever. I don't know why he chose me but he said I had nice eyes. His parents were older too, so we had that in common.

'He started buying me little presents; nothing expensive, just a few small ornaments and a bit of cheap jewellery. My mother was a snoop and she used to go through my things. She found the presents he'd bought me, even though they were hidden away. She accused me of stealing. Eventually I told her the truth before she hauled me off to the police station. I was forbidden to see Jason again. So I used to sneak out after I'd gone to up to bed. I'd meet him and we'd go to the pictures or just hang around in town.

'His wife worked in a care home and was often out in the evenings, depending on her shift pattern. Eventually he invited me round when he had the house to himself. You can imagine the next development without me going into detail. It was about six months after we started to spend time together at his house that he told me that Candice had left him.

'He was vague about where she had gone, he just said she had left and they were getting a divorce. As he didn't know where she was, we had to wait for her to make contact before we could make plans and marry.

I had dropped out of my A-level course by then. I cut all ties with my parents, moved into his home and we subsequently had Oliver. Attitudes weren't so liberal in those days so I changed my name to Carpenter by deed poll. Finances were a bit tight and Candice had some money left from an inheritance. We lived in London and it wasn't like everyone knew each other, so Jason said I could use her bank card and just sign my name which of course by then was "C Carpenter". I wasn't sure about it but he said it would be fine. Of course I should've realised something was wrong and refused. But I was young and impressionable and very much in awe of him, so I went along with it. I did ask why she hadn't taken the card with her when she left and why she hadn't transferred the account. He said she had probably forgotten about it; so all the time it was available, we could take a bit out here and there and she'd never notice.

'It was only after a relative of Candice turned up out of the blue that things started to go wrong. It was a cousin from Australia who had never met Candice. Jason said I could just pretend to be her as no one would ever know. I said it was a daft idea because why did we need to pretend? After all she'd left him, hadn't she? Presumably her parents knew where she was. Jason said they hadn't wanted her to marry him and there had been a rift ever since, so she wouldn't have gone there. It really didn't seem to add up so I pushed him for answers. We had a terrible argument during which he finally told me what had happened. There had been a fight and she'd ended up going for him. He pushed her away and she hit her head as she fell. He had tried to help her but she died almost instantly.

'As you can imagine, I was horrified. I said if that were the case why hadn't he just explained that to the police? He said he'd panicked and buried her in the garden. I couldn't believe it. I wanted to run but I had a baby and where would I go? My parents had gone to live near relatives in New Zealand, my mum was from there originally; she and my dad had met when he was doing his national service. I thought about trying to contact them to ask for the air fare but we'd been estranged for so long and Jason loved us and would take care of us. I just had to tell a small lie and pretend to be Candice until her cousin left.

'We thought we were out of the woods after the cousin had gone but a few days later the police contacted us. The cousin had taken a photo, unbeknown to me and when he showed it to the rest of Candice's family, they realised it wasn't her. That's when it all fell apart. Jason was livid, he asked how I could have been so stupid as to allow myself to be photographed but I hadn't, not deliberately. It was taken without my knowledge but he wouldn't believe me.

'I'd never seen him like that before. He looked wild; he had veins standing out on his forehead and his neck was bulging and pulsating as he stood over me. He said I'd probably posed for the photo, just to make myself important and show off. He came at me and I really thought he was going to kill me. I remember grabbing Oliver and cowering in the corner of the room begging him not to hurt us as I tried to wrap myself around my baby to protect him.

'If I'm honest, I was quite relieved when the police arrived, as I realised I didn't really know Jason at all. I began to doubt Candice's death had been an accident.' Gloria broke off and looked at her husband and he smiled at her reassuringly.

'He was arrested and a day later, I was arrested also. Oliver was taken into care. The police had established an audit trail of my fraudulent use of Candice's bank account. I thought it was odd that they had found out about that so quickly unless Jason had told them. I started to panic about what else he might have said to save his own skin.

'Sure enough, it turned out he'd said I'd killed Candice and he'd covered for me. So basically it was his word against mine. He told them where to dig and her body was recovered in no time. Obviously a lot of decomposition had taken place but it was clear that she had sustained a brutal beating before she died. Jason was a bodybuilder and very strong. I had always been tiny. The pathologist couldn't say exactly which blow had killed her but his findings shed enough doubt on Jason's story for me to be believed rather than him. He was charged and I gave evidence against him in Court but he maintained I'd been involved all along and it had been my idea to impersonate Candice. He was so besotted with me that he had gone along with it.'

'I see, but the thing is, I don't understand...' Lizzie started but Gloria interrupted her.

'No, Lizzie, let me finish, there's something else; Jason had been on the periphery of a south London gang who were involved in a turf war. I became aware that he was hiding weapons and Class A drugs. All sorts of people used to come to our home. Boys in their early teens were dying and I knew it wasn't right, so I made it my business to find out as much as I could, just in case. In case of what, I wasn't sure but somehow I had a feeling I might need some leverage one day.

'When I found out that he was trying to frame me, I told the police everything I knew about the weapons and drugs and where to look for them. They were traced back to some of the most ruthless people in the country. I was told if I gave evidence and identified some of them I'd be protected for life, so I was taken into the witness protection scheme. The fraud charges were dropped. The officials were kind to me and completely non-judgemental, if they knew what I'd been involved with, they never said anything. It was all very professionally organised.

'They moved me around a bit after the "Hennessy Gangland Trial" as the press dubbed it. Finally, they settled me back in an area of London with which I wasn't familiar, gave me a new name and enabled me to start afresh. They told me to keep my background as simple as possible so I wouldn't be caught out by forgetting some of the stories I was making up. It was all agreed in advance and I was coached intensively before I became Gloria Stanford. After a few months I met Si,' she smiled and stretched out her thin veiny hand to her husband who took it and covered it with his own.

'When he asked me to marry him, I told him the truth. I wasn't supposed to but he's goodness personified. I knew my secret would be safe with him. We've had a very happy life together,' she said simply as she looked at the floor.

'And Oliver, what happened to him?' prodded Lizzie tentatively.

'He was adopted. I thought it was best at the time. Oh, I wasn't coerced, not really, but the social workers did say it would be difficult for me to have him back and I must think about what was best for him. You see Jason was murdered in prison. They said it was an accident but everyone knew otherwise, despite nothing being proven. The Hennessy family knew I was his girlfriend and they punished him for the fact that I gave evidence against them. If I'd had Oliver back, I could have been placing him in danger, in the same way that I placed Si in danger as soon as I married him. Do you know I have a bedroom ready for Oliver at the vicarage? Isn't that crazy? He's grown up now but I still have a small boy's room all set up. Simeon,' she said, turning to her husband, 'I'm so sorry, I've lived in the past for far too long; that room should have been used for a positive purpose. I couldn't contemplate having another child, it would have been like replacing the one I gave away but we could have fostered, couldn't we? We could have made a difference. I'm so sorry; I've been incredibly selfish all these years.'

'You have nothing to apologise for, my love. Even if I lived over again, I would choose the same path.'

They looked at each other, almost, it seemed to Lizzie, through new eyes, their love being reinforced by the revelations Gloria had just made. She felt slightly uncomfortable and on the pretext of visiting the lavatory and then making more tea, left them for a few minutes.

Si directed her outside to a brick building at the back of the property which doubled as a coal shed. After shivering in the cold and dimly-lit outhouse, she made her way back across the paved yard to the kitchen in the gloaming and washed her hands in the sink. She reappeared with a fresh pot of tea which she stood on the coffee table and replenished their cups.

'Thank you, my dear,' said Gloria, as Lizzie handed her a cup. 'And thank you for being so tactful. Now you know why we left Blenthorne. Percival Whitaker had somehow become aware of my identity and that gives me the perfect motive for murder, doesn't it?'

'You weren't the only person who believed it was they whom Percival Whitaker was targeting, Gloria,' said Lizzie, returning her attention to the now rather dry portion of sandwich.

'No, I know that,' she said quietly.

'How do you know that?' Lizzie asked, trying to stifle her surprise.

'Because I was there, at the tarn when he was killed; I saw it happen but who would believe me?' She stood up and walked towards the window.

Lizzie spluttered in a most unladylike way, coughed and almost choked. She had a sip of tea as she tried to regain her composure.

'Gloria, you have the uncanny knack of disclosing shocking revelations in the most disarming way. Firstly, you say your partner's wife was buried in the garden and now you tell me you witnessed Percival Whitaker being killed!'

'Goodness me, do I really? I suppose nothing really shocks me now. As it was, I had telephoned Mr Whitaker and told him I knew he was planning to name me in one of his articles and arranged to meet him at the tarn. I haven't much money so I couldn't pay him off but I was going to try to appeal to his better nature and beg him to stay silent. Now I think of it, I believe he was a bit surprised to hear from me. From what you've just told me though, he was looking for someone else entirely, someone called Jane Macintyre.'

'That's right, he was. He had an old file sent from his office as it seems he thought he'd identified her in the village,' replied Lizzie.

'My word; who is it?' asked Gloria turning back from the window and looking at her intently.

'I was hoping you were going to tell me. You said you witnessed him being killed. So who did it?' Lizzie involuntarily held her breath as she waited for Gloria's answer.

'I was on foot and took a wrong turning but I don't think I was late getting to the tarn; if anything, I was a bit early but as I scrambled between the boulders leading to the carpark, I saw that someone had got there before me.'

'And... who was it?' Lizzie realised she had inadvertently raised her voice in excitement.

'I thought it was possible that Mr Whitaker had arranged another rendezvous. He could be meeting someone else there, at a slightly earlier time.'

'Yes, indeed maybe he did; so who was there, Gloria? Who bashed him over the head?' The suspense was agonising; for goodness sake, why could she not just say the name?

'Oh, I don't know that. You see he had one of those hoodie things over his head and I never saw his face.'

Lizzie wondered if in her whole life she had ever felt quite so deflated. Gloria had witnessed a murder but didn't know who the culprit was.

'Wait a moment; you said "he". What makes you think it was a he?' asked Lizzie sharply.

'You see, that's what has confused me because you've been talking about a woman, this Jane Macintyre. The person I saw was very agile and the force with which he brought down the rock across the back of that poor man's head was more than a woman could have managed, I'm sure.

'No Lizzie, I believe the murderer of Percival Whitaker was most definitely a man.'

*

A short while later, Lizzie left the couple in their cold, bleak cottage, assuring them she would speak to the police in confidence and they should make their way home as soon as they felt it appropriate. They had both expressed their thanks, insisted she take some of the leftover sandwiches for her journey, along with a flask and promised they would be in touch when they'd had a bit of time to come to terms with the events of the last few days.

She drove back towards civilisation in the dark and as soon as she had a signal, rang through to Ken Stokes. She promised a full report in the morning.

In turn, Ken told her that Andrea Pearce had been found unconscious in the flat by her daughter, Mia, when she popped back upstairs just prior to starting her lunchtime shift. Andrea was currently in hospital and it was thought to be touch and go as she had taken a large amount of painkillers. They had found no note and presently had no idea if she had attempted suicide. Lizzie didn't enlighten him.

She then phoned Gary for her expected ticking off. However, he professed himself just to be relieved that she was okay. Her emotions had lurched from optimism to something akin to despair in a matter of moments and she couldn't wait to get home.

Whilst Gary had been unsure of the correct course of action, she hoped he now recognised that there was no way he could possibly be the conduit for criminal proceedings to be initiated against Andrea. But was it too late for her friend?

Chapter 12 – Back to the Drawing Board

'So Gloria believes Percival Whitaker's killer is a man. Did Lizzie believe her; I mean she could have done it herself, couldn't she?' Ken put his paper down and laid his pen across the crossword. 'Do you fancy a fry up this morning?'

'Certainly not; your good lady would be horrified if she thinks we've been leading you astray. If Gloria killed Whitaker then why admit to being present at all, there's nothing to link her to the crime scene, is there? No, I think she was at the tarn and has accurately described her impression of what she saw. How about having some Muesli?'

'No, I'll have eggy bread, if that's okay. Nevertheless, we're going to need to speak to Gloria either as a suspect or a witness. Hopefully they'll come home so that we don't have to go after them. I know we've been warned off but being in the witness protection scheme doesn't make her exempt from questioning about an unrelated matter; she's either perpetrated or witnessed a crime.'

Ken rose from the kitchen stool and made his way towards the hob. Gary got eggs from the fridge and gave them to his guest, who was having no difficulty at all in making himself at home.

'They know that; Lizzie impressed upon them the need to return before their absence is noticed by the villagers because once that happens, the press will get wind of it. The anonymity they have spent so many years preserving will be lost overnight. She told them to imagine what would happen if a friendly journalist offered to buy Colleen Plumley a drink. Their business would be all over the tabloids the next day. She thinks they'll come back later today.'

Lizzie appeared at that moment.

'Morning, Lizzie; eggy bread?' enquired Ken, holding the frying pan in his left hand as he attempted to wrap his dressing gown around his body with his right.

Lizzie grimaced and poured herself a mug of tea, shooting Gary a glance as she did so.

'How much did Gloria tell you about her past, Lizzie? I know I've been warned off but is there anything that could have given her a motive?'

Lizzie took a stool on the other side of the breakfast bar and gave Ken a summary of her meeting with the vicar and his wife the previous day, without going into too much detail.

'She was certainly frightened about what Percival Whitaker had discovered and was worried she was to be the subject of his next publication. On the face of it, I suppose she had a motive but I believed her when she said she wanted to talk to him to explain that his interference could put both her and Si in danger. She said she wanted to appeal to his better nature,' said Lizzie, shaking her head.

'I very much doubt that he had one. You know, the more I think about it, the more I think it must be someone he upset or exposed in the past that did for him. The whole business about Jane Macintyre's identity and subsequently the confrontation with Helen Anderson in the pub were in both cases, coincidence.' Ken turned on the hob before breaking his eggs into a bowl and stirring in a little milk and seasoning. He dipped some bread into the mixture before placing them into the hot pan. He turned to his hosts as his breakfast sizzled;

'I think we've just spent the last few days barking up the wrong tree; we were looking for a woman in her mid to late-forties, now it appears the killer is a fit chap, twenty years younger. Do you have any ketchup?'

'How did you get on with Dawn Sanchez? Ketchup's in the fridge or there's chutney if you prefer,' said Gary.

'What; chutney on eggy bread? Gary, really, there's something seriously wrong with your palate if you think that's appropriate for breakfast,' said Ken, clearly disgusted at the suggestion. 'Got any bacon?'

Gary shook his head, making sure to make no eye contact with Lizzie.

'Gina more or less worked out the Dawn Sanchez mystery through hypothesis. She thought maybe Dawn had come here illegally and when it was put to her, she admitted it. It turns out she was trafficked here from El Salvador when she was ten. She was kept in various locations and passed around at the sort of parties where wealthy men are prepared to pay a lot for an underage girl or boy. She escaped when she was sixteen and got the sort of black market work where no questions were asked and no national insurance numbers necessary. After a variety of jobs in what might loosely be described as the "entertainment and hospitality" industry, she finally met a chap who had contacts and he arranged for her to get the necessary documentation. She knew it was forged but she didn't ask any questions. After that, she worked in a bookmakers' until she met her husband, Mario. I think there was a bit of a furore over their relationship and the ex-Mrs Sanchez threatened to go to the authorities and report her, no idea how she found out, but there it is. Seems they've been paying her off for years instead of making enquiries with Immigration regarding Dawn's status. At least that can be sorted out now.'

'Dawn is certainly quite athletic,' mused Gary, thoughtfully. 'So we know that she too thought Whitaker was referring to her that night in the pub; maybe she or Mario did it?'

'But neither fit Gloria's description, do they? No, my friends, we're back to the drawing board,' said Ken as he served his breakfast and turned to the drawer to extract a knife and fork.

'I don't think it's quite that bad, we know it was Gloria Humphries that Percival Whitaker was planning to meet at the tarn; it's just that someone got there first. Now the question is; who knew about their meeting?' observed Gary.

'The vicar, presumably, but Gloria would have recognised him even if he had his head covered and he's not exactly young and lithe is he? Plus of course, she wouldn't incriminate her own husband,' said Lizzie thoughtfully.

'It's a long shot but Percival Whitaker's family; are there any grudges there?' asked Gary as he finished his cereal.

'No, whatever else he was, he was a good provider who took his responsibilities seriously. He paid his ex-wives on time and the children's school and university fees were covered. In addition; we can't find a connection to any of his past cases but we may have to have a closer look if we draw a blank here. If you're putting some toast in, I'll just have one slice after this I think, maybe with some marmalade on it.' He thought for a moment then continued;

'The other person we can't ignore is Andrea Pearce. Did she attempt suicide or was it an accident? Is her overdose connected to this case or not? We know she can't be Jane but after all, she did kill her husband, albeit under extreme provocation.'

Gary wrestled with his conscience for a few moments then made a decision.

'I think it highly unlikely her overdose was anything other than an accident. She has suffered from severe migrainous pain since her head injury. She gets muddled at times and it could well be that she accidentally took her medication more than once. Mia normally regulates her dosages but if she didn't realise her mother was poorly, then there would have been no reason to suppose she would need to take any painkillers. No, I'm sure if she intended to kill herself, Andrea would have left a note; she's a very methodical and considerate person.'

Lizzie smiled at her partner and nodded slightly as she silently mouthed "thank you".

Gary marvelled at the speed with which Ken had devoured his eggy bread as he took the toast from the toaster and gave one slice to Ken who helped himself to sunflower spread and marmalade.

'I don't believe she had anything to do with Percival Whitaker's death. As you said, she can't conceivably be Jane Macintyre. Besides, she wouldn't physically be capable of carrying out such a crime.'

'No, I'm sure you're right, Gary, but all the same I'm going to need to speak to her, when she's up to it of course,' commented Ken.

'How is she, do you know? I tried Jono but he didn't answer,' asked Lizzie.

'They've pumped her stomach or whatever they do these days and I think she's recovering slowly. Her daughter's with her. I'll be in touch later in the day. Dinner's on me tonight, if you'll both join me. I want to try the turbot. Oh, I'll get some maple syrup and we can have pancakes tomorrow morning,' said Ken happily, as he wiped his mouth on a piece of kitchen roll and turned to go upstairs in the direction of the family bathroom.

'I don't mean to be inhospitable and anyone is welcome to a bed here but really, Gary, how long is he staying?' hissed Lizzie in a hushed tone.

Gary spread his hands in a gesture of placation and smiled at his partner, before kissing her briefly, grabbing his jacket and making towards the front door.

He understood Lizzie's frustrations with their self-invited houseguest and found himself wondering how long the case was going to last and if their gastrointestinal systems were up to the challenge of Ken's continued presence.

*

To begin with, there were muffled voices far, far away then gradually, they got closer. Where was she? Was she dead? Were the angels whispering? Wait a minute; that was highly unlikely as she had killed Stuart, so there was no way she was going to heaven, even if she had tried to atone. Then she was aware of a dull ache in her arm, she tried to open her eyes but her lids were so heavy. Birds were singing nearby; was it early morning? What day was it? She heard a familiar voice; it was Mia speaking to someone else in the room, she had no idea who, but it did mean she wasn't dead. Andrea tried desperately to open her eyes, she was speaking but no one was listening to her. She sat up and tried to get off the bed. She had something sticking out of her arm; an intravenous drip? Maybe she hadn't moved at all, maybe her mind was playing tricks; then she remembered something. Yes, it was the thing she had to tell Gary. She had to make them understand she needed to see him urgently. She was literally shouting but no one took any notice.

'She seems agitated, doctor; is that normal?' Mia sounded concerned.

'I'm okay, my love but I need to see Gary Carmichael; it's very important,' she yelled but Mia ignored her.

'Her body has had a shock, she needs to rest. I'll give her something to make her sleep for a while. The canteen is open; go and get some breakfast.'

'No, no, no, don't go, Mia,' Andrea shouted; 'I need to speak to Gary now!' She suddenly felt drowsy; oh alright then, maybe just a little sleep.

*

Gary was on his way to the adventure holiday office when his mobile rang. It was Jono who explained he was still at the hospital but just leaving.

'Andrea's out of danger but very groggy. She has been treated with something called N-acetylcysteine to counteract the effects of the overdose. It's too soon to know if she's suffered any permanent damage to her liver or kidneys but they hope not. I'm on my way home to change and I'll be at work by ten o'clock at the latest,' Jono said a little breathlessly.

Upon ascertaining he had been at the hospital all night along with Mia, Gary told him to get some rest and not to worry as he would man the fort until lunchtime. After which he planned to visit Andrea himself.

This was a very fortuitous turn of events as Gary was wondering on what pretext he could gain access to Andrea's work terminal to delete the Anderson file and now he had the perfect opportunity. He wasted no time in accomplishing his mission. He took a few enquiry calls in the morning and ascertained that the walking party arranged for the day had the two guides necessary for the trip. He left the office just before one o'clock, having diverted the phone to Jono's mobile number.

At least when he saw Andrea he could tell her there was nothing to worry about regarding the letters she'd written. He knew she was devoted to Lizzie but just to what extent had been a revelation. He couldn't let her suffer for that. He of all people knew the effect Lizzie could have on those she came in contact with.

He was confident that he'd done the right thing for Andrea even if he'd broken the law in the process.

*

The darkness was lifting and she could feel warmth from the sun coming in the slightly open window with a light breeze accompanying it. She opened her eyes; they still felt heavy but not as bad as previously. She turned her head a little and saw a figure standing by the window. It was clearly a man but she couldn't quite make out if she knew him. Then he turned around and she saw it was Gary.

Gary had come to see her, now wasn't that kind. She was surprised she wasn't more pleased to see him and wondered why she was vaguely disappointed that it wasn't Jono. How very strange. Dear Jono, so dependable and so decent and she'd wasted all this time thinking she loved someone who would never be hers, even if she hadn't done that terrible thing. Oh dear God; that must be why he was here. Maybe the police were outside. Tears began to form in her eyes and try as she might, she couldn't stop them from escaping down her cheeks.

'Andrea, it's okay, you're going to be fine. No, don't try to speak I'm sure it's difficult with all the invasive procedures you've had to endure. I know how I felt when I came round after having my appendix out, I could barely speak after the intubation. I know they have to do it to keep the airways open but even so, it makes the throat sore for days,' said Gary, his voice full of concern.

'Gary, I'm so sorry,' she started but he interrupted her.

'No, I'm sorry. I should never have left you at the flat after we discussed… what we discussed. I know you must have thought I was going to act upon what I'd discovered and I did seriously consider it but I didn't and I won't. In fact, the evidence has been expunged. Whoever wrote the letters to Helen Anderson is now probably long gone and it never needs to be mentioned again. I just wanted to tell you that you have nothing to worry about.

'I won't tire you further, you need to rest. Mia's waiting outside, I'll tell her to come in. I'm going back to the office now as I think Jono is champing at the bit to come back to the hospital. He was here all night apparently. He's the most dedicated boss anyone could ever have! Get well, Andrea, we want you home, where you belong.'

He touched her hand and made to leave the room, turning just before he got to the door.

'Oh, by the way Ken Stokes will want to talk to you in a few days. I've told him you can get a bit muddled with your medication at times, so we will all need to be diligent to make sure an accident such as this never happens again, right?'

She smiled thinly and raised her hand a little. He really was a very nice man but he was a remote figure, like a soap actor or film star; out of reach and therefore safe. She suddenly realised what she had been doing all this time, fixating on someone from afar so she couldn't be hurt or abused as she had been by Stuart. In fact, it had taken something this dramatic for her to accept that escapism had its place but now she wanted to live in the real world again. Maybe that's why she had been so reticent with Jono, because a fantasy was safer than reality; well she could put that right. She suddenly realised she was alone. She hadn't even noticed Gary leave the room.

She lay back on the pillows and relaxed, breathing a small sign of relief as if a great weight had been lifted. No one would ever know what she'd done. A niggling thought suddenly hit her. For crying out loud! Now she remembered what she wanted to tell Gary and he was right here a moment ago. Her blasted memory; what a prize chump she was.

But at least she was a living chump and not a dead one. Thank heavens for small mercies.

*

Gary found Mia in the visitors' room with her hands wrapped round a disposable cup filled with coffee. She smiled as he approached and sat down next to her.

'How are you bearing up?' he enquired solicitously.

'I'm fine; I just keep reliving what might have been, if I hadn't gone upstairs when I did, the outcome could have been so different. I've been terribly blasé about mum. I convinced myself that she's fine and I've been leaving her overnight. If this had happened say one evening when I was with Connor, I can't bear to think of the consequences.'

'I think we should see this as a wake-up call, Mia; no more. I'm sure your mother herself realises how close a shave she's just had, so we all need to be diligent but at the same time get on with our lives, particularly you, she wouldn't want you to sacrifice your relationship for her.'

'Not sure about that; she never says anything but I know she's not keen on Connor.'

'Since when did the opinion of parents make the slightest bit of difference when it came to the choosing of partners?' Gary smiled ironically.

'You're right, she doesn't say much but her concerns are sort of there in the background. Small silences when I say I'm staying over at his, that sort of thing. I suppose it's natural for a parent to be protective.'

'Yes, I'd go along with that. You said "concerns" why did you use that word in particular, Mia?'

'Why do I always feel like every conversation I have with you is a cross-examination?' smiled Mia, not altogether in jest, thought Gary with a small amount of dismay. Did he do that?

'To answer the question, I think she was worried because Connor has a bit of a past but then he's not the only one is he; the same could be said for a lot of people in Blenthorne.'

Gary thought how prophetic Mia's comment was with all the revelations that were coming out in the village. Who could have thought the quiet unassuming residents could have such complex backgrounds? Presumably there were more to come before the identity of Percival Whitaker's killer was unmasked.

'A criminal past?' asked Gary directly.

'Goodness no, he wouldn't have got the job at the school if he had a record. No, he's just struggled to find the right niche for himself and he fell out with his family before he came here. I don't think he's in touch with them, even though I've encouraged him to try to make amends.'

'Make amends for what?'

'Okay, I'll tell you but please keep it to yourself. He took some property from his parents and sold it to a shop; he couldn't see the harm as it wasn't used and in fact was all bundled up in the attic. Guitars and amplifiers; stuff like that. His father reported it as theft but then when he found out it was Connor, he told the police it had been a mistake; he went to the shop and bought back his things. He said Connor had to repay him out of his earnings. He did, at least he told me he had, but he left home and I don't think they've been in contact since. His father said it was a matter of trust and I said he needed to show his family that he'd turned over a new leaf. He got the job at the school and additional work at the hotel. He needs to get in touch and tell them how well he's doing. I'm sure they'll forgive him because that's what families do, isn't it, they forgive each other?'

Something Mia had said stuck in Gary's mind. He made his excuses and said goodbye. As he walked to the hospital carpark, he rang Jono to say his return to the office would be delayed and then rang Ken to outline his germ of a theory. It was a long shot but sometimes a word here or there and a bit of a hunch paid dividends.

*

An hour-and-a-half later Gary and Ken met up at Fell View Hotel. They walked up to the desk where he found Helen Anderson checking in a guest.

'Hello, Helen, unusual to see you on reception,' said Gary lightly.

'Tell me about it, Karen's gone sick. Now of all times; we still have journalists crawling out of the woodwork offering to pay above the odds for every room. In fact, I could rent out the room that Percival Whitaker had for five times the nightly rate. I wanted our occupancy levels to be healthy for when Robin and Mark get back but I think it's a case of be careful what you wish for! Now, what can I do for you, are you okay?' She gave all her attention to Gary, seemingly not even noticing Ken was present.

Gary ignored the personal enquiry. 'Is Connor around? He sometimes works here after he's finished at the school, I believe?'

'Yes, he's our night porter several times a week and also helps out at the gym now and then. Why do you want to see him?'

When neither Gary nor Ken answered, Helen walked to the telephone and made a call. She suggested they wait in the lounge and said she would arrange some afternoon tea.

Ken's eyes lit up at the prospect of cake but if he was disappointed that when it arrived "tea" actually just meant a pot for two, he said nothing.

Connor arrived after about five minutes. He looked a little apprehensive as he sat down in a chair at right angles to the two sofas occupied by the detective sergeant and the retired detective inspector. He was wearing dark tracksuit bottoms with a white polo shirt bearing the hotel logo. He had a lanyard round his neck with a whistle attached. If nothing else, he certainly looked the part of a gym instructor.

'Connor, good to see you, how's things?' enquired Gary conversationally, although Connor had never been big on small talk.

'Yeah, I'm okay thanks. Ms Anderson said you wanted to see me? Why?' Connor looked uncomfortable.

Direct and to the point; maybe that was a good thing. Ken took the initiative.

'I'm wondering if you can tell us where you were on the day the journalist, Percival Whitaker, was killed?'

'I was at work at the school in Rowendale. Why?'

'You were there all day, from early morning? You didn't take a break at any time?'

'Not that I can remember; if I need materials for repairs then I'll go and get them, often before school starts. I have a petty cash fund for small items but larger things have to be purchased through official suppliers. If I needed screws or something, I may have gone out but I don't know, off hand.'

'You see that's a bit strange, Connor, because when something significant happens, people usually know where they were. It sort of seals a moment in the memory but you're telling me you can't remember.'

'Sorry, I didn't know the guy; I never met him so why would I be bothered that he died? He was a conceited self-important tosser by all accounts so I don't suppose he'll be missed.'

'So during his stay here your paths never crossed? He didn't come to the gym?'

'Did he look like he worked out?'

'So you knew him by sight?' said Ken quickly.

'Yeah, suppose so, I saw him around but I never spoke to him, why would I?'

'So he never needed anything from reception when you were on duty as porter during the night?' persisted Ken.

'Not that I recall,' said Connor to his feet.

'Were you present the night Percival Whitaker spoke to Helen Anderson in the pub?' asked Ken.

Connor turned to Gary. 'You know I was. I usually have a drink or two while Mia's working, if I'm not here at the hotel.'

Gary nodded but said nothing. It wasn't his call.

'Didn't you have a word with Mr Whitaker one night when you thought he was coming on to Mia?'

'I would have a word with anyone who did that,' said Connor sulkily.

'So you did speak to him,' persisted Ken.

'I might have done but that doesn't mean I killed him.'

'Would you mind if we had a look at your place, Connor?' asked Ken gently.

'Why do you need to do that, are you searching everyone's gaff or am I getting special attention because I'm an outsider?'

'What makes you think that, Connor? You work locally, your girlfriend lives here and you're a regular at the Blenny,' said Ken, looking keenly at the young man. 'I would say you're very much part of the community.'

He shrugged and pushed his dark hair away from his forehead.

'Would you be prepared to take part in an identity line up? There's not much to it really, you don't have to appear in person behind a screen or anything like that, it's just a quick video appearance and will only take a few moments,' asked Ken taking out his notebook.

'Why?'

Ken answered the question candidly. 'Because we have a witness, someone who was present when Percival Whitaker had his skull smashed.'

'If that's true and you really believe I killed him, you'd be making an arrest and not asking me to appear in a video. Now if that's all, I need to get on as I have a client waiting,' challenged Connor.

When neither of the men said anything, Connor got up and walked away back towards the gym.

'He's more astute than he looks,' remarked Gary.

'Yes indeed, my feelings exactly. So what do you think?' asked Ken.

'He fits Gloria's description, he's fit and athletic. He "doesn't remember" where he was at the time of the murder. Would getting a bit cheeky with Mia be enough for Whitaker to get himself killed? I would have thought if Connor really took exception to any comments or behaviour, then he would have used his fists. So, if it is him, we've yet to establish a plausible motive.'

'Good point, however I think your hunch about Mia's comment has merit,' added Ken. He opened his notebook, turned a couple of pages and looked at his notes. 'It's possible that she was theorising when she said; *"he has a bit of a past but then he's not the only one is he*; *the same could be said for a lot of people in Blenthorne"*. However, if she was being literal, then from Connor's defensive demeanour just now, I think he probably did say something along those lines to Mia. If so, it's reasonable to assume he's seen the contents of the laptop and knows what Whitaker was working on.'

'In which case, there are only two possibilities, either Whitaker left his laptop unattended at the hotel when Connor was around which sounds highly unlikely or Connor took it from him at the tarn; if we accept the latter, then it looks probable that Connor Robson is our killer,' said Gary, logically.

'We'll put a tail on him; if he has the laptop, he'll get rid of it quick smart now we've spoken to him. As it stands, we don't have enough for a warrant. Also we need to have a word with Mia but that's difficult with Andrea being so poorly,' said Ken realistically.

Gary was about to speak when his mobile rang. He took it out and spoke for a few seconds before replacing it in his pocket. 'Good timing; that was Mia. Apparently, there's something that Andrea wants to tell me so I'd better get back to the hospital before visiting is over for the day.'

'I'm going to sort a bit of background on our friend Connor and get the tail organised. Gina loves doing that so it'll be a special treat for her. See you and Lizzie for dinner,' confirmed Ken.

Gary nodded and they parted company. He found himself wondering what it was that Andrea suddenly needed to tell him.

He got back to Andrea's side ward just before six o'clock, having stopped at a petrol station to pick up some flowers. Mia was in the visitors' room and she told him that her mother was being assessed by a representative from the acute care mental health team. After a couple of minutes, one of the nurses stuck her head round the door to say Andrea's visitor had left so they could go in. When they arrived, Andrea seemed to be surrounded by literature which Mia joked would be a little light reading before going to sleep.

'Sweetheart,' croaked Andrea to Mia, 'do you think you could give us a moment, there's something I need to tell Gary; go and find a nice vase for these beautiful flowers, there's a love.'

'Andrea whatever it is, don't you think it should wait until you're feeling better as it's clearly quite difficult for you to speak at the moment,' said Gary, his voice filled with concern.

'Yes, I know but this can't wait. After I took the pills, just before I lost consciousness when you found out about what I did, I realised something of huge significance and I thought damn it, now no one will ever know. But then when I realised I wasn't dead, it had completely gone out of my mind. As you left…' she again paused, this time to sip some water and cough a little to clear her throat. 'As you left I remembered, so I asked Mia to contact you.'

'You obviously think it's important so what is it?' Gary wasn't anticipating anything earthshattering but what she told him shocked him to the core and for a moment he was completely lost for words. He thanked her and left, making a call on his mobile as he did so.

Could this be the smoking gun they were looking for?

Chapter 13 – The Cornered Rabbit

Ken Stokes made his way back to the parish hall after the interview at the hotel, where he instructed his assembled team regarding the new angle of their enquiry and background searches were immediately commenced into Connor Robson. Initial information revealed that he'd been brought up by adoptive parents who moved from County Clare to Doncaster and he had a good academic record. He had been accepted onto a university course to study sports science but instead had decided to travel. He had moved around, finally ending up in Rowendale, working at the primary school which had accommodation attached. The school were pleased with his work and this was echoed by Helen Anderson at the hotel who said he was popular with hotel guests and the locals who attended the gym.

Gina had allocated the first watch to two other team members but told Ken she anticipated nothing would happen while he was at work. If he had a laptop to dispose of, it would be done later in the day or during the night.

Ken met up with Gary and Lizzie for dinner as planned and Ken enjoyed his eagerly anticipated turbot with a sorrel sauce, accompanied by green beans with parsnip and potato mash. He informed them happily, as he shovelled in the last of his main course, he'd stopped off earlier to purchase some maple syrup ready for their morning pancakes.

If he was wearing his policeman's hat, he would probably have noticed the look of disgust Lizzie shot Gary but as it was, his concentration was fully focused on choosing his dessert.

Just after eleven o'clock, he got into bed and looked at the crossword before switching off the light, unaware that his night's sleep would be cut rather short and his planned morning pancake feast considerably delayed.

*

He jumped when he heard a fire alarm while he was at the cinema and the audience were all made to leave. They filed out into the street and still the alarm was ringing. Presumably it would carry on until the fire service arrived. Then there was a banging noise and for some reason Gary was there. Goodness knows what Mrs S would make of him tagging along to watch the film. Then Gary was shouting at him.

'Ken, wake up! Your phone's been ringing on and off for several minutes.'

'What? Oh, sorry did it wake you?' asked a confused looking Ken.

'It's a good thing it woke one of us. It's Gina by the look of it,' he said as he handed Ken his mobile.

Ken took the call, feeling a little bleary eyed and dyspeptic; definitely wishing he'd heeded Gary's advice and passed on the treacle pudding with crème anglaise.

'Gina, intercept at your discretion. Wait for back up if you're unsure, don't put yourself at risk.' He terminated the call. 'What do you know,' he said as he pushed back the duvet to get out of bed. 'Our friend is on the move. Connor Robson is heading north.'

'I'll go to the hall and monitor things from there. Coming?' asked Ken as he disappeared towards the bathroom with his clothes in his arms.

'I shouldn't really, should I?' asked Gary, clearly hoping to be overruled.

'You're someone Connor trusts so I think we can stretch a point,' called Ken from behind the closed bathroom door.

'You saw him earlier, he doesn't trust anyone other than maybe Mia,' replied Gary quietly.

Ken opened the door slightly. 'Your local knowledge will be invaluable and if we don't need that, you can make the tea; go and get dressed but try not to wake Lizzie. We need to see Mia but we'll let her rest; the girl's got enough on her plate for now. We can speak to her later.'

Gary obviously didn't need any more encouragement and made towards the en suite. Lizzie was awake when he came out but he made her promise to stay at home.

*

The two men left the house and drove the short distance to the parish hall. Once inside, Ken wasted no time in trying to contact Gina for an update. He told Gary he had decided against placing a call to his commanding officer, feeling it could wait until morning when hopefully they had some positive results to impart.

'He appeared to be going towards Lanksworth but he must have clocked us. He turned off in the direction of… what's it called?' she was clearly consulting her colleague. 'Boss, he's now on foot and heading for the range known as Melton Pass? Does that mean anything?'

Ken looked at Gary. 'Melton Pass; do you know it?' he asked as he switched to speakerphone.

'Yes, Jono's company takes advanced groups there. It's pretty treacherous in places, even in daylight. It's not for the inexperienced climber. Hope he's not going to attempt to get over the top and drop down the other side. Of course, he's pretty fit so if he manages that, and it's a big if, he would be near to Hobden's Creek. It could take days to flush him out from there, that's assuming he doesn't disappear in the labyrinth of gullies and hidden paths. Either way, you're going to need some airborne assistance to track him.'

'Gina, did you hear that? Robson might be heading for Hobden's Creek but that would necessitate him getting over the top of Melton Pass which is pretty dicey even in daylight according to Gary. If that's the case, don't pursue, repeat don't pursue… can you hear me?'

There was no reply from Gina Williams, despite Ken's repeated request for her to acknowledge his instruction.

'Signal's probably weak,' suggested Gary.

'Or more likely she's just refusing to respond so she can be a hero. You know, at times I think she has the making of a good or even outstanding cop but she's a maverick. One day she'll get herself or someone else killed.'

'You're concentrating on worst case scenario; it really might just be that she can't hear you,' reasoned Gary.

'Maybe, we'll give her the benefit of the doubt for now. So we need the chopper you think? Great, there goes the budget!' said Ken as he blew out his cheeks and called the chief inspector with his request.

While they waited, they passed the next hour and a half drinking tea and Ken filled Gary in on Connor's past.

'Adopted you say? Do you think he could be Gloria Humphries' son, Oliver? If so, that would explain his motive. He thought Percival Whitaker was going to expose his mother's past, so he killed him.'

'Yes, it's definitely possible,' conceded Ken.

'Theoretically possible but not the case, Detective Sergeant Stokes,' said a soft voice from behind the two men who both jumped, not realising they had left the hall door unlocked.

'Connor's my son. I heard the commotion with the helicopter overhead and then I could see the lights were on in here from my bedroom window, so I knew something was wrong. This has to end. He did it for me, you see.'

Gary pulled out a chair and Hilary Cole slid her tall, slender frame onto it.

'Hilary; um… would you like some tea?' asked Gary gently.

She nodded.

'Are you prepared to make a statement, Miss Cole?' asked Ken quietly.

'Yes, of course. What else can I do?' she folded her hands neatly in her lap.

'There's no doubt it was my fault; everything that has happened in Connor's life can be traced back my actions. The "nature versus nurture" debate; I failed him whichever way you look at it.' She took her tea gratefully and smiled her thanks at Gary.

'I was fourteen when I became pregnant, I managed to hide it for several months but when my parents found out they were horrified. We lived in Derry but I was packed off to Galway in the Irish Republic; out of sight and out of mind. My father had a distant cousin there and I stayed with her family for a while. She was a nice lady, married to a welder. They had seven children but in spite of that, they said they would bring my child up as their own. My father was supposed to be a man of God but there was no compassion in his soul; he wouldn't hear of it and I was sent to a home for "unmarried mothers" just before the birth. I was made to give my baby away and it broke my heart; I kicked up an almighty fuss, I can tell you, but to no avail. Then my maternal great aunt took pity on me and invited me to live with her in Carlisle. She'd lost her husband in the Great War; they'd only been married three months. By now I was beyond redemption as far as my father was concerned, having shown no remorse for my sins so he was happy to let me go.'

Hilary sipped her tea.

'My aunt was so kind, she said my baby would be brought up by a family who would love him and give him a wonderful life. I went back to school and studied very hard to pass my exams. Afterwards I went to work in a bank and continued to live with her. I never went back home.

'When my aunt died, she left me her estate and it was sufficient to buy my cottage here. I worked in a building society in Keswick to begin with and when a vacancy arose in Blenthorne, my application for the Post Office job was successful. It was perfect for me, just along the road from my home. I contacted my parents once to let them know where I was, as I thought it was time to hold out an olive branch and ask if they might like to visit but I never received a reply. I don't even know if they're still alive but I suppose they must be or I would have been notified, wouldn't I?'

She lapsed into a momentary silence then continued in a tortured voice;

'I still think about what I did. I spend every night trying to reconcile my actions with their outcome. Would things have been different if I had somehow managed to keep my boy? He was never far from my thoughts. I had a photo of him by my bed; it was taken just before I gave him away. I kissed it every night and prayed for him to be safe. It was very strange when he found me; I'd thought about the possibility, obviously, but somehow when it happened, it was surreal. This would be getting on for two years ago now.'

'So he contacted you?' asked Ken.

'Yes, I'd registered with the appropriate organisation and when he registered too we were put in touch through an intermediary; we exchanged correspondence for a while. When we finally met, I'm not sure what he thought of me, I imagine he was rather disappointed. I understand that adopted children often make up stories about their natural parents. He was probably hoping I was a successful businesswoman, actress or singer and to find I was a rather frumpy village post mistress must have been something of a let-down.

'He visited me several times before he told me he'd applied for a job locally. I was so excited to think he'd be close by. We decided to let things develop slowly; neither of us being ready for a great public revelation as to our relationship. You see it may not have worked out. We might have discovered we couldn't find any common ground.

'As it was, he worked at the school and subsequently also got some part-time work at the hotel, as a night porter. I have been helping him a little financially as he wants to be a personal trainer so he's studying in his spare time for the qualifications he needs. The hotel have been very supportive and given him some extra work in the gym, mainly just helping out the instructor but at least he is gaining some experience.

'He was doing well and when he met Mia, he said he was happier than he'd ever been. Auntie had suggested he would have a wonderful life with adoptive parents but the reality was his parents had a child naturally a year after they had decided to adopt. His brother apparently outshone him in everything he did and as a consequence, Connor felt unwanted and unloved. The family moved from Ireland to Yorkshire when Connor's adoptive father got a new job. Connor had problems adjusting and found it difficult to make friends. His parents arranged counselling at one point and he was diagnosed with Imposter Syndrome, which is apparently a condition which means he couldn't accept or take credit for his own accomplishments. I don't think he responded well to therapy and by his own admission, he became rebellious. He was offered a university place but was wracked by self-doubt. His parents were terribly disappointed when he decided not to study for a degree. Now I know there are two sides to every tale, so maybe they would tell a different story; he told me there was a terrible misunderstanding about some property belonging to his father and I think that was the last straw for Connor.

'Meeting someone who made him feel really special was so important for his self-esteem and confidence. Mia's a lovely girl and she been a calming influence in many ways. He has always seemed to me a little impetuous, so her support has been invaluable.'

'Does she know you're Connor's mother?' interjected Ken.

'I don't believe so. As I said, we haven't rushed things. It may well be in time we would have told everyone but it's not like a normal mother son relationship. We have only got to know each other as adults. I wasn't there to guide him through his formative years. Who knows, he might have rebelled even if I had been. However, we were on the right track I think, that is, until now when that odious man arrived and ruined everything.

'We both knew it was us to whom he was referring that night in the pub. He said he had "other fish to fry", clearly that would be Connor and me but for what? How had he found out? I was sure I'd never met him previously in spite of his assertion about knowing me in the past. Connor had been born in the Irish Republic so it was unlikely Mr Whitaker had stumbled across a birth record by accident. I'd never committed any crime yet for some reason he wanted to hound me for his "Back in Time" series. I expect the headline would have been something like; *"The Past of Miss Prim from the Post Office"*. His primary intention was to cause hurt, pain and distress. He was doing that before he even submitted his article. Connor said he would have a word with him and I said best to leave it because they had already had a small contretemps regarding Mr Whitaker's overfamiliarity with Mia. I know Connor was seething and planning to approach him again.

'Then an opportunity presented itself to Connor when he was working as the hotel night porter. He overheard Percival Whitaker arranging to meet someone when he was checking the corridors during his shift. Mr Whitaker was setting up a rendezvous at Dark Tarn. Of course he had no idea whom the journalist was going to meet but he told me he planned to be there to witness the meeting, just to see what he could ascertain. I told him not to go. I begged him not to do anything provocative.'

'When he arrived, he found Mr Whitaker alone and took his chance when he saw it. He told me it wasn't premediated; he was just so angry with the man for causing me so much anguish that he had a rush of blood and hit him with a large stone.' She paused, blew her nose and then continued;

'Connor didn't mean to kill him but couldn't get him out after he fell into the tarn. He knew he'd done something heinous and he turned up at my cottage with a rucksack. It contained both Mr Whitaker's laptop and mobile phone. We smashed the phone easily and were going to destroy the laptop but then I noticed a word on the inside of the lid written on a sticky label, so I tried it, in case it was the password. Amazingly, it actually was! Can you believe someone would be silly enough to do that? Anyway, I accessed the files without difficulty as they had no protection whatsoever. We realised very quickly that we'd been wrong. There was nothing about us, he was pursuing someone called Jane but I didn't look too closely once I realised he wasn't interested in Connor and me. He also had information in a file about Helen Anderson but again, I didn't do more than glance at it.

'I know I should have persuaded Connor to turn himself in immediately but my somewhat belated discovery of maternal instinct dictated that I would do anything to protect him. I knew we had to destroy the evidence linking him to the crime with as much expedience as possible, so I deleted the files but believe they can still be forensically retrieved so to be on the safe side I smashed the hard drive with a hammer. I still have the pieces if you want them?' She volunteered, disarmingly.

Gary found himself remembering something else Mia had said when he talked to her at the hospital. She'd said something along the lines; "*that's what families do; they forgive each other, don't they*", and that was certainly true in Hilary's case. The love she had for her child had been suppressed for so long and was now unequivocal.

'But why did he take such drastic action? I mean no offence but being a single parent is no longer a shameful thing,' Ken looked at her intently.

'That's true enough but in my day there was definitely a stigma attached if one had had an upbringing such as mine. However, as you say, it might have caused a bit of gossip for a few weeks but soon enough people would have found something or someone else to talk about. But Connor didn't see it that way. I was his mother and he was going to protect my reputation and anonymity. He wouldn't be swayed by anything that I said. He believed we shouldn't allow ourselves to be victims.' She paused for a while and then added almost as an afterthought; 'of course I didn't call him Connor. I called him Peter; Peter Andrew Cole. They changed his name when he was adopted.

'Please, Sergeant Stokes, get him back safely, I know he's done something unforgivable but he's my child; he's all I have.'

Both men looked at each other, presumably hoping the other would think of something appropriate to say.

'Hilary, if he's sensible and gives himself up, all will be well. He'll be charged of course but at least he'll be safe,' suggested Gary finally. 'Mitigating circumstances and character references...' his voice trailed off.

She nodded as she wiped her eyes and blew her nose on a tissue she produced from her left sleeve.

Ken walked away from the desk and tried Gina again on the mobile.

This time she answered. 'Boss, I can hear you. He's nearing the top of Melton Pass and to be honest I think the lights from the chopper are guiding his path.'

'If you get close enough, tell him his birth mother is here with me and wants him safely home.'

'His birth mother… who the…?' questioned Gina.

'I'll explain later,' interrupted Ken quickly.

'I'm not close enough to shout to him, there's the noise of the chopper, the wind and he's pretty damned agile. He's way ahead and I doubt we'll reach him before he's over the top. The path is far from clear even with torches. We are picking our way very carefully.'

'I hope you carried out a risk assessment before you set off,' commented Ken wryly.

'Realistically, we aren't going to get anywhere near him unless he stops.'

'Can you relay a message to the helicopter; maybe they can hail him.'

'Yes, certainly worth a try; oh shit…'

'What's happened, Gina… what's happened?'

'I don't know; the helicopter is circling as low as it can go. I can't see Connor. I'll call you back.'

'What's happened?' asked Hilary, who had risen and was standing a few feet from Ken when he turned around.

'We don't know yet, Miss Cole. I think it best you go home and I'll contact you immediately we hear anything, I promise.'

As if on cue, there was a light rap on the hall door and Lizzie Lockwood appeared with her coat over a sweatshirt and a pair of jogging bottoms.

'Lizzie! You promised you'd stay at home,' said Gary reproachfully.

'I didn't actually, you asked me to and I didn't answer. I just wanted to check that everyone was alright,' said Lizzie innocently.

'I'm glad she's here, Gary. I've never had many friends; Lizzie and latterly Dawn, have been kind to me.'

Lizzie hurried over and engulfed Hilary in her arms. Hilary dissolved into uncontrollable sobs.

'My boy is out on the fells, Lizzie, the police are pursuing him. He could get himself killed.'

Lizzie nodded. If she was surprised that Hilary Cole had a child, she gave no indication as her countenance didn't change. Hilary would need all the support she could get in the coming days, whichever way the night's events unfolded; she couldn't be in better hands Gary thought, suddenly awash with pride.

Hilary allowed herself to be led away by Lizzie who said she would stay with her for as long as necessary.

Just before they reached the door Hilary turned and faced Ken.

'I want to know, Sergeant Stokes, even if it's the worst possible outcome, even if he's dead, I have to know immediately, please.' There was an imploring tone to her voice that even the most hardened police officer couldn't ignore.

Ken nodded. 'I will come to see you myself with whatever news I have, I promise.'

Ken's phone rang.

'Are you alone, sir?'

Ken looked at the retreating figures as they left the hall in the direction of Hilary's cottage, Lizzie's torch throwing a beam ahead of them as they walked.

He answered in the affirmative and again switched over to speakerphone.

'He's fallen, it looks like he was in a gully and tried to haul himself up on to the next ledge but the overhang was too steep and he lost his grip. We're making towards the spot now. We'll need the rescue team and a doctor.'

Even if Gary hadn't heard every word of Gina's commentary, he would have experienced an overwhelming sense of foreboding from the slope of his ex-colleague's shoulders when the call was terminated.

The next few minutes were spent co-ordinating the emergency teams to reach Melton Pass without delay. It was getting light so the conditions for the mission would be easier as dawn broke.

'Poor woman, she had a child briefly all that time ago and then again for the last couple of years. Connor's main crime was to love his mother enough not to want to see her shamed in public. Like anyone would have cared now,' Ken shook his head.

'Yes, but when he knew the game was up, he didn't have to run. He could have pleaded guilty to manslaughter and served his time. He would have been out in a few years. There was no premeditation. And Percival Whitaker was a prize arsehole.' Gary paused then continued. 'Damned shame Hilary told us about the laptop and phone though because if she hadn't, there wouldn't be anything to connect her to Connor's crime; as it is, she's an accessory. I mean, I suppose you did write that bit down?'

'Whatever are you suggesting? Of course I wrote it down! Being selective with information-gathering is anathema to me and I would have thought you, of all people, would know that. Where does it end? Down the slippery slope to corruption, that's where!' Ken shook his head, as he looked steadily at Gary.

He waited for a few moments before breaking the awkward silence that followed.

'Right; now I need to collect the laptop debris to see if we can put any of it together, however that's highly unlikely if as she said, they took a hammer to the hard drive. For what it's worth, I think the prosecution service will be pretty lenient. She's lost enough.'

'We can't be sure he's dead yet,' murmured Gary more in hope than expectation. He was still smarting from the rebuke delivered by his friend.

Ken's phone rang again and he pressed it to his ear. From his responses, Gary realised the news wasn't good.

'He fell about twenty metres to the path below and it appears died on impact, having hit several rocks on the way down.' He swallowed deeply. 'Stupid little sod, he didn't need to run.' He removed his glasses and rubbed his eyes.

'Do you want a drink?' asked Gary.

'No, I promised Hilary I'd go straight round there now. Worst part of the job, this. Then I'll come back and start on the paperwork.'

'Knowing Lizzie as I do, she'll stay with Hilary for the rest of the night and probably for the foreseeable future if she feels she's doing some good.'

Ken nodded.

'What about Mia; do you want me to tell her? She isn't directly involved so it doesn't have to come from a police officer,' asked Gary.

'Yeah, probably better if it comes from you; poor girl, first her mum and now her boyfriend,' Ken said, shaking his head.

'Ken, sorry about earlier,' said Gary sheepishly.

'What about earlier?'

'Suggesting that you could maybe forget Hilary's part in this,' said Gary rather bashfully.

'I've no idea what you're talking about. I don't think we're going to make breakfast are we. Maybe we could have the pancakes after a fry up for lunch?'

Gary smiled.

'Strange how things turn out,' murmured Ken. 'We were determined to link this crime to Helen Anderson or Jane Macintyre and yet neither were involved in any way. Life is full of bizarre coincidences, isn't it?'

Gary didn't answer as Ken's words hit home. He had been pursuing his own line of thought over the last hour. Maybe life wasn't so full of coincidences after all…

Chapter 14 – Secrets and Lies

'Not the best outcome, obviously, but we've done our job. Good to work with you again!' Ken said as he picked up his overnight bag.

'No offence but I'll be glad to get back to my day job,' smiled Gary.

'Yes I'm sure. I don't like loose ends though and we never established any sort of link between the murder and the poison pen letters, did we.' Ken held out his hand and Gary shook it warmly.

'I suspect they weren't connected and whoever did that probably got bored. Same with Jane Macintyre; she was a complete red herring. If she is living here, none of us will ever be any the wiser. She clearly didn't kill Whitaker so best we don't dwell on her possible identity.'

'If I know you, you'll find out sooner or later,' said Ken shrewdly.

'If I do, it'll be accidental,' replied Gary.

'What will be accidental?' asked Lizzie, appearing in the doorway as she took in the scene of devastation that was once her kitchen.

Gary explained as they both waved Ken off.

Lizzie yawned; she'd been at Hilary's since Connor's death and was planning to pop back later. Dawn was there currently and suggested Lizzie should go home to get her head down for a while. As it was, she was far too wound up to sleep and turned her attention to the room.

'I thought you were possibly the most untidy man I'd ever met but Ken Stokes has given you a run for your money. I mean, look at the mess you've made between you; it resembles a doss house! Now I'm finally home, fill me in on the bits I missed on the night of Connor's accident.'

Lizzie listened without interruption, which was a rarity in itself. She was deep in thought. 'I really can't believe how badly I let Hilary down. I should have drawn her out of her shell ages ago. She said she thought of me as a close friend; some friend I've been over the years, I only ever chatted to her briefly over the post office counter.'

'You're far too hard on yourself, Lizzie; you can't take everyone under your wing, much as you'd like to.'

Lizzie wasn't convinced but turned her attention to other matters.

'So you covered up for Andrea and asked Ken to overlook Hilary's aiding and abetting an offender. Some might say I'm a bad influence,' said Lizzie as she smiled at her partner.

'It's not you; I'm going soft in my old age,' said Gary quietly as he held Lizzie's gaze. 'Now, I need to go to the hotel but see you at home for dinner about seven o'clock? It will be great, just the two of us.'

'Isn't that the truth,' said Lizzie with a smile and small sigh.

He walked to the hotel, utilising the time to make a call on his way. He noticed the police team packing their equipment into a waiting van outside the parish hall. He waved to Gina as she got into her car.

He reached the hotel foyer and a voice he knew well greeted him.

'Hi, Gary; I hear you've had some excitement while we were away.'

'Hey! Hello, Mark, good to see you. Did you both have a relaxing break?'

'Yes, it was wonderful but my goodness what's been going on here? Helen seems to have coped magnificently. I really don't know what we would do without her; she's an absolute brick.'

'Yes, that's certainly one word for her. Is she around; I'd like to see her, if that's possible?'

'Oh really; she's in the office but I'm sure she will be delighted to see you,' he said, looking intrigued.

Gary wasn't so sure that would be the case for long.

He declined refreshment and went into the lounge to wait for Helen. He stood at the window, looking over the garden to the fells beyond. He didn't realise she had entered the room until she spoke to him.

'Gary, my goodness, what a lucky girl I am. To what do I owe the pleasure today? I suppose it's too much to hope this is purely a social call and you want to invite me for dinner,' she said, with a slight hint of sarcasm, or was it optimism, in her voice.

'No, it isn't a social call, Helen,' said Gary gravely.

'You surprise me! What have I done now?' she said almost mockingly as she sat down gracefully on the edge of a sofa, crossing her legs at the ankles.

'I don't want to talk about now, I want to talk about the past,' he replied, sitting down opposite her.

'Good God, you're not raking up Malching again! For crying out loud; how many times can I say it? I was stupid and gullible but I've paid for that and moved on. I came here hoping you would be happy to see me. I believed we had a connection; I saw very quickly that as far as you were concerned, we didn't. I haven't pestered you and thanks to Robin and Mark, have embarked on a new career. However, I might remind you that we were close for a short while in Devon and whilst I know that now embarrasses you, it's not something to be taken lightly. So tread carefully, Gary, before you accuse me of anything,' a glint of anger flashed across her eyes.

'Actually, it has nothing to do with Devon. It was way before that. I've been doing a bit of digging over the last couple of days; I'm not sure of the exact details as yet but I've just contacted the police team in Malching who investigated the deaths at Folly End Farm.'

'But you just said it had nothing to do with Malching.'

'No, but the Devon team will liaise with officers in Sussex, I believe.'

'Will you stop being so theatrical; why are the police in Malching liaising with a team in Sussex? You profess to be disinterested, yet you just can't leave me alone, can you? Please believe me when I say I want to move on.'

'I'm sure you do, Helen. Move on and have a future; it's just sad that the residents to whom you had a duty of care weren't afforded that opportunity.'

'Jeremy Sampson manipulated and blackmailed me. I was naïve but that doesn't make me a murderer.'

'You see, I believed that at the time. I was convinced by your performance. But I was wrong.'

'Okay, so you aren't interested in me, it was a brief passing moment about which you wanted to forget, so when I turned up here it was a shock. But you have to admit I've been nothing but discretion itself and if things stay on an even keel, I have every intention of remaining so.'

'Yes; I can't fault you for that. That's why I'm here, I suppose, to forewarn you of what's about to happen. Then it's up to you what you do about it. Stay here and face the consequences or start afresh in a place where no one knows you. In fact, if you hadn't come to Blenthorne, none of this would have come to light.'

'There you go again, talking in riddles. Has anyone ever said that you really do like the sound of your own voice?'

'Indeed, my ex-wife, countless times. No, I want to talk about something that was said to you rather than me. It was the night of your unexpected encounter with Percival Whitaker. He baited you for a while according to those present, letting you think he was pursuing someone else, which of course he was. When you relaxed a little he leaned forward and whispered something to you. Do you remember?' he paused to allow Helen to answer but she said nothing.

'At the time you suggested you didn't recall the incident. Subsequently, Andrea Pearce told Lizzie that she was walking past when she overheard what she thought he had said to you. She thought he had whispered someone's name; "Trevor Gill" and when I asked you about it, you said he was an old boyfriend, "Trevor Gilham", going back to when you were a teenager. Unfortunately, no one of that name has been traced.'

'That's not a complete surprise is it? I mean, it was years ago, he's probably long gone, he could be anywhere, he could have left the country or I suppose he could be dead.'

'The problem with that scenario is it presupposes one thing; that he actually existed in the first place,' said Gary very quietly as he looked closely at the woman sitting opposite him.

'No, he didn't exist, I made him up. I'm a fantasist. What the hell do you want me to say?'

She looked a little flushed and was certainly agitated. Last time she had got the better of him and he wasn't about to let that happen again.

'For once, Helen, how about you tell me the truth? I know honesty is an alien concept when you've spent years spinning yarns, so I'm sure it can't be easy but just try it,' his voice was steady and emotionless.

She stood up; 'I've had enough, I've lots to do and this is clearly going nowhere, so I'll say goodbye now.'

She made to move away.

'I could shout this across the lounge but I think you might prefer to come back to hear what I have to say in private then you can do with the information what you will. It isn't a person, is it?'

Helen stopped, turned to face him and walked slowly back to sit down on the sofa from which she had just risen.

'Andrea gave me the answer herself. Her memory is not great and there are times when she can't find the right word or remember names or places. She thought she'd overheard Percival Whitaker saying someone's name but just recently she remembered something important. Suddenly an image of a policeman riding a bicycle came to her. He was a local bobby in a lovely tranquil location in Sussex near a caravan park where she spent holidays as a child. Somewhere from the recesses of her memory the name of the village came to her. Then she realised she had inadvertently mislead us. It wasn't a person at all, it was a place. Ring any bells, Helen?'

Her jaw was set tight but still she remained silent.

'We weren't looking for someone called "Trevor Gill" or "Gilham" we needed to look at a small hamlet, a few miles from Eastbourne by the name of "Trevon Ghyll" - spelled "GHYLL". Most people have never heard of it, it consists of about twenty properties and has a wood close by with a ravine which is popular with walkers and picnickers. There is a pub there too and an old manor house which was converted into a nursing home in the seventies. Does that sound familiar?'

Helen still said nothing. Her head was now bent towards her lap, her hands were clasped and her knuckles white.

'Do you want to fill in the rest or would you like me to carry on?'

Helen shook her head defiantly. 'You can do and say what you like. I've worked at several nursing homes over the years. There's no proof that anything untoward happened during my time in Sussex.'

'Maybe not, but the police are going to be looking closely at past records of the home and any possible untimely deaths of residents. It's just possible that when questioned, some of the relatives will do as they did in Malching; find their consciences too much to bear and break their silence regarding how much they paid you to dispose of their kinfolk. Whilst you got away with Malching, I don't think anyone would be naïve enough to believe that Trevon Ghyll was a coincidence, do you?'

Helen looked out of the window far into the distance, seemingly detaching herself from what she was hearing.

'What will your defence be this time? In Malching it was Dr Jeremy Sampson; was there a doctor in

Trevon Ghyll who manipulated and threatened you too?'

Helen's eyes shone brightly as her face drained of colour.

'That's what Percival Whitaker was suggesting, wasn't it?' Gary continued. 'Onlookers described you as blanching ashen white, much as you've just done now. Did you fear he was going to produce one of his infamous articles relating to the events in Trevon Ghyll?'

'Are you going to suggest I killed him and it wasn't Connor Robson after all?'

'You have no alibi for the time of his death, apart from your sudden love of walking and exploring isolated places. But no, I don't think you killed him; nonetheless, it was convenient for you that he died wasn't it?'

Helen didn't reply.

'How much did you pay him?'

'Pay who? You're talking in riddles again.' she said impatiently.

'Am I? The more I think about it the more it makes sense. Connor Robson had a motive for killing Whitaker, albeit rather a flimsy one. Would he kill to protect his mother's reputation? It seems pretty unlikely from what I know of him. On the other hand, would he kill if he were offered a large sum of money? Yes, probably.

'You worked with him at the hotel and in all likelihood got to know him quite well. You probably flattered him and praised his abilities. Someone of questionable self-esteem like Connor would respond to that. You have a reputation for focusing on people's vulnerabilities; Mark told me how you "helped him decide" that he wanted to go back to hairdressing. Your motive of course was to be appointed to the hotel management team. So when Whitaker posed a threat, you saw in Connor the perfect patsy and turned your attention to him.'

'And your proof is... where?' asked Helen, looking up defiantly.

'I have none. I'd be amazed if there's an audit trail as you're much too clever for that. So no, Helen, I have no proof, it's just a hunch. Did Connor tell you that he'd overheard Whitaker making plans to meet someone at Dark Tarn? Did you tell Whitaker you would meet him at an earlier time in the same place? Was he expecting you, when Connor turned up? Did you collect Connor from the rendezvous afterwards? Did you tell him to take the laptop and then destroy it; after all, you couldn't risk being caught with it in your possession could you?'

'I'm not even going to dignify your absurd allegations by responding.'

'As you wish, Helen; I think you'll find the Malching police will want a word soon after liaising with their Eastbourne colleagues regarding Trevon Ghyll. As to whether my theory regarding Connor can be proved, I doubt it but I'll be putting it to Ken Stokes later today. I'm just giving you prior warning. What you do about it is up to you.'

'Why?' she asked, suddenly looking him straight in the eye.

'I'm not sure. I suppose it's because if I'm honest, you once meant something to me. Although I suspect your feelings for me were an act to deflect my attention away from your enterprise at the nursing home. You only looked me up again because you were desperate. Also, I suppose I'd like to think that maybe you're not rotten to the core and that given the chance, you could become a decent human being.'

He got up and made towards the door.

'Gary,' called Helen from her position on the sofa.

He looked towards her over his shoulder.

'Thank you for the heads up and for what it's worth, it wasn't an act. But then again, how can you believe anything I say?' The smile was back, genuine or otherwise.

He turned without reply and walked through the foyer where Mark was still hovering expectantly. He didn't linger to satisfy the hotelier's curiosity and continued purposefully towards the front door.

He shouldn't have warned her. He should have let any official investigation take its course and if evidence was found, then the due process of law should be brought to bear on a serial killer because that's what he now thought she was, even if she didn't get her own hands dirty.

Had she colluded with Dr Sampson in the murder of Zlata Bocharova, the elderly lady who knew too much in Malching? If so, maybe it wasn't such a big leap to suspect she'd orchestrated Percival Whitaker's demise too, working on the weak and impressionable Connor Robson to do her bidding.

He had been honest when he said his theory was no more than a hunch but her reaction told him he probably wasn't far off target. He wondered if he'd tell Lizzie about what had just transpired between him and Helen; he thought on balance, probably best not. Leave it so that life could get back to normal, if indeed life with Lizzie Lockwood could ever be described as normal…

*

Helen excused herself before lunch and went to her room. It didn't take long to collect her possessions. She had explained to Mark that she had received a call from her dear uncle who had just been given a terminal prognosis so she had to leave the hotel temporarily to be with him. She would be in touch just as soon as she knew when she would be back, but she would understand if they couldn't keep her position open.

Mark assured her she could return whenever she wanted and her job would always be there. He proffered the generally accepted platitudes and told her to stay in touch. She promised she would.

It seemed like she'd been here for years, so quickly had she settled but it was only a few months. After she arrived, she had quickly discovered the identity of the petty pilferer; who better positioned to steal from the hotel and guests alike than the night porter? He had the run of the place and worked autonomously, well almost. She unmasked him without difficulty and he expected to be dismissed, however that wasn't her plan. She liked to play a longer game. Connor became an ally and forever in her debt.

She didn't know how she would use him to begin with, probably in a scam of her own in the fullness of time. When that damned journalist turned up, Connor's allegiance took on a new significance and she worked on him in the same way she worked on Jeremy Sampson in Malching when Zlata Bocharova needed to be dealt with.

Zlata had started asking far too many questions about her friends and peers who were dying rather unexpectedly at Folly End. She hadn't worked out what was going on but Helen was beginning to feel uncomfortable.

The doctor readily agreed to help, probably because he'd already fleeced the old dear out of the money she'd intended for the parish church and she kept questioning him about it. It was a shame she had to die but there was no choice once Gary Carmichael arrived and started digging around into Doug's death. Zlata obviously trusted him; she was the one person who could expose the doctor but what if she also confided in Gary her suspicions regarding the deaths at the nursing home?

She was dismayed to find that Gary had been almost spot on with his hypotheses as far as they went, sadly he knew her too well. Thank goodness he was gullible enough to believe she could change; fat chance.

Gary was wrong in his assumption that she had paid Connor. He wasn't supposed to kill the hack at the tarn. Just scare him witless and take the laptop. But Connor was unstable, impulsive and above all, unpredictable; she hadn't factored that into the equation. Whitaker might need to be removed permanently at a later date if he didn't take the hint. Had that been the case, his demise would have been planned meticulously and she most certainly would have had an unbreakable alibi. Bashing his brains in was clumsy, crude and amateurish.

She had promised to give Connor a thousand pounds for the mugging and more in time if she needed his services again. When he asked her what he should do after being questioned at the hotel, she'd told him to wait until dark and then scarper, pronto; she'd be in touch. Thankfully, getting himself killed had solved the problem. At least sometimes things worked in her favour. After all, what were the odds against the mouse-like Andrea hearing what Percival Whitaker had said to her and knowing about Trevon Ghyll?

She placed her bags in the boot of her convertible and climbed in behind the wheel. Mark and Robin were at the door to wave her off.

'Come back soon,' called Mark.

She nodded and wiped a tear from her eye. Stop being so soft, there was a whole world waiting out there. A proper change of name this time and no stupid emotional stuff, like falling for anyone.

Now she thought about it objectively, Gary never really fit the bill; he was nowhere near wealthy enough, yet for some strange reason, she wouldn't have minded. She tried to remember if she had ever seen him look truly happy. Even on that last day in Malching. She should have known then, the sanctimonious prig. After the last night they spent together, he couldn't wait to get away. She had thought him enigmatic; in reality, he was as dull as ditch water.

Enough of this self-indulgent nonsense; head not heart from now on, she resolved, as she put her foot down and headed south; maybe London this time or the continent?

Silly little place, Blenthorne.

*

At the same time as Gary was seeing Helen Anderson at the hotel, Lizzie was thinking about the conversation she had had with Hilary Cole as they waited for news of Connor on the night he died.

'Lizzie, I didn't tell the police but there was something about you on Whitaker's laptop.' Hilary held out a piece of paper to her friend.

'Me?' said Lizzie in surprise.

'When his investigations into Helen Anderson were complete, he was going to look at the circumstances of... um, some things in your past which may need a bit of explanation.'

Lizzie had taken the note from Hilary, stuffed it into her pocket and muttered something noncommittal. The problem was, she kept thinking about it.

She absentmindedly collected up the detritus Ken had strewn everywhere. For heaven's sake, he'd left whole supplements behind; no wonder his wife nagged him unmercifully. She collected all the papers into a pile and was about to take them out to the recycling bin. She glanced down at a half completed crossword, started either by Ken or Gary; Ken from the look of the handwriting. In spite of herself, her attention was drawn to an anagram. She looked at some of the letters that had been scribbled around the edge of the page. She found herself sitting down and grabbing a pen. It took less than a minute for her to work out the answer. Lizzie felt extremely pleased with herself! That's the funny thing with anagrams; sometimes you could suddenly just see them.

Sometimes… she gasped involuntarily. Good Lord…

She wrote down some letters and crossed them off as she made two new words. That coupled with the scribbled note found in Whitaker's room; *'The Leopard That Changed Its Spots"*. Yes, of course, she could see the significance now.

She left the house and got into her car. She travelled the short distance to Barton's Farm and took a right turning towards the museum.

As she approached the entrance, Tim Carney was sitting just outside with a piece of pewter in his hands and what looked like a scalpel.

'Hello, Tim, lovely day,' said Lizzie as she walked towards the museum assistant curator.

'Yes, isn't it? We're not open today so we're in catch up mode. If you're looking for Colleen, she's gone over to Rowendale to see someone who has a large number of artefacts to ascertain if any of them are suitable for display. She's always on the lookout for complete collections as you can imagine and we are getting quite choosy now. Some valuable pieces are in pretty bad condition; that doesn't matter if they're salvageable but it takes time. Nevertheless, it's very rewarding work. It gives one plenty of time for contemplation.'

Tim showed Lizzie the pewter jug and how he was painstakingly dislodging some of the encrustation.

'Pewter dates back to the Bronze Age; did you know that? This one is oxidised so I'm treating it accordingly. I've dipped it in a solution first to try to soften the coating a bit, as it has years of grime attached. The end result should be amazing. I have heard that once clean, the best way to keep pewter in pristine condition is to rub it with cabbage leaves! Isn't that extraordinary? Some of the old methods are still the best according to Colleen.'

'Is it a valuable piece?' asked Lizzie.

'I'm not sure yet, not as valuable as silver plate. We have someone who comes round occasionally to see what the entire collection is worth. Only problem is, the insurance goes up accordingly!'

'Ah yes, I suppose it would. Actually, Tim, it's you I've come to see.'

'Me? I can't imagine why,' Tim looked curious.

'Can't you really? You must have heard the gossip going round the village. I know Colleen has and she must have discussed it with you. The identity of Jane Macintyre, that's been the local mystery of the moment, hasn't it.'

'As I say, Colleen isn't here and if you want gossip, she's your girl.'

'Okay; sorry to have bothered you, I just wondered if there was anything you knew about Jane that's all. The Whitaker case is over, she's totally in the clear.'

'Is she though?' Tim said sharply. 'Will she ever be totally free of allegation and insinuation? I mean, firstly there was the suggestion she had murdered her entire family and now more recently she was the prime suspect in this case. The papers will get hold of it I'm sure and then they'll start digging. Wherever she goes and whatever she does she will never be completely free of the suspicion of guilt.'

He remained silent for a moment then continued;

'*"The lingering stench of death"*, that's what he called it. How melodramatic. Whitaker was an evil man and I'm glad he's dead. Mind you, it's only a matter of time before the next one comes along. Another hack trying to make their name with no thought of the damage they're doing to people's lives.'

'If they do, they'll get no help from us; we look after our own here in Blenthorne. I think if Jane has a new identity, is living happily and productively in society, then no one from this village would ever want to ruin that for her... or him.'

'How did you know?' Tim put down his jug but held on to the scalpel.

'I didn't. It was only this morning when I was tidying up after Gary and Ken that I worked it out; I found a discarded crossword and solved an anagram which had clearly foxed the pair of them. Then I suddenly started thinking about anagrams in general and saw it; "Tim Carney" is an anagram of "Macintyre". That's quite clever.

'As I was driving over here, a couple of other things then fell into place. I remembered Colleen had said that during a conversation with Whitaker, he had asked her about Jane and then changed the subject to ask about you and the museum. What if he wasn't just idly chatting? What if he was trying a different angle; namely to question Colleen about Tim rather than Jane?

'Finally, there was something that I had forgotten and was reminded of a few days ago when I was visiting a friend in Scotland; a trifling thing and of no significance on its own but during his diatribe, Whitaker had said where better to *"reinvent"* oneself than a sleepy little village. I mean *"resettle"* or even *"re-establish"* but *"reinvent"*? It seemed a bit incongruous and only accurate if he was referring to something entirely new; not just a change of identity but a whole new person. Did he just use the wrong word? Surely as a journalist, a wordsmith, he wouldn't have done that.' She paused. 'Was it difficult to come up with a name?'

'Not really. I always wanted to be called Tim even when I was a small child. I never played with dolls or wanted to dress in "appropriate" clothes. I tried dating a boy once; total disaster! During my gender reassignment I had a lot of time to think about what I wanted my name to be; Tim obviously, then the remaining letters in my surname made Carney so it all made sense. More to the point, now I make sense; I know who I am, I'm happy in my own skin and I've built a life for myself here. Whitaker wanted to ruin that.'

'Did he contact you?'

'Yes, it was one night after choir practice. A group of us were walking back to the village and there must have been something about my choice of words or cadence which he recognised in spite of the intervening years. Apparently, a contact in the police had let him have access to the interview tapes when I was questioned about the death of my family; can you believe that? A corrupt officer being bribed by a journalist; isn't it just my luck? It's still quite a connection for him to make though, because my voice is several octaves lower than before my hormone treatment. Still, he was good at his job, I'll give him that; he realised who I was and made contact the next day.

'His latest exposé was to be called; *"The Leopard That Changed Its Spots"*. He found that highly amusing. I told him to go ahead, what had he got on me? I was never charged with anything when my family died and what was there to know since? I had been female, now I was male and it appeared that was his big scoop.

'He seemed to think unmasking me as Jane Macintyre would bring him in a fortune. Colleen said not to worry, we would face whatever was thrown at us. I think it frustrated him to find I didn't appear half as bothered as he thought I should be. I told him if he had new evidence, he should take it to the police. I was confident any subsequent enquiry would exonerate me.

'I was bluffing of course. I was petrified that he would expose me and my life would be turned into a circus but in the short term, my strategy seemed to work. I think that performance in the pub was bravado because in spite of all his digging he had no new story, no huge explosive revelation, so he was trying to provoke a reaction. Obviously, he did that but clearly not in the way he intended, as he got himself killed.'

'So Colleen knows?'

'In the beginning she only knew that I was transgender. Difficult when you share a house to hide the fact you're on medication. I told her the truth when Whitaker was pursuing me. Did she say anything to you?'

'No, she can be discreet when she wants to be but she did say something which at the time I didn't fully appreciate. She said that it wasn't often that men wanted to buy her drinks these days, other than you but that was "different". She quickly qualified the remark by saying it was because you were housemates but I also thought she might mean because you were young enough to be her son.'

'Of course, I'm not that much younger than her, certainly not young enough to be her child. Jane would be mid-late forties now, so I'm also that age chronologically but reassignment from female to male can sometimes result in the male looking younger than his female counterpart. I didn't start shaving until a few years ago so my complexion makes me appear quite youthful.

'To be honest I've also had a bit of work done; a silicone implant in my chin area and a couple of small ones to change my cheekbones, so I think the plastic surgeon took the opportunity to tighten everything up a bit.' Tim pointed to the appropriate areas on his face.

'I was always rather tall and awkward as a female but as a male, I'm just shy of average height. Plus, of course, I've kept myself in shape; I've worked on my biceps and core muscles. Many men tend to carry a fair bit of timber as they get older, don't you think? Not Gary of course, he's kept himself trim but the policeman who came with you to see Colleen the other day, he could certainly do with shifting a bit.'

Lizzie smiled. 'Ah yes, that explains it. I wouldn't have put you more than mid-thirties. Anyway, I hope you don't mind me coming along to see you, just wanted to quench my curiosity I suppose.'

'Not at all, Lizzie; I know I can rely on your discretion,' Tim smiled thinly and looked at Lizzie pointedly, twisting the scalpel tip into his left palm.

'Oh gosh yes, that goes without saying; we'll never mention it again. Now, how about coming along tomorrow night for a drink at the pub? I'm sure you won't have to twist Colleen's arm. Andrea's being discharged today and Jono's bringing her home. It would be good for her to be among friends; it won't be a long drawn out affair as I'm sure she'll want to rest but just to let her know we're all rooting for her.'

'Yes, that would be nice. Maybe see you then,' Tim smiled as he leaned forward and hugged Lizzie. 'Thank you,' he said softly. She gave his arm a squeeze as she left.

*

As she drove away, Lizzie wondered briefly if she would tell Gary she'd solved the Macintyre mystery. She thought on balance, probably not. That wasn't the only thing she didn't plan to tell him.

She was still thinking about Hilary's laptop revelation as they waited for news of her son.

'I was looking for references concerning Connor and me; however, an entry about you caught my eye, Lizzie. It was quite a list and I copied it before I destroyed the hard drive, as I thought you should have it. I doubt Whitaker had started any sort of investigation,' Hilary added, optimistically, as she handed Lizzie a page of lined paper covered in her neat handwriting.

"Lizzie Lockwood: Secrets of the Benefactress of Blenthorne."

'Look at that list of bullet points! What sort of sick mind would even entertain such thoughts? A truly vile man,' Hilary had said, shaking her head. 'I had no idea you had encountered so much tragedy throughout your life, Lizzie, how very unfortunate. It's no one else's business, obviously, and I won't tell a soul, you can rest assured.'

Lizzie had thanked her. She had no reason to believe that Hilary wouldn't be true to her word, however, what would happen if not? Lizzie would definitely make much more time for the lonely post mistress from now on. Yes, she would have to keep a watchful eye on Hilary.

An old, familiar feeling rushed through her veins, her heart pounded and a small shiver ran down her spine as long shadows from the past reached out to claim her. What next for Lizzie Lockwood?

*

Tim had returned to his task after Lizzie left. His hands worked methodically as his mind raced. Yes, very nice to have friends who would rally round; lucky Andrea. If only Jane had been so fortunate.

His left hand was sore. He looked at the palm and noticed he'd drawn blood with the scalpel. It was a good thing Jane wasn't present this morning he thought grimly. Pressurising her in the way that Lizzie Lockwood had pressurised Tim might have led to a whole different outcome. Her mother could attest to that.

'You don't belong here,' she had said.

Jane had tried to conform, but nothing she did made any difference. The putdowns continued until one day during a particularly nasty argument, her mother made a fatal mistake.

'You're not normal and I don't want you anywhere near my children.' She shouldn't have said that. Jane pointed out that she was one of Pat's children too but Pat had laughed.

'You steal, you lie and this other business; dressing in boys' clothes, bandaging your chest, you're disgusting, a freak of nature. I'll never know what I did to deserve you.'

'We were happy, before Larry came along.'

'We were broke, Jane; we were barely existing on tick and waiting for the bailiffs to bang on the door. I wanted more than that; a life, a nice home and…'

'And nice children; the ideal family unit with no room for "a-freak-of-nature" like me,' she'd shouted with tears streaming down her cheeks.

'You're right; there isn't room for you!' She would never forget the words that spewed out of Pat's mouth. It was the last thing she ever said to her daughter or indeed, anyone else.

She'd looked down in disbelief when Jane had plunged the knife into her flabby abdomen; she'd flailed around a bit, knocking things over so Jane stabbed her again and again… Amy was a spoilt pampered child but it was a shame she had to die; sadly, there was no choice because she had seen what Jane had done. Killing the two boys, who teased and taunted her every day egged on by Larry, had been easy. They slept at the top of the large solidly built detached house so had no idea what had happened downstairs. She knew just where to plunge the knife for swift, optimum effect.

She'd always had an interest in real life crime. She'd read up extensively on anatomy and the most efficient ways of killing people, so she could write stories and dream of becoming a famous novelist. Even now, every time Tim got rejected by a literary agent or publisher he wanted to scream at them, tell them his plot ideas worked because Jane had proved it, she'd committed the perfect crime; but how could he without incriminating her? No, he had to smile at each rejection and continue to try. At least Jane's mother would never reject anyone again. She was in a nice place with her nice children.

Larry had been more of a challenge but Jane had eventually caught up with him in Wales. Boating accidents were always a possibility for the inexperienced sailor, particularly if one was careless with the dead man's switch. Poor Larry; all tangled up in the rudder after somehow falling from the craft. He'd screamed like a pig, begging Jane to save him. It was rather ironic that whilst she was already a strong swimmer, he'd paid for the lessons that had enabled her to become exceptional. This, in turn, empowered her to extract the ultimate payback for all those years of emotional cruelty, humiliation and exclusion.

What was the saying; *"revenge is a dish best served cold"*? In Larry's case it was so true; watching him slowly drown in the swell of the bleak grey sea, surrounded by his own blood. As she trod water just off the coast, it was possibly one of the most satisfying moments of her life.

Once she'd disposed of everyone who'd caused her misery, she could move forward. She washed her hands of Jane's deeds and became Tim.

Tim loved his life, he could use his natural artistic flair in a positive way at the museum, helping Colleen make the best of her collection and he could fulfil his desire to write. He enjoyed performing in the choir and making friends. He wanted that to continue. No one had ever rejected him in Blenthorne – not yet.

Tim sucked his palm; savouring the taste and breathing in the metallic smell. Blood could always evoke so many disturbing memories. He waited patiently for his heartbeat to return to normal as he too contemplated the future.

Acknowledgements

I would like to thank everyone involved in the production of this novel:

Nia for proofreading
Jo for the cover design
Emily for advising on the clinical bits
Clive for uploading the manuscript

And special thanks to Stacey for giving me the confidence to get #ProjectPublication off the ground.

Finally… a heart-felt thanks to you for reading **Reasonable Doubt?** If you have enjoyed it, please would you mind taking a moment to leave a review on Amazon and or Goodreads.

About the Author

Julie is a former NHS medical secretary/administrator who lives in West Sussex and also spends a lot of time wandering the fells of the Lake District. 'Reasonable Doubt?' is her third novel and when she isn't mingling with pretend people who intermittently take over her life, she works as a church verger, volunteers for the National Trust and reviews the work of other authors.

She is married with three children and, to date, five grandsons.

Previous books by this author:

Long Shadows
Evil Echoes

Find her at:

https://jhbooksblog.wordpress.com/

https://www.facebook.com/juliehaiseldenbooks/

https://twitter.com/juliehaiselden

https://www.goodreads.com/author/show/13607989.Julie_Haiselden

Printed in Great Britain
by Amazon